Late N

By

Allison Creal

To my lovely friend
Di
Much love from
Allison
x

Chapter 1

Christian Hambridge was a popular businessman with a sunny disposition and ready smile. He was well respected, kind hearted and would always be the first to help a friend in need; the type of man any mother would have been proud to have as a son. At thirty-eight years of age he had been enjoying the prime of his life, until he was tragically killed in a motorcycling accident. A thoughtless drunk driver had veered his van onto the opposite side of a winding country lane and, in one fatal second, Christian's life had ended in a head-on collision.

News reports of his untimely death had dominated the front page of the Hanford Recorder. Christian had been the only son of a wealthy local estate agent. He had taken over running the family business after his father's sudden death the previous year. Christian had been a principled man and had relished the challenge to help dozens of townsfolk who had struggled to find a home to rent. He had worked tirelessly with landlords and tenants to achieve a fair deal for all, and his hard efforts had made him a local hero. His father's agency, Thomas Hambridge & Son, had thrived, and Christian became well-known for his charity work in the town. On the day of his accident the benevolent businessman had been returning from delivering Christmas presents to a children's hospice with a local group of bikers. Following his tragic death, the local newspaper's family announcements pages had been filled with notices from hundreds of people lamenting the sad loss of their friend, colleague and the people's champion.

Christian's funeral was attended by many mourners; all giving their heartfelt condolences to his distraught young widow Diana and grieving mother Elisabeth. A procession of motorcyclists had followed the cortege of black limousines through the town on their solemn journey to Hanford Town Crematorium; bringing other traffic to a halt. Locals and shop keepers had bowed their heads and festive decorative lights were dimmed as a mark of respect for the likeable family businessman, as the sombre cavalcade of cars and bikes had slowly passed along the crowded high street.

One of Christian's friends had set up a memorial page on a social media site called FriendsBag to give others an opportunity to leave their messages of condolence. It was quickly supported by well wishers and friends who flooded the newsfeed with thoughtful words of sympathy.

During the weeks that followed the funeral, the outpourings of grief turned to posts of happier memories of the well-loved young man, his friends choosing to share amusing stories and photographs to celebrate Christian's life. It was easy to see that he had been an amazingly popular colleague, a caring son and loving husband who had everything to live for.

#

Timeline: Monday 6th June 2016, 08:30hrs
Six Months Later.

Elisabeth Hambridge browsed through the pages of her family's photograph album. It was a heavy book bound in red leather and filled with fond memories of her late husband Thomas and their son Christian. The smiling pictures and newspaper clippings were a glowing testament to the Hambridge men's strong bond and their successful business partnership. It had been six months since Christian's funeral, and the wealthy widow had a daily ritual of poring over the contents of the album each morning. She was determined that the precious memories of her loving family would never be allowed to fade, and she would always start each day sitting at her ornately hand-carved writing desk in her study with a china beaker of freshly brewed coffee and a lingering look through the laminated pages.

Elisabeth was an elegant woman in her late sixties, whose impeccable appearance belied her advancing years. As the young Liz Blake in her twenties, she had enjoyed a rewarding career as an air stewardess. A highly dependable member of the team, Elisabeth successfully climbed the airline's career ladder

2

to take a much coveted place as part of the First Class cabin crew. She met businessman Thomas Hambridge on a supersonic flight to Bahrain. After a whirlwind romance, the couple married during the summer heat wave of 1976. She left the airline to start a family with her new husband and quickly settled into comfortable suburban life.

Despite placing her glamorous career on hold to become a full time housewife and mother, the instilled habit of being constantly well-groomed never left her and she still took great pride in how she looked. Elisabeth's long ash blonde hair was usually swept up into a chic French plait and she carefully applied make-up each morning. Her clothes were always immaculate, even the ones she wore around the house. There were no scruffy T-shirts or tatty trousers in Elisabeth's wardrobe; just a smart collection of high quality tailored garments. Her friends would often playfully tease that she didn't know the meaning of casual dress, and what she wore to do the gardening in wouldn't look out of place at a Royal garden party.

Elisabeth and Thomas Hambridge's marriage had been a loving and happy one, but despite their dreams of having a large family, Christian had been their only child. The wealthy couple had doted on their son; believing that one day he would marry a socialite, settle down and they would then be blessed with beautiful grandchildren. Elisabeth had supported her husband's dream of expanding his business and Thomas always planned that Christian would one day take over the reins. The aspirational estate agent had mingled with Hanford's high fliers at all available opportunities by joining the golf club, Rotary Club and Masonic Lodge. Elisabeth had been an active member of the Inner Wheel and she had played an important part in nurturing her husband's convivial reputation; the Hambridges' dinner parties and soirees became legendary throughout the town's business community.

The estate agent's wife had also been instrumental in raising funds to launch the town's first computer club for the local under sixteen-year-olds. Elisabeth had spent a lot of time online researching exotic dinner party menus and this had given her a good understanding of how the internet worked. She knew first hand how powerful knowledge could be. Her husband's company supplied the first few terminals to the computer club and paid for the internet connection at the local village hall. That generous donation helped dozens of underprivileged school children to realise their full potential by giving them access to the world wide web of information. The after-school club had recently celebrated its fifteenth anniversary and Elisabeth had been proud that the facility had kept many an idle teenage mind occupied. Thomas Hambridge's legacy had even helped some to follow a lucrative career path into computer programming.

Following the sudden death of her philanthropic husband a year earlier, Elisabeth had largely withdrawn from public life, choosing to have only the minimal contact with friends. Since Christian's motorcycle accident six months later, the elegant widow had become more reclusive. The only regular visitor she saw was her daughter-in-law Diana, who came to take her out grocery shopping once a week.

Elisabeth turned a page of her photo album and gazed at a group photograph that had been taken at her son's wedding ten years previously. Although in the picture she appeared to be the cordial happy mother of the groom, the grieving woman hadn't exactly been bosom buddies with Christian's young wife over the years. She knew her son had always wanted to start his own family, but Diana had been unable to become pregnant. Elisabeth had desperately longed to be a grandmother; to fill her house with the cacophony of playful children that she had missed out on in her own marriage. Consequently she had secretly felt a little resentment towards her daughter-in-law in what she regarded as the young woman's failure to give Christian the family he so clearly craved.

After a few years of trying for a baby, it appeared to Elisabeth that Diana had easily given up on any dreams of motherhood. Diana always refused to be drawn into any conversation about treatment for her apparent infertility and instead had chosen to focus all of her energy into pursuing her own successful career in property sales at Thomas Hambridge & Son. Elisabeth had been bitterly disappointed by her daughter-in-law's lack of maternal spirit. What she viewed as

Diana's petulant refusal to even consider the medical options available had once led to an over-heated argument between the two women. Christian had been forced to intervene and bravely told his mother that she had to accept once and for all that there would never be a grandchild and she should stop harassing his wife. Consequently whenever the couple visited the Hambridge family home, everyone knew that the subject of babies was not up for discussion.

Even though Elisabeth knew that Christian and Diana had loved each other dearly, a small selfish part of her wished that her son had married someone else; someone able to give her grandchildren. During the past six months she often thought that if he had done so, then at least now she would still have a part of Christian to hold in her arms. Maybe the responsibilities of fatherhood would have curbed his thrill-seeking ways and he would not have been out riding such a powerful motorbike on the fateful day of his accident.

Elisabeth was a master at hiding her true disdain for people and always coped in a crisis with the utmost professionalism. Her cool almost icy demeanour had once earned her the nickname of 'Swan Blake' among her colleagues when she worked at the airline. They knew that no matter how demanding the young Liz Blake's passengers had been, or how flustered and upset she felt inside, the consummately professional flight attendant would always remain calm and composed on the outside, like a seemingly unruffled swan who was furiously paddling beneath the water line. Elisabeth carried the same trait into her private life too as, despite her underlying resentment towards her daughter-in-law, she had always remained serene and civil towards Diana.

In the months following Christian's death the two women had grown a little closer and their previous frostiness had recently thawed towards a genuine respectful fondness for each other. The warmer relationship between them had initially been borne out of their shared grief, but it had mainly grown from Elisabeth coming to realise that Diana was also alone. The old woman felt slightly ashamed that, at first, she hadn't given her daughter-in-law's feelings a second thought. Diana must have been truly devastated that her loving husband had tragically

5

died and she didn't have Christian's child; she too had no one to hold in her arms. Both women hoped that, in time, coping with their bereavement would get easier, but for the time being they would try to get on with their lives as best as they possibly could, and be there for one another when needed.

Elisabeth took a sip of coffee before turning another page of the leather-bound photo album to look at a few snapshots that had been taken during Christian and Diana's honeymoon; her mind was instantly taken back to waving off the happy couple after their wedding reception, as they rode off into the sunset on Christian's Harley Davidson. The newly-weds had gone on to spend three weeks motorcycling around Europe and most of the photographs featured panoramic scenery in the French Alps and shots of Christian and Diana posing with dozens of new-found friends they had met on their travels. Suddenly Elisabeth's trip down memory lane was rudely interrupted by the buzz of her house intercom.

"Who on earth is that?" said Elisabeth aloud.

"I'm not expecting Diana today," she tutted at the intrusion.

The Hambridge family home was a large detached Georgian building located in the highly desirable area of Hanford, called Himley Fields. The imposing cream-rendered property was set behind wrought iron electronic gates on a private road named Clover Croft. Being one of the largest houses on the quiet tree-lined avenue, it was a seven bedroom executive home befitting the status of the town's most successful estate agent. In reality the mansion was far too large for one person to rattle around in and Elisabeth had begun to consider downsizing, but for now she had decided to remain in the property surrounded by the precious memories it gave her of her late husband and son.

The elegant woman stood up from her writing desk and made her way out of the ground floor study into a wide marble-tiled hall. She picked up an intercom receiver that hung by the front door and peered out of a small downstairs window. Elisabeth could see a man wearing a pale blue shirt, red gilet and dark blue trousers was standing outside the wrought iron gates at the end of her gravel drive. He had a large red canvas satchel idly slung over one shoulder and a clipboard in his hands.

"Hello, can I help you?" asked Elisabeth.

"Delivery for Christian Hambridge?" replied the chirpy voice on the other end of the line. Elisabeth was startled at hearing the name. It was the last thing she had expected.

"Christian . . . err . . . he isn't here at the moment," she faltered, as she felt a lump in her throat begin to choke off her words. She couldn't bring herself to admit the awful truth to the stranger that her beloved son had recently passed away.

"It's just something that needs a signature?" replied the postman after pausing for a couple of seconds. Elisabeth noticed he raised his sentences at the end, as if asking a question. Such an unnecessary upward inflection was one of her pet hates, and she had often scolded her son when he had developed a similar habit in his late teens. Elisabeth pressed a button to open the electronic gates. She watched the man walk over the crunchy gravel drive as she opened her front door. The elderly woman vaguely recognised what looked like a Royal Mail logo printed on an ID badge hung loosely around the man's neck.

"Nice day for it?" smiled the postman as he hurriedly handed over his clipboard and pen to Elisabeth.

"Right then, Christian Hambridge where are you?" mumbled the man as he began to rummage through his delivery bag and search through a small stack of mail.

"Ah, there you are," announced the man victoriously as he pulled a cellophane wrapped envelope out of his bag. The grieving mother was momentarily startled by the unexpected mention of her late son's name again; it was as if for one split second Christian was still alive. Although the postman was totally oblivious to how much pain his innocuous comments had caused Elisabeth, he realised the dazed woman needed prompting to sign for the delivery.

"I've had a few of these this morning. It's just a letter that needs to be signed for. I'm afraid it's been caught up in the postal system for some time." The postman smiled again as he helpfully pointed at the relevant empty space on his list that was awaiting a signature.

"And to make matters worse my electronic gadget thing has given up the ghost this morning, so we're back to old fashioned

7

paper and pen today I'm afraid," he added, still tapping next to the space alongside Christian's name.

Elisabeth's hand shook as she silently signed the docket sheet and the man handed over the small packet. He nodded to indicate all was present and correct, turned away from the door, and began to cheerfully whistle an out-of-tune rendition of Summer Time as he headed back across the gravel driveway. She closed the front door before carrying the mysterious package back through the hall.

Elisabeth inspected the curious delivery. The original handwritten envelope was sealed inside a clear plastic bag. An official-looking sticker on the outside of the wrapper apologised for the item's delay in the post. The label had a Royal Mail verification stamp with the previous day's date on it; the original date printed across the second class stamp on the old cream coloured envelope inside was from 10th June 1996; two decades previously. The letter had been delayed in the post for twenty years.

'I wonder who it was writing to Christian all those years ago?' thought an intrigued Elisabeth, as she picked up the plastic bag and slowly slid her finger along a perforation line to open up the cellophane wrapping.

Inside was an accompanying letter of apology from Royal Mail. It explained that a local post office had recently closed down and the building was undergoing a re-fit. A builder had found a small bundle of old envelopes trapped behind some filing cabinets. The letter gave a telephone number for the recipient to ring should they need any further clarification. Elisabeth decided whatever contents lay inside the old cream coloured envelope, it was a precious connection to her only child, and she was determined to give it all the reverence it deserved.

She went into the kitchen and made herself a second cup of strong coffee before carrying it through to the warm sanctuary of her downstairs study. She placed her china beaker on a drinks coaster that sat on top of the green leather-bound writing desk and carefully positioned the unopened letter alongside. Elisabeth picked up a silver bladed letter opener from her desktop organiser and stared at the old envelope for several minutes.

Opening a private letter that had been addressed to her son all those years ago just didn't feel right to her, but there was only one way to find out if it had been important or not. With great trepidation she took in a deep breath and picked it up. The paper outside was a little crumpled and scuffed around the edges; the unfamiliar handwriting on the front was delicate and had been carefully written using a ruler to keep the lines straight.

'No going back now,' she thought as she slit along the top edge with her paperknife. Nervously she opened out the neatly folded piece of matching cream coloured notepaper that had been inside; its contents hidden from the world for twenty years.

The letter was from a girl called Charlotte Rook.

Dear Chris,

I have tried to meet with you lots of times over the past few weeks but you haven't returned any of my calls and it feels like you're avoiding me. I know it was only ever meant to be a drunken one night stand, and you wouldn't normally look twice at a girl like me, but I think it's only fair to let you know I am pregnant and I am going to keep our baby. I can't come to your house because I'm scared about meeting your parents and I quite honestly don't know how they'll react. When college finishes for the summer I have a job in France to go to and I'll stay there to study for my degree. So I'll leave England at the end of the month. I'm giving you one last chance to get in touch. Please meet me at the college library at 1pm on Friday (14th June) so we can talk about it. If I don't hear from you before I leave, then I'll understand you don't want to have anything to do with me or the baby. I will leave and you won't ever have to see me again.

Much love,

Charlotte Rook.

Elisabeth gasped and then slumped back into her office chair, shaking her head in stunned silence. She felt a rush of

9

blood pump through her veins as she read the letter over and over again. With each carefully written word from the past, a hot flush of anxiety stung through her chest like a surge of electricity. Her hands trembled as she checked the date stamp on the front of the envelope. The grieving mother knew Christian had been an eighteen-year-old engineering student at Hanford College in 1996 but she couldn't remember him ever mentioning a girl called Charlotte. She smiled warmly as she thought of how he had been such a popular and good looking young lad, that he could have had his pick of any girl he fancied.

Elisabeth knew her son had played the field a little but he had always been a sensible boy; she had warned him often enough about the dangers of unsafe sex and she had brought him up to believe it was wrong to sleep around. Christian had gone out with quite a few girls at college and Elisabeth knew she had probably only been introduced to half of his dates. She felt a heavy pang of disappointment as it seemed her motherly advice may have gone unheeded and her son had not been as sensible as she had been led to believe. The girl in the letter had said it was a one night stand. Christian may never have known about the baby or given the girl a second thought.

Apart from her daughter-in-law, Elisabeth had no other family left alive. The sudden and unexpected news of a possible grandchild flooded her brain with a tsunami of mixed emotions that brought both pleasure and pain. If she was able to track down the mysterious Charlotte Rook then she may be able to at least hold a part of Christian in her arms once more; but how would his grieving widow take the news? How could she explain who the child was to Diana? It would surely break the young woman's heart to know that another girl had successfully borne her husband's baby all those years ago.

To Elisabeth, the idea that she could have a grandchild out there somewhere in the world was suddenly all consuming. She imagined the child could once have been a young boy with Christian's sparkly eyes and cheeky sense of adventure, climbing trees and playing with his friends. He would now be a strapping nineteen-year-old young man. Maybe Charlotte's baby had been a little girl instead; she would now be a beautiful young lady about to embark on her own adult life. A whole host of different scenarios played out in Elisabeth's imagination. She thought of nothing else for the rest of the morning.

'It's no good; I really need to find this Charlotte woman,' thought Elisabeth. She carefully folded the precious letter in half, placed it back inside the old crumpled envelope and slipped it into the top drawer of a dark mahogany bureau that stood next to her leather-clad desk. She went into the kitchen and made a fresh cafetiere of coffee before returning to her study to thoroughly think through what to do. She needed a plan to deal with any fallout from the unexpected yet very welcome addition to the Hambridge family.

Elisabeth decided, for the time being, that she would keep the letter a secret until she had established all of the facts. It would not be worth upsetting her daughter-in-law until she knew all of the details. Diana would know nothing about Christian's baby until Elisabeth was certain that Charlotte had actually gone ahead with the pregnancy and given birth to her grandchild.

#

Timeline: Monday 6th June 2016, 14:30hrs

Elisabeth sat in her study and nervously picked up her mobile phone. She believed her best course of action would be to first establish where the mysterious letter had been posted and how the envelope had become lost in the postal system for twenty years. The grieving mother had practised for a couple of hours what questions to ask. She took in a deep breath before hesitantly punching in the number listed in the explanatory note from Royal Mail found with Charlotte's letter. After a couple of rings the call was answered by an enquiry clerk.

"Hello, postal enquiries. Robin speaking. How can I help?" said the young man's voice at the end of the line. He had a slightly camp tone and his office sounded very busy with an intrusive gaggle of voices and ringing telephones in the background.

11

"Oh, hello. I've received a delayed letter in the post today and I was wondering if you could give me some more information about where it was posted," replied Elisabeth, her careful opening statement was well rehearsed.

Robin asked for the reference number on the postal company's letter and Elisabeth heard him tap the code into a keyboard. She could hear office workers merrily chatting near to the enquiry clerk; all totally unaware of the gravity of her query. Eventually the man said he had found the information attached to the reference. He explained that the letter had been discovered during the demolition of an old post office in Lye Heath. Elisabeth knew the area; it was a run down housing estate in Hanford town where some of Christian's college friends had lived. Robin said there was a note on the system to say that the letter had been found with a few other envelopes and postcards, behind an old metal filing cabinet. The system confirmed that the letter had been posted locally in the town and first processed on 10th June 1996. Elisabeth quickly scribbled down notes as the enquiry clerk continued to give her more details.

"Our investigations team have been looking into this issue and they have added quite a few notes on the system since forwarding on the delayed mail," said Robin.

"It says here that in the nineties, the old Lye Heath sub-postmaster's shop was a central gathering point where postmen from the Hanford district used to drop in for an early morning break. They would then set off on their rounds all over the town. Some letters must have slipped out of one of their delivery sacks unnoticed and become trapped all those years ago. Your letter was one of half a dozen others found in the bundle," explained Robin quickly in an unemotional matter-of-fact tone. His voice reminded Elisabeth of the way one of her gay male colleagues used to contemptuously deliver passenger safety announcements on board the aircraft; blankly read from a script with the undercurrent of a haughty sneer.

"I'm sorry for the delay. I hope it wasn't anything too important," he added, still without true conviction or any sympathy in his voice.

Elisabeth couldn't begin to explain the significance of the letter to the clerk and instead simply thanked him for the information and hung up the phone. She realised it was probably going to be a lot more difficult to track down the mysterious Charlotte than she had first thought; but at least Robin had been able to confirm the letter had been posted in the local area. That was a start. It seemed to fit with the girl being a student at Christian's college.

Elisabeth felt an overwhelming surge of energy flow through her body; she could feel the small shoots of hope beginning to grow in her heart. For over a year she had buried herself in the grief of losing her family. She had only just started to re-build her life following the cruel and untimely deaths of her husband and son. If nothing else, tracking down her only grandchild would give Elisabeth something positive to focus on; some invigorating optimism for the future.

Suddenly Elisabeth's feelings of hope were replaced with the unwelcome return of the daunting prospect of having to break the unexpected news of Christian's baby to her daughter-in-law. She knew that Diana was also still grieving the loss of her husband. How would the young widow react to seeing his sparkly eyes and cheeky smile in the face of another woman's child? Would she ever be able to accept the situation and allow Elisabeth to enjoy being a grandmother?

Elisabeth pushed her wavering loyalty to Diana towards the back of her mind. Despite her blossoming relationship with Christian's wife, she decided that she had no choice but to go ahead and track down her only grandchild. Whichever way Diana chose to cope with the bombshell, they would simply have to deal with the fallout later. The most important thing in Elisabeth's mind was to let the mysterious Charlotte know her child would be cherished by a loving grandmother. After meeting him or her, Elisabeth would find a way to break the heartbreaking news to Diana; until then she would carry out a little secret detective work. All she had to do was find someone called Charlotte Rook with roots in Hanford twenty years ago and links with France.

#

13

After an afternoon spent online, Elisabeth's internet searches for Charlotte's name had returned numerous lists of results; many of which linked to profiles on social media sites. Another hour of digging later, she had a shortlist of half a dozen people on Link-Zone and FriendsBag who best matched her criteria. Elisabeth began to narrow down the results. The profile photographs of the first three women looked too young to have been at college with her son; another two were in Australia. The last one on the list featured a photograph of a woman who looked to be in her late thirties. She was located near Cannes, in the south of France. Anxiously, Elisabeth clicked on the thumbnail image to open up the woman's FriendsBag profile.

Immediately Elisabeth saw a large cover picture appear across the top of the screen that featured a sunset from what looked like a typical Mediterranean coastline. The calm sea was a vibrant shade of azure blue; the sand golden yellow. A couple of rowing boats in the corner of the picture were gently lapped by the water and draped in fishermen's nets. A small artisanal hand-painted sign at the side pointed the way to a local 'Poissonnier'; a French fishmonger. The small profile image was of a smiling blonde woman with high cheek bones who wore her hair in a sophisticated chignon. Her name was listed as Charlotte Benoit; née Rook.

"Oh it's a French beach," gasped Elizabeth. She imagined the cover photograph had probably been taken on a family holiday. The woman's maiden name was a perfect match to the one in the old letter.

'Could this be the mother of Christian's child?' she thought as she felt a flush of excitement began to fizz through her veins.

'Had it really been that simple to track her down?' A small flicker of doubt fluttered through Elisabeth's mind.

'But everything fits with what she said in her letter about leaving to live in France twenty years ago. She must have stayed there and got married. Gosh, finding her was easier than I thought it would be though.' Convinced that she had found the mother of her only grandchild; Elisabeth gave herself a small self-congratulatory smile, but her initial excitement soon turned to frustration as the woman's profile gave very little other information.

Madame Benoit had her privacy options set to high and only shared her personal information and online photo albums with friends. As a member of the general public, it was impossible for Elisabeth to gain any further insight other than Charlotte's name, location and a few comments about where the cover photograph had been taken. If she wanted to find out more about the mysterious woman, she would have to contact her directly or send her a friend request and hope that it was accepted.

Elisabeth hesitantly allowed her cursor to hover over the friend request button. The gravity of her actions was not lost on the grieving widow. She knew that if Charlotte was the mother of Christian's child, with one small click she could be opening Pandora's Box; there would be no going back and it could potentially change the course of all of their lives forever. She closed her eyes, took in a deep breath and nervously pressed the button to send. Now all she could do was sit back and anxiously wait for a reply.

#

Timeline: Tuesday 7th June 2016, 08:30hrs

The next morning Elisabeth was disappointed to see Charlotte had not responded to her friend request. There had been no acknowledgment at all. Her sleepless night had been spent thinking about the contents of the old letter. Thoughts had continually buzzed in her head as her stomach churned with the exciting prospect that she may only be a few steps away from finding her grandchild. She had convinced herself that the Charlotte Benoit she had found on FriendsBag simply had to be Christian's Charlotte Rook; everything seemed to fit.

As she emptied the last dregs of coffee from her cafetiere into a tall china mug, Elisabeth's impatience grew. Her initial delight at having tracked down the woman she believed to be the mother of Christian's child had begun to dwindle with each passing moment; her laptop computer lay tauntingly silent with no acceptance of the friend request in sight. Suddenly Elisabeth had another thought of how to make contact with the mysterious Madame Benoit. She would send her a personal message to introduce herself and ask if the woman in France had known her son Christian twenty years ago. Of course she couldn't run the risk of going into too much detail, just in case it wasn't the same woman as the one who had written the letter, so she kept her carefully worded message brief and polite.

Dear Mme Benoit
Please forgive the intrusion. I see your maiden name was Rook and I am writing to ask if you knew my son Christian Hambridge? He went to Hanford College in 1996.

Sadly he passed away recently and I was sorting through some of his old paperwork when I came across your name. I've been trying to locate as many of his old friends as possible to let you know about his FriendsBag memorial page. If you knew him then maybe you'd like to follow the page. If you didn't know him, then please accept my sincerest apologies for having troubled you
Elisabeth Hambridge (Mrs)

Chapter 2

Another twenty-four hours had passed and still Elisabeth waited for a reply from Charlotte. She was growing increasingly frustrated and could not understand why the young Madame Benoit had not responded. Her initial surge of excitement and optimism had begun to fade. Elisabeth believed that if she had found the right person then she would have heard back from her by now. She reluctantly clicked open another browsing window on her laptop and began a new search; resigning herself to the fact that her first attempt to find the elusive mother of Christian's child had failed.

Unwilling to be deterred by the setback, the calm and collected Elisabeth began to look at the search from another angle. 'Maybe she calls herself Charlie or Lottie instead,' thought Elisabeth with renewed hope. She began by entering a new search term, featuring all the possible abbreviations of Charlotte's name she could think of. Unfortunately the same old list of familiar results kept appearing.

Eventually, after hours of fruitless searching, Elisabeth reluctantly began to accept defeat. It had been a long day and she was no closer to tracking down the mysterious woman who had written the letter. She rubbed her tired eyes and let out a long loud yawn before going back to the kitchen to make yet another cafetiere of coffee. As she stood waiting for the kettle to boil, Elisabeth heard the sudden sound of a beep come from her laptop in the study. She skipped back into the room and saw that she had a FriendsBag personal message. Excitedly Elisabeth clicked on the link to open it up. It was the eagerly awaited reply from Charlotte Benoit.

Hello Mrs Hambridge.
Thank you for your message. Yes I knew someone called
Christian Hambridge at college. He was there studying

engineering when I was doing my A levels in Art, English and French.

'Hammers' was always such a lovely and popular guy. I was very upset to hear the sad news about his death out of the blue like that. Please accept my condolences. Thank you for letting me know about his memorial page.

Best regards
Charlotte Benoit

Elisabeth was delighted to discover she had at least found the right woman, but she was bitterly disappointed that there was no acknowledgment anywhere in the returning message about Charlotte's relationship with Christian twenty years before, and absolutely no mention of a baby.

#

Timeline: Wednesday 8th June 2016, 20:30hrs

Charlotte's non-committal reply had weighed heavily on Elisabeth's mind all evening. She felt sure that she had found the right woman; after all she had referred to her son with his old school nickname, Hammers. Also, what was the possibility that anyone else with the uncommon first name of Charlotte would have been at college in Hanford at the same time as Christian? Elisabeth thought she simply had to be the same woman as the one who wrote the letter.

Despite the overwhelming temptation to reply with an intrusive list of questions about Charlotte's presumptive teenage pregnancy, the ever-pragmatic Elisabeth realised she would have to take a hold of her own emotions and handle the situation very carefully to avoid alienating the young woman. She would have to be patient. 'Swan Blake' would never allow herself to wallow in the negativity and disappointment that there was no mention of a baby in the FriendsBag message. Instead she would choose to be encouraged by the reply. The calm and poised Elisabeth would take a deep breath and calmly regard this initial response as a positive thing. Now that contact with the elusive Charlotte had been established, it would be the beginning of the adventure and a strong foundation to build upon.

Elisabeth methodically replayed all of the past few days' activities in her head and mentally placed herself in the young woman's shoes; to try to view everything from another perspective. It was then she came to understand that Charlotte had probably been startled by the message out of the blue; she could even have been upset by the unexpected news of Christian's death. Elisabeth assumed that the young woman had more than likely built a whole new life for herself since her days as a student at Hanford College. Maybe no one knew about Charlotte's relationship with Christian. Dredging up a twenty-year-old secret lover from a person's past like that could take a few days to come to terms with, if ever. It was therefore perfectly understandable why there had been a delay in her reply. It must have been quite a shock for the young woman.

'But why hasn't Charlotte mentioned anything at all about her own son or daughter?' a nagging doubt pecked at Elisabeth's brain.

'Why was she being so detached and matter-of-fact in her reply? The grieving woman's calm composure slowly evaporated in the over-bearing heat of emotion that began to swirl inside her mind.

'That's not the sort of response I would expect from the mother of Christian's baby. I'd have thought that she would have at least been a little curious to find out more about her child's grandmother.' Elisabeth's heart began to quicken as she felt a sudden surge of blood pump through her veins.

'Did she even have the child?'

The serene and understanding Swan Blake would soon take flight; she would no longer remain calm. Anger raged through Elisabeth's body at the dreadful thought that hadn't crossed her mind until now. Maybe Charlotte had not gone through with the pregnancy all those years ago.

"Oh God, no!" she gasped at the realisation that her fleeting chance of being a grandmother could have been cruelly snatched away from her.

Elisabeth carried her laptop and Charlotte's letter into the lounge. She had spent all day and most of the evening sitting at the desk in her study and she now felt stiffness creep across her neck and shoulders. She opened a bottle of brandy and poured a large comforting glug into the remnants of coffee in her china mug. Elisabeth gulped down the warming liquid and promptly poured another large measure. The grieving mother sat down on one of the leather sofas in her lounge and opened up Charlotte's letter again. She read through the desperate words that had been written by a confused and upset teenager twenty years before, as a salty tear trickled down her cheek.

"Oh, Christian, why didn't you know about this?" cried Elisabeth, as she raised her head up to gaze at the ceiling.

"Things would have been so different if only your father and I had have known." More tears flowed down her tired face as she took another gulp of Brandy and lifted the lid of her laptop open. Elisabeth logged on to FriendsBag again and opened up Charlotte's profile. She was still unable to gain any more information from the listing as, even though Charlotte had replied to her personal message, her friend request had still not been accepted.

A couple more brandies later, Elisabeth had summoned up enough courage to prompt Charlotte into action with a short and friendly returning message.

Hi Charlotte.
By the way, I just wondered if you received my friend
request?
Elisabeth :)

Elisabeth was beginning to get a little impatient and the alcohol started to kick her imagination into overdrive.

'Why wouldn't you accept a friend request from your child's grandmother straight away? Why would you need to be prompted?' she asked sadly.

'Oh no, maybe I'm coming across as a bit of a stalker or something,' she mused. The brandies were beginning to take affect and Elisabeth allowed a small smile to flicker across her face. The silly idea that anyone would ever accuse the level-headed Elisabeth Hambridge of being so infatuated was quite amusing to her.

Suddenly, another thought crossed her alcohol charged mind; a darker more evil scenario that could only be imagined after all other outcomes had been thoroughly examined. Maybe Charlotte's baby had been a sham. Had the desperate student lied in a simple attempt to trap the eligible Christian Hambridge all those years ago? The grieving mother's sadness slowly began to turn to brooding anger. She knew it wasn't unusual for young women to ensnare suitable men after one night stands. During her time serving as cabin crew, the young Liz Blake had often known other flight attendants cruelly use invented pregnancies to trick airline officers into relationships or marriage.

"Have you forgotten that Christian was one of your conquests?" slurred Elisabeth as she stared accusingly at Charlotte's profile photograph.

"Is that why you're ignoring me now? You've forgotten who you tried it on with all those years ago haven't you, you little strumpet."

Christian had been a popular young man with an assured future ahead of him. He had once dreamed of becoming an architect and studied design engineering at Hanford College. But it was a well-known fact that he was the son of the town's most successful estate agent, and all of his friends knew that he would one day take over the family business and inherit his father's fortune.

"You dirty little tramp trying to hook my lovely innocent boy with your lies," raged Elisabeth as she began to recite Charlotte's reply.

"Yes I knew someone called Christian Hambridge at college," the scornful woman continued to mock Charlotte's message by reading aloud in a young girlish voice.

"You only remember *someone* called Christian, not the man called Christian who fathered your child then?" she repeated incredulously.

"I was doing my A levels in Art, English and French," she continued with a childish sing-song tone.

"Well whoopi doo for you," chided Elisabeth as she poured more brandy into her china mug.

"What you mean is you came crawling out of your council estate without a bean to your name and thought you'd sink your chavvy dirty fingernails into my beautiful son and his golden future didn't you?" Tears began to stream down the grieving mother's hot cheeks.

"And then, next thing we know, you've only gone and managed to get yourself pregnant by the richest, best looking boy in the whole college," slurred Elisabeth sarcastically as she took another gulp of brandy.

"You probably tried that old chestnut on with so many of the other lads in your year that you can't even remember the lies you wrote to Christian, you filthy little gold-digging whore."

Elisabeth angrily slammed the lid of her laptop shut and slid it onto a coffee table in front of the sofa. The upset woman angrily picked up Charlotte's letter and furiously screwed it into a tight ball, before throwing it into a waste paper basket in the corner of the living room.

"Well, goodbye to bad rubbish," she cried, before slumping back down onto the sofa. Elisabeth swallowed the final dregs of brandy in her mug, before drifting off into a tearful and drunken restless sleep.

#

Timeline: Thursday 9th June 2016, 08:00hrs

At eight o'clock in the morning Elisabeth was rudely awoken by the sound of the postman roughly pushing a bundle of junk mail into the letter box on the gate at the end of her drive. The heavy rap of the metal lid on the box had startled a small puppy in the front garden of a neighbouring house. His repetitive yapping quickly became an unwelcome audible intrusion. Slowly Elisabeth opened her sore eyes and realised she was still lying down on the settee. Her head was propped awkwardly against a cushion and her right arm was feeling numb from where it had been raised above her head for most of the night. Slowly she sat up and began to shake her hand to try and restore the circulation to her arm with a stinging flow of pins and needles. Her neck was stiff and she had a very dry mouth. Elisabeth rubbed her fingers and palms of her hands over her tired face as she felt a surging headache begin to throb in her temples. She stood up unsteadily from the sofa and immediately felt dizzy; as if her brain had been shaken loose inside her skull. Elisabeth looked down to see her skirt and blouse were crumpled from where she had slept in her clothes. Her tights were snagged and she could feel her bra had become twisted and now uncomfortably bit in to the skin beneath her bust.

'God, how much did I drink last night?' she thought, as she caught sight of her laptop next to the half empty brandy bottle on the coffee table in front of her. She slowly made her way upstairs to her en-suite bathroom.

The invigorating zest of lemon hair shampoo helped to soften the edges of Elisabeth's hangover. She breathed in the heady aroma as she stood in the shower beneath the massaging jets of water. She tried to piece together her thoughts from the previous evening; to try and make sense of how she felt about Charlotte's cordial reply. A couple of Paracetamol tablets began to quell Elisabeth's foggy headache as, in the sober light of day, she decided there could only be three possible scenarios to explain Charlotte's failure to mention her child. Either Charlotte had been a silly young girl who had tried it on twenty years ago and attempted to trap the eligible young Christian Hambridge with a wicked lie, or she really had been pregnant and sadly lost the baby. Alternatively she could have given birth to the child and re-built her life with no one knowing anything about the whole sorry episode. Maybe she had given up the baby for adoption? That outcome would be the most difficult to accept, as Elisabeth knew if Charlotte was unwilling to speak about the pregnancy mentioned in the twenty-year-old letter, she would have no way of tracing where her grandchild was. The gracious Swan Blake would have to use all of her calming powers of persuasion to coax the reluctant young woman to come forward with any information.

Refreshed by her shower, Elisabeth dried her hair and got dressed ready for the day ahead. A soft veneer of carefully applied make-up belied how tired and washed out she was really feeling. Her headache was now just a dull sensation at the front of her forehead but it was nothing that a couple of slices of wholemeal toast and a glass of chilled freshly squeezed orange juice couldn't fix.

After breakfast Elisabeth made a fresh pot of coffee and carried it through to the study. She opened up her laptop to review a list of emails waiting in her inbox. Nothing seemed to need her immediate attention, so that left her free to spend the morning focussing on the more important issue at hand; establishing just what had happened to her grandchild.

With renewed vigour Elisabeth logged onto her FriendsBag account and immediately noticed Charlotte had accepted her friend request. A warm glow of excitement fluttered through Elisabeth's heart as she also saw that the young woman had sent her another personal message.

Hello Elisabeth.

Thank you for your friend request. I'm very sorry it took so long for me to accept it but I have to be extremely careful about whom I have as friends here on FriendsBag. My old account was completely hijacked at the beginning of the year by a hacker who managed to trick me into befriending them. I lost everything on that profile, contacts, photos, the lot! Since then I've had a terrible time having to start a whole new profile from scratch and it has made me very wary about befriending people on here that I don't know.

Anyway, as I know you're Hammers' Mother, I hope we can keep in touch. I really was very fond of your son.

Warmest regards
Charlotte x

Elisabeth filled her china mug with more coffee and re-read Charlotte's friendly message. She was encouraged by the fact that the young woman had accepted her friend request and the undertone suggested she wanted to keep in contact. The grieving mother was beginning to feel a little ashamed that she had been so quick to judge her new friend so badly and she had allowed her drunken imagination to run away with her the night before. Charlotte appeared to have a perfectly legitimate reason for being so hesitant in accepting Elisabeth's friend request. She had obviously suffered a bad online experience and needed to be on her guard. The old woman was elated that her perseverance had paid off and she secretly hoped that her actions hadn't made her appear to be too much of a stalker. Maybe, in time, Elisabeth would have an opportunity to broach the subject of what was written in the letter, to once and for all establish if she really had a grandchild.

#

Timeline: Thursday 9th June 2016, 14:00hrs

Diana Hambridge sat behind a desk in her large open plan office. She was an attractive yet very thin young woman with long dark brown hair that hung loosely around her bony shoulders. Diana had always been slim, but the stress of coping with her recent bereavement had begun to leave its mark; her once petite and delicate features were now gaunt and pale. She had been a senior negotiator at Thomas Hambridge & Son for the past five years. Following her husband's death six months previously, the young businesswoman had inherited great responsibility when she had agreed to take on the mantle as Managing Director. Diana fully understood the enormity of the challenge that lay ahead as Thomas and Christian Hambridge would be difficult acts to follow. She had only recently returned to full-time work following compassionate leave, but the stress of being at the helm was secretly beginning to take its toll. Unfortunately she could no longer afford the luxury of self-pity, as the grieving widow knew the livelihoods of a dozen other people employed by the company depended solely on her ability to keep the estate agency running efficiently.

She had spent the whole morning catching up on a mountainous pile of paperwork and replying to a seemingly never-ending list of impatient emails and telephone calls. By lunchtime the pace of enquiries had begun to slow and Diana was able to take a short break. She picked up her mobile phone and went to the staff room to make a cup of tea. As she waited for the kettle to boil Diana idly logged onto FriendsBag to check for any new personal messages. A notification in her

25

newsfeed said her Mother-in-Law had become friends with a woman called Charlotte Benoit.

'I'm glad the old biddy is starting to make new friends,' thought Diana as she poured boiling water into a mug.

'It must be difficult for someone nearing seventy to meet new people,' she mused as she dunked and swirled a tea bag around the cup with a plastic teaspoon.

'It's probably just what Elisabeth needs to take her mind off the tragedy of losing Tom and Christian.'

#

Elisabeth sat fidgeting at the leather-clad desk in her home study. She was finding it difficult to contain her overwhelming desire to bombard Charlotte with a barrage of interrogation. She had so many questions that needed to be answered, but the grieving mother knew Christian's illegitimate child would be a highly sensitive subject that would require delicate handling.

'I can't just go barging in and ask hey, did you have my son's baby nearly twenty years ago?' lamented Elisabeth. She was afraid such an approach would upset the girl and lead to her ending the fragile online friendship quicker than it had started. The frustrated old woman realised she would have to be extremely patient. Until she had the opportunity to talk to Charlotte properly and gain her trust, the only avenue open to her was to see what information she could gain from her new friend's limited FriendsBag profile.

Elisabeth trawled through Charlotte's page, searching for photographs and information about any children; any crumb of evidence that she had given birth to Christian's baby. But it was obvious the profile was relatively new; it had only a few recent images within its short timeline and brief personal information.

'Damn that bloody hacker,' thought Elisabeth. She knew Charlotte's original profile would have made it much easier for her to find out what she wanted to know. There would have been so much more information for her to go on. If only she had received the letter a few months earlier; before Charlotte had been forced to create a new FriendsBag profile.

Elisabeth felt a little uneasy as her cursor hovered over the tab to open up Charlotte's friends' list. Deep down she believed delving through a stranger's profile was a bit like snooping, if not a little stalkerish. However, any doubts she had about the ethics of nosiness were quickly dispelled as she convinced herself that she was perfectly justified in exploring every facet of information on the young woman's profile.

'Wouldn't Charlotte have blocked my access anyway if she didn't want me to see her friends' list?' thought Elisabeth. Given the possibility that she could be about to find a precious connection to her only grandchild, Elisabeth took in a deep breath and clicked the button. In the middle of a dozen names she spotted a link to the profile page of a young man called Luke Benoit.

'Could that be Charlotte's son?' she gasped excitedly.

'My grandson?'

Elisabeth's heart throbbed loudly in her chest; the palpitations sent a pounding beat of blood storming through her brain. She took a long drink of strong coffee to quell her nerves and hesitantly clicked on the link to open up Luke's page. Immediately the smiling face of a good-looking eighteen-year-old boy came into view. The privacy settings were set to public and she was able to access all of the information within the profile.

Luke was an extremely popular and well-loved young man. The page had hundreds of followers and it was filled with dozens of messages written in French with heart shaped emojis. Elisabeth had a rudimentary knowledge of the language from her days as cabin crew, but she decided to skip reading the text; it would be much more fun to look through the lad's photo albums first.

Most of the pictures featured a sun-tanned Luke with groups of friends enjoying camping trips, racing speedboats, riding motorbikes, bungee-jumping and skiing adventures. He was a handsome boy; an adrenaline junkie with a loyal bevy of beautiful young girls in his friends' list.

'An action man just like Christian was at that age,' thought Elisabeth, as an unexpected tear of pride welled in her eye.

27

She turned her attention to the words written by Luke's friends on his timeline. Elisabeth was bemused that many of them seemed to be lamenting the passing of a much loved friend. She needed to check that what she thought she was reading was accurate. Unsure of her own translation skills she copied and pasted some of the text into an online language converter. She felt a hot surge of adrenaline burst through her heart as the unwelcome words appeared on the screen. Elisabeth's worst fears were confirmed; Luke Benoit had tragically died in a skiing accident a year previously in the French Alps; on his eighteenth birthday.

Shocked by the unexpected discovery, Elisabeth slumped forward over the desk and began to cry uncontrollably. Her fleeting chance to become a grandmother had been cruelly snatched away from her. She would never be able to hold that precious piece of Christian in her arms. She would never be able to see his sparkly eyes and cheeky face smiling back at her. The grieving grandmother's hope of kindling any relationship with her teenage grandson had been firmly crushed; her dreams were in tatters with the stinging realisation that all three generations of the Hambridge men were now gone.

"Oh Charlotte," whispered Elisabeth.

"You poor woman," she murmured with a dull ache of guilt in her heart. The death of Charlotte's child was a tragic fourth scenario she had not envisaged in the shower that morning. Elisabeth realised that she had practically hounded the young woman for the past few days and her mention of Christian's name had probably whipped up a whole hurricane of emotion for everyone involved.

"God I've been so bloody selfish," she thought.

Elisabeth noticed her family album was perched on top of the mahogany bureau next to her desk; she reached over to pick it up and consoled herself within the laminated sleeves of photographs and mementoes. She needed time to think about how best to handle the situation. Elisabeth slowly turned the pages in the album and came to the final entry; a newspaper cutting from the Hanford Recorder that featured an article about Christian's funeral. It was then the lamenting mother decided that the heavy leather-bound book of memories should include a complete history of her brood; it should be updated to include every chapter of the Hambridge family story. If Luke Benoit was Christian's son, then Elisabeth was determined her grandson would be given his rightful place in the final episode.

She spent the rest of the afternoon trawling the internet for more information; printing off photographs of Luke, translating and reading through various articles that reported his untimely death. Dozens of memorial notices had appeared in a French newspaper, all reflecting how much the young man would be missed.

Luke had been a popular teenager with a bright outlook on life and a promising future. He was the only son of a couple of university lecturers and had lived in the south of France with his parents Charlotte and Eric Benoit. Despite his academic upbringing, the young thrill-seeker had a passion for adventure sports and had been a keen snowboarder. His family and friends had gone on a short break to the French Alps to celebrate the young man's eighteenth birthday. On the first day of the skiing holiday, a trip to go off-piste and race his new snowmobile had ended in tragedy. Luke and his fellow adrenaline junkies had ignored all warnings that the weather conditions were extremely dangerous that day. The previous night's snowfall had not compacted sufficiently and the vibrations from their racing engines had created an avalanche. In one fatal minute, Luke's life had ended beneath a crushing blanket of asphyxiating ice and rocks.

Elisabeth printed off every small piece of information that she could find; carefully collating the sheets of paper into chronological order. It was then she understood the reason behind Charlotte's guarded attitude and initial hesitance in accepting her friend request.

If Luke Benoit had been Charlotte's secret illegitimate son, then her failure to mention him to his biological grandmother could be totally understandable. After all, the poor woman had effectively been abandoned by the father of her child almost two decades ago; Charlotte had then lost her son in a tragic snowmobile accident and had unwittingly become the victim of an online hacker. Then, quite out of the blue, she had been contacted by a total stranger who appeared to be Luke's

29

estranged stalking grandmother. On top of coping with the death of her beloved son, stirring up the memory of Luke's biological father had probably been too much pain for the young woman to bear. Additionally Elisabeth had no idea whether or not Charlotte's husband, Eric Benoit, knew any details about the conception of his wife's baby.

"Oh Charlotte, you poor thing," whispered Elisabeth as she clipped her print-outs into a cellophane wallet at the back of the Hambridge family photo album. Elisabeth knew exactly how the young woman would be feeling and she could fully empathise with such heart-wrenching loss. The remorseful emptiness felt after the death of any loved one was almost impossible to cope with; but she knew that heartache could not be compared with the all-consuming pain of losing one's own child. Elisabeth began to cry again. The grief-stricken mother's sadness had been secretly compounded. Not only had she lost her loving husband and son, but also an innocent grandchild that she hadn't even known existed.

It was obvious to Elisabeth that during the past twenty years Charlotte had successfully built a new life for herself in France with Eric Benoit. The newspaper articles only ever mentioned the French couple as being the tragic teenager's parents. There was no mention of Luke's biological father. It seemed no one else knew about the one night stand with Christian Hambridge and it had become an old buried secret. Elisabeth desperately needed to speak to Charlotte, but the last thing the old woman wanted was to cause Charlotte any more upset by raking up the past. However, the overpowering compulsion to find out more about her grandson was like an itch that needed to be scratched. She would have to summon her inner Swan Blake to find a way of diplomatically broaching the subject with enough sensitivity and compassion to avoid completely alienating her new friend.

Chapter 3

The following day Diana Hambridge drove her bright red Mini through the open wrought iron gates onto the gravelled driveway in front of Elisabeth's house. She was a punctual woman of habit and always arrived promptly at two o'clock every Friday afternoon to take her mother-in-law shopping. Diana leaned across to the passenger seat of her car and opened up her briefcase. Inside was a large bunch of keys that had belonged to Christian. The collected pieces of metal charted all aspects of her husband's life. They included his house keys and the ones for his cars, motorcycles, shop, office and safe; along with a set for his parents' house and a small electronic remote control box to operate the wrought iron gated access. A small leather key fob featuring the Isle of Man flag hung from the ring. It was a memento from the Hambridge's trip to watch the TT motorcycling a couple of years previously. Diana smiled at the memory of the short holiday and how she had proudly watched her husband valiantly cross the finishing line on Mad Sunday. She quickly searched through the clunky bunch of metal and found the key to unlock Elisabeth's front door.

Diana got out of her car, walked to the entrance and let herself into the house. She announced her arrival with a cheery 'hello' and made her way towards the kitchen. The young woman filled the kettle with water and began to make a pot of tea. Such informality was a comfortable arrangement for Elisabeth, as she knew her daughter-in-law would always be able to gain access to the house in the case of an emergency. Helping Elisabeth was a convenient coping mechanism for Diana, as their weekly shopping trips gave both women an unbridled opportunity to talk about Christian for endless hours. The young widow's friends positively encouraged her to talk about anything other than her late husband and they always avoided any subject remotely connected to motorcycling; whereas Diana's mother-in-law was more than happy to indulge. The two women would frequently enjoy a pre-shopping cup of tea whilst burying themselves in their memories of Christian.

"Hello Diana," said Elisabeth as she walked into the kitchen and gave her daughter-in-law a warm hug.

"Hello Mother. How has your week been?" Elisabeth was slightly startled by the innocent question, as she realised she could not begin to explain any of the emotional roller-coaster trip she had been on during the past few days. She could not bring herself to mention anything about Charlotte's letter and her newly discovered grandson; that would surely be too much pain for her grieving daughter-in-law to bear.

"I noticed you're making some new friends on FriendsBag," continued Diana as she poured hot water into a china tea pot.

"Oh, yes," said Elisabeth hesitantly.

"Well, you know, I thought it was about time I got on with life," she continued. Diana smiled warmly; she was pleased that the old lady was beginning to move on. Making new friends online would be a good place to start. Elisabeth walked back out of the kitchen, into the marble hallway and made her way towards the downstairs cloakroom.

Diana placed the pot of tea, two china cups and a milk jug onto a round floral tray and carried them through to the study. She carefully placed the tray on top of the bureau and sat down on one of the leather swivel chairs as she waited for Elisabeth to return. The young woman noticed the lid of Elisabeth's laptop was still open and she glanced at the screen. A page from an ancestry search website was still open; a small online form had been partly completed with the Hambridge family's details. Intrigued by the discovery, Diana turned the laptop to face her and clicked on another open tab in the browser bar. That page opened up a map of the south of France. Suddenly she heard the lavatory flush and the gushing sound of water from the tap in the downstairs cloakroom. She knew Elisabeth would soon return to the study, so she quickly clicked back to the ancestry page and returned the lap top to its former position on the desk.

"Are you thinking of creating a family tree?" asked Diana casually, as her mother-in-law walked into the study. A slight wave of panic arose in Elisabeth's chest. How could her daughter-in-law possibly know anything about that?

"What do you mean?" she asked, flustered by the unexpected question.

"It's just that I noticed you've been filling in an online ancestry form," replied Diana, giving a cursory nod towards the open laptop.

"I'd be happy to help you do the research if you like."

"Oh that," replied Elisabeth with a small nervous laugh, as she desperately searched through her brain for a reasonable explanation.

"You know what those annoying things are like on websites," she said, stalling for time to regain her composure.

"You go to click on something, the screen jumps, then hey presto an advert has bounced across the screen and before you know it you're visiting a site you never intended to see." Elisabeth continued dismissively, as she sharply pulled her laptop towards her.

"So why did you start to fill in the form?" smiled Diana, a little surprised by Elisabeth's curt response and defensive move.

"Well, just for a silly moment I thought I'd give it a go and see what this ancestry thing is all about, and then you arrived and I forgot all about it." Elisabeth was clearly agitated and protectively closed the lid of her laptop, pushing it towards the back of the desk. She could not run the risk of her daughter-in-law finding out about Christian's illegitimate child just yet.

"It's okay, I understand," soothed Diana as she poured steaming hot tea into the two china cups.

'I very much doubt that,' thought Elisabeth as she settled back into her swivel chair, relieved that she had managed to put the young woman off the scent for now.

Diana began to reminisce about the time she had met and fallen in love with Christian. Her heart had always known he was the one for her from the first moment they set eyes on each other at the local pub quiz night. Elisabeth sat and nodded, quietly sipping her tea, as Diana confessed to bitterly regretting she had never been able to get pregnant and Elisabeth had been denied grandchildren. With both of the Hambridge men gone, it was perfectly understandable if her grieving mother-in-law

33

wanted to trace her ancestry and connect with other members of the family.

"There's no need to get all defensive about tracking down the Hambridge roots you know. I guess a wealthy widow like you needs to make sure your Will is in order; after all you may have a long-lost niece or nephew out there somewhere," said Diana helpfully.

"Anyway, Mother, it might be fun to see if there are any skeletons in the family tree anywhere." The young woman laughed, totally oblivious to the irony in her off-the-cuff remark.

Elisabeth forced a smile to hide her fear of Christian's secret being unveiled, as the two women finished their tea before heading out to the supermarket.

#

Timeline: Friday 10th June 2016, 21:30hrs

It had been an emotionally exhausting week for Elisabeth Hambridge and she had decided to go to bed early. The sorrowful woman lay propped up against a couple of large feather pillows at the centre of her king size bed, and idly flicked through a long list of emails on her laptop. She desperately needed something to stop her from thinking about the tragic catalogue of events that had recently unfolded. She had convinced herself that her son had fathered Charlotte's child all those years ago, a child she would never meet. Elisabeth could not believe how a twenty-year-old delayed letter had stirred up such a hornets' nest of burning questions that would now remain unanswered. She had reluctantly accepted that her grandson was dead and there was little to be gained in pursuing Charlotte. Luke's biological father had obviously been kept a secret from the world. Whether or not Eric Benoit knew was another matter so, apart from simply opening up old wounds, the revelation could potentially ruin the young woman's marriage.

Elisabeth idly signed into her FriendsBag profile to catch up on the daily messages of support posted by well meaning friends in her newsfeed. Thought provoking memes, funny photographs and videos of cats in amusing predicaments were interspersed with positive messages of love and encouragement for the grieving mother. Suddenly, Elisabeth noticed Charlotte's name pop up in a chat window. Intrigued by the unexpected opportunity, she could not resist the urge to enter into an online conversation with her new friend. She sat up on the bed and repositioned herself on the pillows; if Charlotte was willing to talk then she could be in for a long night. The two women exchanged pleasantries and made polite conversation comparing the British weather with the climate on the French Riviera. Before long Elisabeth felt comfortable enough to carefully broach the subject of children.

"I did have a son," wrote Charlotte.

"But he died last year." Elisabeth felt a fat salty tear run down her face at the realisation of how difficult those words must have been for the young woman to write.

"I don't know if Christian ever told you that we actually had a bit of a thing at college once?" she continued. A sudden surge of adrenaline shot through Elisabeth's chest. Was this going to be the confirmation that Luke had indeed been her grandchild? Was she prepared for a full confession direct from the horse's mouth?

Charlotte slowly explained that her liaison with Christian Hambridge had been a one night stand after a college disco. The evening had ended in fumbled hurried sex in her parents' front room. The young woman continued to say she had a boyfriend at the time called Eric Benoit. He was a foreign exchange student who had visited England a year earlier. Eric had returned to France but kept in contact with Charlotte. Over the months their long-distance friendship had blossomed and she realised that she had fallen in love with the Frenchman. At the college May Ball she had felt alone and jealous as she watched all the other young students come together at the end of the night for a slow smooch. As the other teenagers awkwardly groped each other on the dance floor to Seal's Kiss From A Rose, she realised that all she had was a handful of letters from her boyfriend who lived a thousand miles away.

Christian had seen Charlotte tearfully watching the other couples enjoy their hot sweaty embraces on the dance floor. He had been a true gentleman and had comforted the upset and lonely young girl at the bar. She admitted she was flattered that he had given her any attention at all as she had been a bit of an ugly duckling. Charlotte explained that when she was a teenager puberty had not been kind to her. She had suffered with bad acne and her horn-rimmed National Health spectacles had made her the butt of many students' jokes. When Christian approached her to ask her to dance she had been totally swept along by the moment. Elisabeth felt tears of pride well up in her tired eyes. Her son had been such a nice young lad; always the first to help a friend in need or come to the aid of a damsel in distress.

Charlotte continued her account of that eventful night. She admitted that by the time Christian walked her home at the end of the evening she knew he had a beer-goggled view of the world. Six pints of lager had more than likely dulled his senses. Why else would he have shown an interest in her? She knew she should have stopped herself; she realised it was her fault. He was drunk and she had led him on. She knew that it had been wrong to take advantage of him, but the lonely lovesick teenager had desperately needed to feel the heat of a man that night.

Charlotte admitted her regretful one night stand with Christian had been a foolish mistake and she had tried to move on and forget the indiscretion. However, a few weeks later the positive result of her pregnancy test changed everything. Charlotte had been a virgin before sleeping with Christian and she was shocked to discover that she had become pregnant during her first time of having sex. A month later, as college finished for the summer, she had tried to contact Christian but his course had ended earlier than hers and he was no longer around. She understood that he was probably trying to avoid her as he was more than likely embarrassed and regretted the intoxicated liaison even more than she did. Charlotte had felt ashamed. The scared teenager didn't have the nerve to visit Christian's parents' house; she could not face the prospect of turning up unannounced to explain the situation. The

Hambridges were a well-known respectable family; Christian was an eligible young man with a bright future and fortune ahead of him. No one would have believed the claims of the spotty-faced bespectacled girl from the Lye Heath council estate. Charlotte simply couldn't summon up enough courage to stand on the imposing doorstep of the Clover Croft mansion and tell Christian's family the embarrassing news. Writing the letter seemed to be the least confrontational course of action. Christian could then choose whether to do the decent thing or not.

Charlotte said that she had never heard back from Christian and that she assumed it was because he wanted to forget all about their drunken fling. She knew most of the girls at college were in love with him and that he could have had his pick of any woman he wanted. Why would he want to become a laughing stock and lumber himself with the college joke? After all, she knew that he had only drunkenly slept with her out of pity.

Elisabeth sat in bed slowly shaking her head as she read Charlotte's heartbreaking words. If only she had known back then, if only that damned letter had arrived in time. Of course Christian would have done the right thing; he would have stood by the girl. Yes Thomas and Elisabeth would have erupted in a blazing row; yes they would have probably made empty threats of totally disowning their careless son, but the family would have still stood by the girl. This momentous revelation was too much for the grieving grandmother to read; her head ached and her eyes were stinging with tears. The two women agreed that if they were going to continue the conversation it would be better done via a video link instead. Elisabeth opened up her video calling app and waited for Charlotte's face to appear on the screen.

"Bonsoir Elisabeth." Charlotte's voice was softly spoken with the warm hue of a slight French accent. The young woman had an attractive face; her hair was pulled into an elegant chignon that accentuated her high cheekbones. She wore an understated cream coloured blouse with a single string pearl necklace. She was every inch the epitome of an elegant French lady. Behind her was a backdrop of gold Fleur de Lys wallpaper with matching floral curtains; typical of a chic French boudoir.

"Hello," replied Elisabeth trying to stifle a tear. Charlotte couldn't help but notice that the older woman's eyes were red and puffy from crying.

Charlotte continued to explain how a couple of days after posting the letter she had gone to the library on the last day of term. She had waited all afternoon and Christian hadn't shown up. She had assumed that he didn't want to have anything to do with her or the child, and the pregnant teenager had panicked. Soon afterwards Charlotte left England and went to live in France with Eric, the French exchange student. Convincing her boyfriend that the baby was his had been easy; he knew his girlfriend had been a virgin and he had no reason to suspect that wasn't still the case. He totally believed that he was her first lover and that he was the father of the child. They married in the autumn, the unwitting Eric always believing that Luke was his own premature son.

"Oh my God, it must have been so very difficult for you to cope with such a thing. At such a young age too," said Elisabeth warmly. Charlotte agreed that she had at first bitterly regretted her one night stand with Christian, but over the years, as Luke had grown into such a beautiful young man, she had felt blessed to have him in her life. Charlotte's voice began to waver as she brushed back a small tear. She began to explain more about how Elisabeth's grandson had tragically met his untimely death.

Eric Benoit had been a wonderfully doting father and he blamed himself for Luke's addiction to adrenaline fuelled activities. Eric was a bookish university lecturer and had never taken part in dangerous sports, but he had been keen to encourage Luke's passion for adventure. Luke had displayed a natural talent for motorcycling and he was a keen amateur racer. Eric had bought his son a surprise eighteenth birthday gift of a snowmobile that arrived at the Benoit home the day before the family's annual skiing trip. Charlotte explained how Luke couldn't wait to share his excitement of riding the new machine with his friends on the first morning of their holiday. He rode it out into the mountains, racing across pistes and valleys, cutting through the powdery soft blanket of snow; blissfully unaware of the fatal consequences that would follow.

Elisabeth's heart was torn apart by the bombshell confession. Luke had so clearly inherited Christian's thrill-seeker genes; but it seemed that his zest for danger had been instrumental in his death. She knew daredevil adrenaline flowed through the Hambridge DNA; her own son had been just the same. Poor Eric Benoit had wrongly blamed himself for supporting the young lad's adventurous spirit, but it was clear to the grieving grandmother that Luke's passion for dangerous sports had not been due solely to Eric's encouragement. The studious academic could never be spared his misery; he could never be told the truth about Luke's paternity. Eric could never know about his wife's deception. Such a guilty secret that he wasn't Luke's biological father would surely destroy the couple's nineteen-year marriage.

Elisabeth slowly began to understand Charlotte's initial reluctance to accept her friend request and why she hadn't exactly been willing to come forward and engage in conversation. It was only because of that damned letter from two decades ago that Elisabeth knew her grandson and his mother existed. The woman felt a small knot of guilt twitch in her stomach as she realised she had mercilessly hunted down Charlotte, selfishly pursued her and pushed her into talking about Luke; all of which had driven the emotional young woman to tearfully confess her secret. Elisabeth decided that Charlotte had suffered enough following Luke's death, without having her marriage to Eric ruined into the bargain. She recognised that the poor woman must now be living in constant fear of her husband finding out the truth; all because of that desperate letter written by a scared teenager twenty years before.

Even though Elisabeth longed to shout the news of her grandchild from the rooftops, the grieving grandmother understood exactly what would be at stake for Charlotte should anyone ever find out who Luke's biological father was. She felt her heart would burst with pride that Luke had been so like Christian, but she knew she could never tell anyone about her beautiful grandson. Reluctantly Elisabeth agreed to be sworn to secrecy, as she knew she had another reason to promise never to reveal that Luke was Christian's son; she needed to protect Diana and the Hambridge family's reputation from the scandalous truth.

Elizabeth realised she had become firmly entangled in Charlotte's deception and she would never be able to get the idea of her grandson out of her head. Luke had been a piece of Christian, his flesh and blood, and the grief-stricken woman was determined she would never lose her precious connection to him.

Chapter 4

Thursday 23 June 2016, 13:30hrs –
Two Weeks Later.

Over the weeks that passed Elisabeth and Charlotte engaged in daily online messaging and chats. The elderly widow was always delighted to see her friend's smiling face appear in her video call window. She was encouraged that Charlotte appeared to be more relaxed each time they spoke, as the once guarded young woman began to open up and share more details about her life in France.

The Benoit family lived in a comfortable villa in a small hamlet on the outskirts of Cannes. Their house had once been the village bakery and flour mill that had been abandoned by a Jewish family during the Second World War. Eric was a history lecturer who held classes at the area's leading university and colleges; most of his time was spent travelling between Nice and Cannes. Charlotte had been a freelance English teacher but she had tired of her hectic work schedule and seemingly endless commuting between schools. In 2005 she decided to address her work life balance. Buying and renovating the old bakery had given her a new project to focus on. Over the years Charlotte had lovingly converted the run-down honey coloured stone building into an elegant property and the young woman proudly uploaded a collection of photographs of the plush interior to her FriendsBag album. Renovating the old mill had given the family a beautiful home that they would otherwise not have been able to afford. Charlotte now possessed a new set of creative skills that she hoped would one day help her to launch her own interior design consultancy and photography studio.

Elisabeth had been very impressed by Charlotte's positive outlook on life and clearly recognised her new friend was one of life's go-getters; the kind of person who seizes the day to achieve their goal, no matter what life throws at them. The young woman had indeed had her fair share of challenges along the way but, after each hurdle, she had always managed to step up, dust herself down and re-build her life for the better.

"If only you and Christian had been given the chance to get together," lamented Elisabeth.

"My God what an absolute force of nature the two of you would have been."

#

Timeline: Thursday 23rd June 2016, 14:00hrs

It had been a particularly busy morning for Diana Hambridge. The estate agency had recently seen a healthy increase in new business; it seemed as if the summer sunshine had brought a whole host of prospective house buyers out of hibernation. Most of the young businesswoman's day had been spent showing people around a collection of properties for sale close to her mother-in-law's home at Himley Fields. Diana's one o'clock appointment had been at a bungalow in the adjoining road to Clover Croft. The meeting went well and Diana smiled as she got back into her car. The house hunters had been suitably impressed with the property and promised to call later that day with an offer. She drove the short distance to the Hambridge family home; bathing in the warm glow knowing that Christian would have been so proud to see how she had successfully taken the reins at the company. The young estate agent had been forced to postpone her lunch until after the viewing, so she decided a quick sandwich at Elisabeth's would save her having to travel back into town before her next appointment.

Diana pulled up outside the house and pressed the button on Christian's electronic key fob to open up the wrought iron gates, before driving her red Mini onto the gravelled driveway. Diana got out of her car and walked across the paved path towards the front door. It was a very hot sunny afternoon and she noticed that Elisabeth had opened many of the ground floor windows in an attempt to encourage any hint of a summer breeze to flow through the house. As Diana put her key in the door lock she could hear that her mother-in-law was talking to someone in the study. Diana quietly entered the hallway and decided not to interrupt Elisabeth's absorbing conversation; instead she stood and waited for a suitable break. She could hear two women chatting and it quickly became clear that they were discussing Christian's thrill-seeking love of motorbikes and adventure sports.

"It's such a shame Luke never got to ride with Christian, I'm sure they would have both loved that. I can just imagine how proud he would have been, he was such a softy." said Elisabeth joyously.

"Yes, it sounds as if Luke was just like him," replied the young woman on the screen. Diana drew in a short gasp of surprise. She had not expected to hear her mother-in-law comfortably discuss Christian's emotions so frankly with anyone else.

'Who is the old biddy talking to?' she wondered.

Elisabeth suddenly became aware she had a visitor and hurriedly ended her conversation with Charlotte, snapping her laptop shut.

"Hello? Is that you Diana?" she called out nervously from the study, unsure how much of her private conversation had been over-heard.

"Hello Mother, yes it's me."

"What are you doing here?" continued Elisabeth, the tone of her shaky voice sounding a little higher pitched. The startled woman could feel a wave of panic sting through her chest; had the secret of Christian's love child been prematurely revealed?

"I thought, as I was in the area, I'd pop in for a late lunch," replied Diana as she breezed into the study. A sudden rush of blood pounded through Elisabeth's brain as she quickly pushed her laptop to the back of her desk and stood up to greet her unexpected visitor.

"I'm sorry to interrupt your chat," said Diana. She walked over to give Elisabeth a familiar peck on the cheek. The young woman noticed that her mother-in-law seemed to be a little nervous.

"Are you okay? Who was that on your video call?" she asked.

"I'm fine thanks. Erm, it was no one really," faltered Elisabeth, her face flushed.

"She's just a friend from FriendsBag who lives in France," she added, trying to retain her composure.

"It's just I thought I heard you talking about Christian," replied Diana, almost apologising for her unwitting eavesdropping.

"You didn't have to end your call prematurely you know. I would have waited until you had finished talking," smiled Diana as she walked through into the kitchen to switch the kettle on.

"I didn't end the call prematurely," replied Elisabeth cautiously.

"And yes, I probably mentioned my son, I do it all the time," she said with a slight hint of indignation. Inside Elisabeth was frantically scrabbling to explain her abrupt behaviour as a thousand thoughts flooded through her brain. She could not bring herself to tell her daughter-in-law about the circumstances behind the blossoming friendship with Charlotte; it was still too early to introduce the subject of Luke. She would have to quickly think of another excuse.

"My friend has a bit of a dodgy internet connection in France and I think her signal went down just as you were coming in. It's always happening when we chat online. I'll call her back later on. What are you doing here anyway?" she asked, in an attempt to change the subject. Diana clearly understood that Elisabeth didn't want to discuss the conversation. Her turning up at the house unexpectedly had obviously ruffled her mother-in-law's feathers and she hated to appear meddling.

"Oh, I've had a few viewings in the local area today and I thought it would be nice to spend a late lunch with you rather than rushing back to the office," smiled Diana, realising that Elisabeth had cleverly steered the conversation away from the subject of the mystery woman on the video call screen. She knew she would have to accept that the old woman was perfectly entitled to her privacy and that she was allowed to make new friends. Diana busied herself in the kitchen by making a pot of tea and a couple of ham and cheese sandwiches. She carried the tray of food into the conservatory at the back of the house.

Elisabeth had opened the windows and French doors and a warm summer breeze fluttered through the room. As the two women made small talk over their late lunch, Elisabeth was relieved that her secret was still safe. She began to think that she had over-reacted to Diana's surprise arrival and her daughter-in-law probably hadn't heard anything to alert any suspicion anyway. Before long their idle chatter returned to their favourite topic of conversation.

"I heard from the stonemason today," said Diana.

"The granite for Christian's headstone has arrived from Italy and he'll start on the inscription next week," she continued. Elisabeth stared back blankly and took a sip of hot tea. Fat salty tears began to well in her eyes. She realised that in a week or two's time there would be a black slab of stone to officially mark the end of her son's vibrant life. It all suddenly felt so final; the closing chapter. The thoughts of how she and Diana had carefully planned the epitaph of gold letters bubbled up to the front of her mind; how long it had taken the two women to finally agree on the few short words that would summarise Christian's full and adventurous life.

"The stonemason said he will let me know the day before it's due to be delivered to the cemetery," said Diana.

"If you like, we can go together to see it in place for the first time before anyone else," she smiled, trying to quell her own tears and remain strong for her mother-in-law's sake.

"Perhaps we could visit before we go shopping in a couple of week's time. We could make an afternoon of it."

\#

Timeline: Thursday 23rd June 2016, 15:00hrs

Elisabeth stood by her front door waving goodbye to Diana. With a feigned watery smile she watched the red Mini drive away. The grieving grandmother waited a couple of moments to ensure her unexpected visitor didn't come back, before pressing the intercom button to close the heavy wrought iron gates across

45

the drive. She quickly made her way back inside the house and returned to the sanctuary of her study. She had patiently waited for Diana to leave and now, almost two hours after the initial interruption, it was time to reconnect online with Charlotte.

'God I hope she's still there,' thought Elisabeth as she lifted the lid of her laptop and logged back onto her video call account.

'I hope she doesn't think I was being rude by simply cutting off the conversation.' A minute later Charlotte's familiar blonde hair and elegant features came into view on the screen.

"Bonjour," said Charlotte. Elisabeth was relieved to see the young woman was smiling back at her.

"Hello. I am so sorry I had to cut you off like that," she replied apologetically.

"It's just Christian's wife turned up out of the blue and I panicked a bit."

"Don't worry about it," soothed Charlotte with a small laugh.

"I understand how complicated it would be to tell her that you've become friends with the mother of her late husband's secret son. That's not something you can get your head around easily. But, by the same token, I can imagine how impossible it would be for me to explain to Eric who you really are, if he overheard our conversations." Elisabeth smiled warmly as the two women continued their online chat. Charlotte was also grateful that Elisabeth had kept her promise and not divulged her deception to anyone else; she still lived with the fear of her husband finding out that Luke hadn't been his biological child.

"We'll have to come up with a decent cover story for when I visit England in a couple of weeks' time though," announced Charlotte. Elisabeth felt a flutter of nerves knot in her stomach.

"You're coming over here? To England?" she asked with a slightly startled tone.

"Absolutely," replied Charlotte.

"Besides it would be wonderful to meet up in person with my son's secret grandmother," she added with a smile.

Charlotte explained that becoming friends with Elisabeth had rekindled lots of fond memories of Christian. She believed that visiting her home town, the old college and student

46

hangouts from her youth would be cathartic. Maybe a trip down memory lane and eventually placing some flowers on Christian's grave would give her the closure that she desperately sought.

Chapter 5

Two weeks later Elisabeth Hambridge stood in her plush marble-tiled entrance hall. The whole house had been specially cleaned in anticipation of her important visitor, and she had just put the finishing touches to a large floral display that filled the top of a glass console table. The elegant widow stood back to admire her handy work as the fragrant aroma of freshly cut roses filled the room. A wave of excitement began to well in her chest at the thought of meeting Charlotte Benoit in person. Elisabeth checked her appearance in the hall mirror and smiled a small self-congratulatory smile. All of her painstaking amateur detective work had paid off; she had come so far. Today was the day that she would finally meet the mother of her secret grandchild. She would at last be a step closer to Luke; the small piece of Christian that had been so precious.

Like an excited puppy anxiously waiting for her master to return home, Elisabeth had bobbed in and out of the hall, passing by the window every couple of minutes to peer out and see if Charlotte had arrived. Eventually, her patience was rewarded when she saw an unfamiliar silver car pull up outside the entrance gates. A stylish looking young woman got out of the driver's side of the car and gracefully walked across to press the button on the gate. Elisabeth eagerly picked up the intercom receiver.

"Bonjour Charlotte, bonjour," she laughed, before her visitor had a chance to speak. Elisabeth pressed the button to open the gates.

"Just come through darling and park on the drive." She clicked the receiver back into its cradle and rushed to swing open the front door. Charlotte waved back and returned to her car before slowly driving through the open entrance and onto the crunchy gravel. Elisabeth's attention was drawn to how the young woman bore a striking resemblance to how she herself had looked in her thirties. Charlotte wore a beige Chanel suit with a smart cream blouse and taupe coloured stiletto healed court shoes. Her pale blond hair was gently swept into a sophisticated chignon. Every inch of her seemed to exude elegance and effortless style. The two women greeted each other warmly with a soft peck on each cheek before making their way inside the house.

"How was your journey," asked Elisabeth as she poured boiling water into a china teapot.

"Not bad at all," replied Charlotte.

"There was a little turbulence on the flight but there were no delays. In fact, the longest delay was waiting for the hire car," she joked, happily making small talk with her new friend.

Elisabeth placed two bone china cups and saucers onto a silver tea tray alongside the tea pot, milk jug and sugar bowl. Next she retrieved a long silver platter of delicately cut smoked salmon and cucumber sandwiches that she had made in advance from the fridge. These were laid out on a second tray next to a cut glass bowl that contained a selection of dainty chocolate biscuits. The two women carried the afternoon tea trays into the living room and continued chatting.

"So now you're back in Blighty, where do you plan to visit first?" asked Elisabeth as she poured the tea.

"Well," replied Charlotte, almost hesitantly.

"I did think I would like to go and visit Christian's resting place this afternoon, if that's okay with you?" She studied the older woman's face carefully, looking for an honest reaction to her suggestion.

"Yes, of course," replied Elisabeth, slightly startled by the idea. Although she fully expected a visit to Christian's grave to be on the young woman's list of places to see, she was not expecting to go there that day.

"We can go to the cemetery after tea if you like."

#

Timeline: Thursday 7th July 2016, 15:30hrs

The journey to the cemetery had taken longer than expected. Elisabeth realised that they had chosen a bad time to travel as

49

they were caught at the end of the afternoon school run. The seemingly endless stop-start traffic came to a halt outside Hanford Nursery & Infants School. Elisabeth and Charlotte gazed out of the car windows to watch a couple of giggling schoolboys skip across the road ahead of their mother towards their parents' car. The twin boys waved childishly painted pictures in the air and excitedly began to recount the day's activities to the man sat behind the steering wheel. The children's babbling went largely ignored, as both parents feigned sparse interest in their children's tales and promptly ushered them into the rear seats of the people carrier. A small tear of regret welled up in Elisabeth's eye as she realised that she had maybe once been guilty of such impatience and indifference to her own child's stories from the classroom. What she wouldn't give to have that precious time once more, to join the other mothers on the school run; to have the opportunity to hear Christian's voice or see his smiling face, as he recounted what he and his friends had done during the school day.

Eventually the pulsing snake of rush hour traffic stopped outside the imposing wrought iron gates of Hanford Town Crematorium. Charlotte turned her car into the car park of the memorial grounds and switched off the ignition. The two women turned and smiled at each other before silently stepping out into the afternoon sunshine. Charlotte walked around to the rear of the car and opened the hatch to retrieve a small posy of pink carnations from the boot.

Elisabeth led the way along a block paved path through the cemetery towards the Hambridge family's plot. The bare mound of earth that had been dug less than a year prior marked where Christian had been buried. A simple wooden cross bearing his name stood in the ground at one end of the grave. Grass had begun to grow on the surface of the raised soil; the faded floral tributes recently left by friends had withered and Elisabeth made a mental note to suggest to Diana that they remove them. Charlotte noticed Christian lay next to his father, Thomas Hambridge. There was space beneath the inscription on the older man's gravestone for another name. Elisabeth's kitten heals sunk into the soft grass at the foot of the grave as she felt an uneasy shiver of mortality run through her spine. It was an unwelcome reminder that one day this would be her own final resting place with her husband.

The women's silent thoughts were rudely interrupted by the un-ceremonial arrival of a small forklift truck. It beeped an intrusive warning alarm as it trundled along the path towards them. Its forks carried what appeared to be a heavy load covered in a Hessian blanket. Two men in blue overalls followed closely on foot behind, as the driver slowly manoeuvred the vehicle up onto the grass and made his way towards where Elisabeth and Charlotte were standing. He stopped the truck at the head of Christian's grave and slowly lowered its forks onto the grass. One of the workmen smiled and nodded his head at the women, as he proudly removed the protective blanket to reveal a large piece of polished black granite beneath. The three men shuffled the stone into its final position as Elisabeth let out a short gasp; she realised that they were the stonemasons delivering her late son's headstone.

"Looks nice doesn't it?" said one of the workmen as he folded up the Hessian sheet. Elisabeth stared silently at the newly erected piece of stone. She felt tears fall uncontrollably down her face as the afternoon sun glinted on the carefully chosen gold lettering; the inscription now seemed to inadequately summarise such a full and adventurous life.

Christian Hambridge
Beloved Son and Husband

Charlotte gave a sad smile and nodded in unspoken appreciation back at the workman, before placing a supportive arm across Elisabeth's shoulders. The two women stood in quiet contemplation as the stonemason's entourage respectfully made their way to the other side of the cemetery.

"It's a shame that he isn't described as a father," said Elisabeth, finally breaking the silence.

"I'm sure he would have been a wonderful dad to Luke had the circumstances been different."

Charlotte remained still and simply gazed at the headstone. Elisabeth could only imagine how many regrets were flooding

51

through the young woman's mind. If only the scared college girl had pursued Christian more; been more forceful, made him understand. If only she had summoned enough courage to confront his high and mighty family all those years ago. Elisabeth would have helped her son with the responsibility of being a father. She would not have let him abandon the mother of his child. More tears cascaded down the grieving grandmother's face as she knew she would never have the opportunity to make it right.

Charlotte knelt down onto the grass and laid her fresh posy of flowers in front of the slab of polished granite. She opened her handbag and took out a small photograph of Luke along with a large smooth pebble.

"There you go, you're with your daddy now," whispered Charlotte, as she gently kissed both items before placing the picture at the base of Christian's headstone. Elisabeth watched silently as the young woman put the rock securely on top of the photograph to prevent it from fluttering away in the summer breeze.

"It's a stone from Luke's favourite beach near Cannes; the place where we scattered his ashes," said Charlotte tearfully as she blew another kiss towards the headstone. The two women left the cemetery and slowly walked back to Charlotte's car.

"Where would you like to visit next?" asked Elisabeth as she sniffed back a tear.

"I don't mind really," replied Charlotte, mindful that it was now approaching four o'clock in the afternoon and she had left it a little late in the day for visiting any other places down memory lane. It had been a very emotional trip and Charlotte thought that the older woman could do with a little cheering up.

"How about we go for a drink?" Elisabeth smiled at her friend's suggestion and the two women made their way to a small wine bar on Hanford High Street.

The warm embrace of Hunter's Bar was a welcome distraction from the solemnity of the visit to Christian's grave. The pub had been recently renovated and featured a retro seventies theme, with a long shiny mirror-backed marble counter and larva lamps. Large posters featuring pop stars and sporting legends from the bygone era adorned the freshly replastered walls. An array of multi-coloured leather bean bags and hammock chairs were scattered artistically on a newly-laid wooden laminate floor. The décor reminded Elisabeth of the trendy London bars that she had frequented in her twenties and she felt very much at home amid the elegant homage to a colourfully gauche decade.

A large photograph of a tall moustachioed man had been proudly placed on a glass shelf, nestled amid the optics and bottles of malt Whisky. It was a small memento to honour the memory of the bar's founder. A few yellowed newspaper cuttings had been framed and hung alongside the portrait and they reported how the businessman had tragically died in a drinking game some eighteen months previously. His family and friends had taken over the running of the bar and they had successfully built on the notoriety that came with such a tragedy. All barmen were made to adopt the same comical facial hair featured in the photograph in tribute to the popular late landlord.

A middle-aged man served Elisabeth and Charlotte their drinks and snacks. Both women giggled uncontrollably, as they secretly thought his long black Mexican moustache made him resemble an ageing seventies' porn star. The friends whiled away a couple of hours in the comfortable surroundings of Hunter's Bar; openly chatting about their sons and exchanging lots of happy memories as they shared a bottle of wine and a selection of tapas.

"Would you like to see more photos of Luke?" asked Charlotte, as she summoned the barman to open up another bottle of Chablis. The young woman switched on her tablet and clicked open a folder of images. Elisabeth eagerly pulled the screen closer to her as she took in every small detail. The photographs charted Luke's life; from when he was a small baby, through school and college to when he got his first moped and developed his love of fast motorbikes and adventure sports. Charlotte re-filled Elisabeth's wineglass and ordered a sparking mineral water for herself.

"These are beautiful Charlotte, simply beautiful," said Elisabeth holding back a small tear of pride. Charlotte placed a supportive hand on the older woman's shoulder.

"Don't cry Elisabeth," comforted the young woman as she passed her a small plastic envelope. Charlotte had thoughtfully created a CD filled with scanned photographs for Elisabeth to keep as a memento.

"I'm only sorry I couldn't give you any original photos of Luke. As you can imagine they're all back home in Cannes and safely housed in the Benoit family's photo albums," she explained.

Elisabeth felt a warm glow envelop her whole body. It was wonderful to know that her grandson had been so like his father. She realised that she was beginning to develop a very special bond with the mother of her grandchild. In the hazy wine-fuelled euphoria Elisabeth believed that she had discovered her kindred spirit. If only the circumstances behind their friendship could be announced to the world and celebrated.

"What did you tell your husband about your trip to England?" asked Elisabeth with a slight slur, realising that she had drunk most of the second bottle of wine on her own.

"Oh Eric probably won't even notice that I've gone away," replied Charlotte dismissively before taking another sip of sparkling mineral water.

Charlotte explained that the grieving Eric Benoit had refused any bereavement counselling; instead he had chosen to deal with Luke's death by throwing himself into his work. He had blamed himself for the tragedy and firmly believed that if he hadn't bought Luke the damned snowmobile then his son would still be alive. Following the accident Eric had returned to work at the university and accepted all the extra lecturing responsibilities that were available; regularly working away from home for most of the week. He had spent many weekends alone in his study, and had virtually cut himself off from the outside world to avoid having to talk to anyone about his dead son.

Charlotte admitted that she had used Eric's behaviour to her advantage and had invented a perfect excuse for escaping on her own for a few days. She had handled her son's tragic death differently from her husband. Charlotte needed people around her and desperately wanted to share her grief. As her husband's reclusive demeanour gave her little solace, Charlotte told him that she had joined an online forum for people dealing with bereavement and she had become friends with Elisabeth Hambridge; a fellow grieving mother who had also recently lost a son. Coincidentally her new friend lived in the same area that she had grown up in before moving to France, so it would be nice to meet up with her and it would be a good opportunity to catch up with other friends while she visited the UK for a short break alone.

Elisabeth poured the last few drops of wine from the bottle into her glass. She was sad to hear how badly Eric had coped with Luke's death, but she couldn't help thinking that Charlotte's inspired white lie about the bereavement forum was a fabulous invention. She smiled inwardly as she realised that there was no reason why she shouldn't use the same cover story if ever she had to explain her friendship with Charlotte to Diana.

The waiter arrived to clear away the tapas tray and empty bottles. He placed a small leather wallet on the table that contained the bill.

"Here, let me pay," said Elisabeth as she offered up three twenty pound notes.

"I wouldn't dream of it," replied Charlotte, firmly closing her friend's hand around the money to gently push it away.

"It's the least I can do to thank you for giving me the opportunity to make my peace with Luke's father."

It was there in the warm sanctuary of Hunter's Bar, surrounded by seventies' décor and watched over by a hovering moustachioed barman, that both women realised they shared the bond of a powerful mutual secret. Neither could tell anyone the truth about the biological father of Charlotte's son; it would cause too much pain for Eric and Diana. Innocent people's lives would be further devastated should the truth ever be revealed.

#

Timeline: Thursday 7th July 2016, 18:30hrs

During the short car journey back to Clover Croft, Elisabeth realised that the warm late afternoon sunshine and chilled wine had made her sleepy and she was finding it increasingly difficult to remain awake. Charlotte pulled up outside the wrought iron gates at the end of Elisabeth's drive and gently shook her friend's arm. Elisabeth was slightly embarrassed by her perceived lack of self-control and immediately blinked her eyes open.

"Oh gosh, I am so sorry. I must have dozed off. What ever must you think of me?" She pulled down the sun visor to check her appearance in the vanity mirror. Charlotte smiled back warmly.

"It's no problem Elisabeth, after all what are friends for?" The two women hugged warmly before Elisabeth got out of the car. She turned and smiled at her friend through the open passenger door.

"If you're in town for a few days then we really should meet up again before you go back to France. Call me," said Elisabeth, closing the door as she mimed holding a telephone next to her face. Charlotte smiled back and nodded as she watched the older woman lazily open the electronic gates. She gave a friendly wave as Elisabeth's kitten heals crunched unsteadily over the gravel drive before she made her way safely into the house.

Elisabeth entered the plush marble hallway and kicked off her shoes before walking into the kitchen. It had been a marvellous day; an emotional day, but a good one nonetheless. She needed a strong cup of coffee to clear her head so that she could savour every beautiful detail. The wonderful mother of her grandson had been there for her today. Elisabeth had forged another bond to her beloved Christian, and now, as she waited for the kettle to boil, she clutched a CD that was crammed full of precious images; more mementos to add to the secret final chapter of her cherished Hambridge family album. Elisabeth switched her mobile phone to silent in preparation of an indulgent evening with her family photographs, but her happy contemplation was suddenly interrupted by the buzz of her intercom.

'Oh, that must be Charlotte popping back for something,' she thought.

"What have you forgotten," asked Elisabeth as she nonchalantly picked up the phone on the kitchen wall and smiled at the CD wallet in her hand.

"What do you mean? I haven't forgotten anything?

Startled to hear Diana's voice, Elisabeth spun around and peered out of the kitchen window. She was disappointed to see her daughter-in-law standing by the gate.

"Hello Mother. I was just passing by and I don't have Christian's keys on me but I wondered if I could pop in for a minute?" Diana saw her mother-in-law at the window and gave a small wave.

"Sorry I thought you were my friend Charlotte, I've just been out with her for a late lunch," explained Elisabeth who was clearly irritated by the unexpected intrusion. Her bubble of intoxicated happiness had been burst and any indulgence in her secret grandchild's memory would now have to wait. Elisabeth reluctantly pressed the lock release to open the electronic gates and Diana got back into her car before pulling onto the gravel drive. Elisabeth greeted her daughter-in-law at the front door with a cordial peck on the cheek before walking back into the kitchen to fill the cafetiere with boiling water.

"The stonemason left me a voicemail on my mobile this morning, but I've been in so many meetings today that I've only just got around to listening to it," announced Diana as she took off her jacket. Elisabeth began pouring coffee into two bone china beakers.

"He said he was going to put Christian's stone in place today, so I thought as it's a nice warm evening, maybe we could pop over there. If we get a wiggle on we could just about make it before the cemetery closes."

Elisabeth felt her heart freeze at Diana's suggestion. How on earth was she going to explain Luke's photograph and Charlotte's posy of flowers being there? She simply had to remove them from beneath the headstone before Diana had a chance to see them. 'Oh God, no it's just too soon for her to find out about Luke,' she thought, as she imagined having to reveal the whole scenario to the grieving young widow. Elisabeth became so lost in her own thoughts that she hadn't noticed that she had over-filled one of the china cups in front of her and coffee had begun to cascade all over the kitchen work surface. Immediately Diana steadied Elisabeth's trembling hand, took the cafetiere from her and grabbed a paper towel to mop up the spillage.

"Are you okay Mother?" asked Diana, noticing how pale and drawn Elisabeth's face had suddenly become; she was also surprised that she could smell alcohol on her breath. The old woman was a little unsteady on her feet and her usual calm demeanour had seemed to evaporate at the mention of the impromptu trip to see Christian's headstone.

"Yes I'm fine thank you. Why wouldn't I be?" she snapped.

"I'd just prefer to leave visiting the grave until tomorrow instead. Okay?" added Elisabeth as her mind frantically scrabbled to think of when she could get to the cemetery beforehand to remove the incriminating evidence.

Diana was surprised by her mother-in-law's curt response and apparent lack of enthusiasm for visiting the grave. The two women had a mutual agreement that they would always attend any landmark events together, and that arrangement included sharing the inaugural visit to Christian's sited headstone. It would be an important event and neither one should go without the other to the first viewing.

"What's the matter? I'd have thought you would want to go and see the stone as soon as possible; but you don't seem to be all that bothered about going to visit your only son." Diana immediately realised her harsh remark was rather snide.

"Not at all," replied Elisabeth defensively.

"It's just my mind is not really on things today. I met up with a friend at lunchtime and had a few glasses of wine and now I can feel a headache coming on, so I'd simply prefer it if we could go tomorrow instead . . . when I've got a clearer head."

"Okay, okay, I'm sorry. We can go tomorrow instead if you like, before I take you shopping," said Diana curtly as she stood up to leave.

Elisabeth noticed the stroppy tone in the younger woman's voice but she was relieved that her daughter-in-law hadn't pushed the point too far. She was pleased her excuse of a headache had managed to postpone the visit to the cemetery.

She would go there early in the morning and remove the photograph and pebble. Diana would be none-the-wiser; Charlotte and Elisabeth's shared secret would be safe.

#

Diana reversed off the drive and pulled away quickly from Elisabeth's house; her car tyres squealed as she sped around the corner at the bottom of the tree-lined avenue. She was furious and her Mini would suffer the full brunt of her anger.

'God what an infernally annoying woman,' she thought, slamming the car into fifth gear as she sped along the road.

"I make a special effort at the end of an extremely busy day to take her to visit her beloved son's grave, and she's spent the afternoon boozing and now doesn't want to go 'cos she's nursing a bloody hangover," spat Diana incredulously.

The young widow had always been careful to placate her mother-in-law. From the first moment that they had been introduced a dozen years ago, she had always been on her guard. Fearful of upsetting or upstaging the senior Mrs Hambridge, Diana had been mindful to never allow her true disdain for the over-protective matriarch to become public knowledge. She knew that her late husband had wanted to make his own mark in the world as an architect. As Christian left university clutching a first class engineering degree his parents had somehow managed to convince him that his future lay at the estate agency; the persuasive tug of his mother's apron strings had been too great for Christian to resist and any thoughts of a different career had been quickly extinguished.

Elisabeth had disapproved of her son leaving the family home to move in with Diana; it was as if she believed there was something shameful about an unmarried couple living together. Her constant niggling about what she always referred to as 'living in sin' had led Christian and Diana to marry sooner than they had planned. This had kept his mother happy for a short while, but soon after the young couple's wedding, Elisabeth had seemed to become infatuated with the idea of having grandchildren. It was as if she didn't think her son's life would be complete without hearing the pitter-patter of tiny feet and someone to call him Daddy. Elisabeth had raised the subject of babies at every possible opportunity. It quickly became obvious to Diana that her mother-in-law believed having children and becoming a stay-at-home mom was a role that most women should strive for.

Elisabeth became almost relentless in her pursuit of having a grandchild; from casual hints about the newly-weds' sex life to blatantly giving her daughter-in-law the names of numerous fertility clinics and specialists. Diana had always graciously turned down the intrusive offers of help. The young couple didn't want any assistance to get them on the road to parenthood. But Diana knew it would be crucial to remain friends with her over-bearing mother-in-law if she ever wanted to forge her own career within the family business. Eventually, Elisabeth's meddling and constant efforts to grind her daughter-in-law into submission became overwhelming; Diana had endured enough interference and one day the young woman's patience had run dry. Heated emotions boiled over and Elisabeth was firmly told that Diana was putting her career first; children could come along later. Sadly, for both women, that dream was crushed on the day Christian lost his life.

Diana's temper cooled as she drove towards Hanford Cemetery. She hated how the belligerent harridan always seemed to sit on a cushion of superiority; as if Elisabeth's needs and feelings were more important than anyone else's. But Diana wasn't going to let a small spat with the old crone totally ruin her plans. This was one of the most important landmark days following the death of her beloved husband and she was determined to visit his grave today; with or without his bloody mother. After all, how would Elisabeth ever know she'd visited there without her?

#

Timeline: Thursday 7th July 2016, 19:00hrs

Elisabeth drank the last drops of coffee and placed her china mug down on the work surface in the kitchen. She allowed herself a small self-congratulatory smile as she thought that convincing Diana they should visit Christian's grave the next day had been relatively easy. She had come so close to her secret being revealed yet somehow Swan Blake had emerged once more victorious. Her thoughts were rudely interrupted by the sharp trill of the landline.

"Hello, the Hambridge residence." Elisabeth's old fashioned greeting was very formal but to her mind it was the most efficient manner in which to answer an unknown caller.

"Elisabeth. Thank God." Immediately she recognised the quiet voice with a feint hue of a French accent.

"Hello my dear, did you get back to the hotel okay?" replied Elisabeth.

"I'm so sorry to call you on your house phone but your mobile kept going to voicemail and I urgently need to speak with you," said Charlotte without answering the old lady's question.

"I simply don't have anywhere else to turn," her voice began to tremble. The young woman was extremely upset; she sounded flustered and was obviously having difficulty getting her words out. Elisabeth remained quiet, calmly taking in every detail as her friend explained her precarious predicament.

Charlotte had carefully disguised her visit to see the secret grandmother of her dead child as an innocent trip down memory lane. She had told her husband she simply needed time away to recharge her batteries; to re-boot herself. This self-help therapy session could be boosted by visiting old places she used to know before she had become a mother; when she had lived in Hanford all those years ago. But, unbeknown to Charlotte, Eric Benoit had been suspicious about his wife's out-of-the-blue solo trip to England. Many of her actions of late had been so out-of-character that he simply refused to believe it was only grief that had brought about such a noticeable change in her demeanour. Instead he had suspected that she was having an affair. His suspicions had festered and engulfed his every waking thought until the day she had left for the airport; the fateful day when his dubiosity had driven him to hack into her emails and FriendsBag account in an attempt to track down her secret lover. It was then he had discovered the secret text chat history between Charlotte and Elisabeth.

Every detail about the innocent young boy he had thought was his own flesh and blood had unfolded on the screen before him. From the sordid details surrounding Luke's conception, to the unrequited feelings of love that Charlotte had obviously held for the man who had fathered her child; the whole grubby account was laid bare in an online chat. His marriage had been a sham; an elaborate deception to convince Eric that he was Luke's father. He had felt used and humiliated on realising he had been his wife's second choice; her life's back-up plan. In his mind, Charlotte had been nothing more than a college whore and she now deserved to suffer for her wicked deceit. The raw emptiness he felt knowing that Luke wasn't his biological son served to compound his immense sorrow. His confusion about why he still felt grief for the loss of another man's child soon grew into un-vented anger.

Eric had spent a tauntingly long twenty-four hours poring over the facts, re-reading the emails and messages. The two women had plotted their clandestine meeting during endless days and nights of messaging; like a couple of witches agreeing to keep their cruel deception a secret beneath a blanket of mutual trust. But now their cosy confidence was about to be revealed, their whole world was about to crumble beneath the fallout of his Gallic wrath; beginning with a vengeful telephone call to his conniving bitch of a wife.

"He said he knows everything about Luke and his real dad and he wants a divorce," sobbed Charlotte.

Eric had delivered his tirade with the final announcement that he had cut off his wife's access to their joint bank account and cancelled her flight ticket back to France. She now had no son, no marriage, no money and no hope of ever being allowed back into the Benoit family home. She had been cast adrift.

#

Timeline: Thursday 7th July 2016, 19:15hrs

Diana drove her Mini into a parking space at Hanford Town Crematorium and sharply snatched on the handbrake. She stepped out of the car and picked up a black bin liner out of the door pocket before hurriedly striding towards Christian's grave. She knew that the grounds men at the Garden of Remembrance closed the gates at seven thirty sharp and it was now just after a quarter past the hour. As she approached the graveside her pace respectfully slowed to a more reverent walk and she took in a few gulps of air to catch her breath. She could see the shiny piece of newly laid black granite standing proudly among the other headstones; the top of it glinted in the hazy summer evening sunshine. As Diana walked nearer a quizzical look grew across her face as she could see a fresh posy of pink carnations lying at the base of the stone.

'That's strange, I don't remember those flowers being there when we visited the other week. They look quite fresh,' she thought.

A shallow trench had formed around the edge of the soil plot and this had now become a collection point for an assortment of paper detritus; from old condolence cards to the odd cigarette butt. Diana shook open the black bin liner and knelt down at the graveside to begin tidying away the rubbish and some of the wilting leaves and petals from a few older bouquets left there by numerous other visitors. Suddenly she noticed something fluttering beneath an unusual large smooth pebble next to the posy of pink flowers at the base of Christian's headstone. She leaned over and pulled at the piece of paper. On the front was a photograph of a young man sitting astride a motorbike. Puzzled by her find, she turned it over to see three lines of hand written text on the back:

"Rest in peace Hammers.
Your ever loving son.
Luke. X

A shocked Diana slumped backwards, the pointed toes of her stiletto shoes dug into the soft grass.

'What the hell is this?' she thought. Immediately she stood up from the graveside and spun around in a full circle, trying to see if there was anyone else around. Had someone simply placed the memento on the wrong plot or was it a cruel joke?

63

Surely no one who knew the family would intentionally leave such an insensitive insult on Christian Hambridge's grave.

Diana picked up the fresh posy of flowers and noticed that there was a small folded piece of card attached to it. The mystified young woman opened it up and read the simple line of text written inside.

With fondest memories of a missed Dad.

The handwriting matched that on the rear of the photograph. Tears welled up in the young widow's eyes.

'Why in God's name would anyone leave this at Christian's headstone?' she thought.

'Someone's obviously put it here in error.' She quickly looked around the immediate area to see if fresh flowers had been left at any of the other graves, or if any names on the other headstones were similar to her husband's. It was a vain attempt to find the correct place for the freshly laid tributes, as all she could see were dried-up bouquets and withered wreaths adorning the neighbouring plots. Diana felt it would not be right to leave the inappropriate offering at the graveside, so she quickly put the incongruous posy, photograph and stone into the bin liner with the rest of the collected rubbish.

The grieving young widow stood back from the grave and read the shiny gold lettered epitaph that had been painstakingly decided on after endlessly fraught discussions with Elisabeth. She remembered the frustration she had felt by the old woman's constant mind changing; how it had taken weeks for her mother-in-law to decide on the colour and shape of the stone and another couple of days to choose the font and compose the final wording.

'You can't rush these things. It's going to be there for decades so it has to be right,' Elisabeth's patronising words floated through Diana's brain as she became slightly irritated by the memory of the old woman's total take over of the proceedings.

She blew her late husband a loving kiss and made her way back to the car; giving a small nod of appreciation towards two groundsmen who locked the cemetery gates behind her.

The discovery of the posy and photograph still burned at the back of Diana's mind as she began her short drive home. She was still unsure whether they had been placed at the headstone as a prank or if someone had made a simple mistake. Whatever the reason behind it, she believed that her solo trip to the grave had now been vindicated. Going there without Elisabeth could no longer be regarded as a defiant or selfish act; she had after all spared the grieving old woman the upset of seeing the unexpected floral tribute.

'Elisabeth's such a manipulative old mare,' thought Diana as she drove her car off the crematorium car park. The young woman always hated herself whenever she quarrelled with Elisabeth. Her mother-in-law always knew which buttons to press and Diana was annoyed. Yet again the snooty matriarch had made her feel as if she was in the wrong, but the young widow felt forced into letting her get away with it. She knew that Elisabeth couldn't help it if she had become belligerent; she was alone in life and was used to getting her own way.

'You're such a curmudgeonly old biddy Elisabeth.' She smiled and shook her head as she turned the car around to head back towards Clover Croft; Diana decided that she would be the bigger person and would call in at the Hambridge family home to clear the air and apologise for her earlier stroppiness.

#

Timeline: Thursday 7th July 2016, 19:30hrs

Elisabeth pressed the intercom release button on the phone in the hall to open the electronic gates so Charlotte could pull her car onto the drive. Quickly the young woman got out of the vehicle and ran over to the comforting embrace of her friend's open arms.

"Eric knows everything," sobbed Charlotte through a flood of tears coursing down her face. The two women stood in the hallway for a few moments before Elisabeth led her visitor into the soothing sanctuary of the living room. They sat together on one of the cream leather sofas as the devastated young woman's story unfolded further. Her husband had discovered her cruel

65

deception and the damning fact that the child he had thought of as his own flesh and blood for almost twenty years was not his biological son.

Elisabeth's mind raced as she realised that the young woman's life now lay in tatters and she felt wholly responsible for her friend's desperate plight. If only she hadn't pursued her so impetuously on FriendsBag and kept on chipping away until she had eventually prised the buried secret out of Charlotte. If only that damned letter had arrived on time twenty years earlier, Christian and Luke would both be alive, they would all be one big happy family and no one would be living through this awful nightmare. Elisabeth took in a deep purposeful breath and hugged the young woman closer.

"Right then. Christian and I got you into this mess," she smiled, gently stroking the top of one of Charlotte's hands.

"The least I can do is let you stay here until it's all sorted out. I've got plenty of room and I simply won't take no for an answer." Charlotte looked back at the strong mature woman in front of her and nodded as more tears welled up in her eyes.

"Just because Eric knows everything, we still can't tell anyone else about Luke though. Promise me you won't say anything to your daughter-in-law just yet," she pleaded.

Charlotte believed that since Eric now knew about Luke's biological father then Elisabeth would be aching to announce news of her grandson to the world, but she begged her not to divulge her secret. The last thing that she wanted was any of Elisabeth's inquisitive family and friends contacting her to ask awkward questions about Luke. She explained that it would only add fuel to the fire of Eric's Gallic wrath. There was also the impeding predicament of how Diana would react to the unwelcome scandal.

"I suppose we'd better get this drama with Eric out of the way first before we create another one by telling Diana the truth and rubbing her nose in it," agreed Elisabeth. Charlotte smiled back, relieved that her friend understood the situation she was in.

"I'll have to handle that one very carefully though, as they had been trying for a baby for years you know," lamented the old woman.

66

"I'm sure it'll make Lady Diana feel like a worthless failure to know that Christian found it very simple to get another woman pregnant," added Elisabeth ruefully. Charlotte noted the indignant nickname that her friend used when referring to her daughter-in-law.

Elisabeth's contemplative mood was interrupted by the unexpected buzz of her intercom. She got up from the sofa and walked out of the lounge into the hall to peer through the window.

"Talk of the bloody Devil!" exclaimed Elisabeth. She could see Diana standing at the gates waving. Slowly she picked up the receiver with no idea of what she was going to say to explain whose car was parked on the drive.

"Hello mother. Can you let me in," smiled Diana.

"I just wanted to say sorry and to make up with you for my rudeness earlier."

"There's no need for any of that," replied Elisabeth cutting off Diana's apology.

"You were probably right and I shouldn't have made you wait until tomorrow to visit the cemetery. But there's no use going over it all now," she added, desperately trying to stall her daughter-in-law.

Diana noticed Elisabeth still hadn't unlocked the gates, and she felt a little snubbed by being held at bay.

"Sorry mother, am I interrupting something? And who does that belong to?" she asked, pointing at the unfamiliar car parked on the drive.

"Oh that, it's just a friend of mine from the bereavement forum," she replied sheepishly.

"She has a bit of a crisis to deal with at the moment, and I'm helping her through it," added Elisabeth, relieved that she had been quick to give a believable explanation.

"I'm sorry Diana, I've got to get back to her. I'll see you tomorrow. The whole world doesn't revolve around you, you know," she said hanging up the intercom phone.

Diana got back into her car, a little shaken by Elisabeth's uncharacteristic sharp outburst. It was the second time that day that she had allowed the old woman to upset her and she wasn't going to wait around for another flare-up.

'What bereavement forum?' wondered Diana.

'I've never heard of that one before.' The squabble with her mother-in-law played on the young widow's mind as she drove the couple of miles home. She couldn't help but notice that Elisabeth had been in a rather frosty and standoffish mood on both occasions when they had met that day. She had been even more aloof than usual, almost as if she was trying to hide something. Diana thought that perhaps it was for the best she hadn't been let in through the gates; at least she would now have more time to work out if she was going to tell her about the posy of flowers and photo left at the graveside.

The more she thought about the mementos the more she believed someone was playing a very cruel joke on the family by claiming Christian had a son. Diana decided to protect her mother-in-law from the tasteless stunt. Despite being an interfering pain in the neck, Elisabeth still didn't appear to be coping very well with her grief and she didn't need any more stress to tip her over the edge.

#

Timeline: Thursday 7th July 2016, 20:30hrs

Elisabeth sat next to Charlotte on a sofa in her living room and gave a nervous smile. She was well aware that Eric Benoit would be an enraged man with a score to settle. She needed to know what he intended to do with the explosive knowledge that Luke was her grandson. She had persuaded Charlotte to call Eric again, but this time Elisabeth asked to speak to the young woman's husband herself in the hope that she would be able to find the right words to calm the situation. Charlotte dialled her husband's number and, after he answered, she quickly handed the phone to Elisabeth.

"Hello Monsieur Benoit, it's Elisabeth Hambridge here," she began.

"Yes, I know exactly who you are," he replied angrily with a very heavy French accent.

"It is your precious son who has totally ruined my life, and if he was still alive I'd come over there to your stupid little

68

country and kill him myself," he added bitterly. Elisabeth felt a sudden sharp pain stab through her heart at the mention of the meaningless threat.

"I can understand how betrayed and hurt you must be feeling right now Monsieur Benoit, but surely there must be something that can be done to work this all out?" she said hopefully.

Elisabeth closed her eyes, tilted her head back and took in a deep purposeful breath as if to summon her inner Swan Blake; the serene flight attendant who had the special knack of calming people down in the most fraught of situations. The worried woman hoped to God that she still possessed her magical gift, as this particular challenge would be far more difficult to deal with than any nervous or drunken airline passenger had ever been. She knew that Eric Benoit had suddenly lost everything he had believed in for the past twenty years; he had no family and his whole marriage had been built on a wicked lie. It would be perfectly reasonable to assume he would seek revenge. Elisabeth realised that she desperately needed to placate him in order to protect her own family from the fallout. Even though she and her daughter-in-law hadn't exactly seen eye to eye in the past, their friendship had begun to grow following Christian's death. Furthermore the whole of the Hambridge business empire was now in Diana's hands and Elisabeth needed to avoid upsetting the grieving young widow. It was a fragile situation that would require careful handling. The last thing Elisabeth wanted was for Charlotte's aggrieved and vengeful husband to somehow break the news before she had a chance to formulate a plan to deal with the aftermath.

Elisabeth continued to talk calmly to the angry Frenchman. Her soothing words began to wash through his brain. He respected the fact that she had not argued with him and she had taken all of his insults firmly on the chin. The woman had quietly listened to his fiery outbursts and even appeared to understand his point of view. Despite the fact that she had been keen to harbour Charlotte's cruel secret, he warmed to her patient demeanour and conciliatory tone. After an hour-long conversation, Eric eventually agreed that he and his wife needed to talk face-to-face to discuss their predicament at a more personal level. He ended the call and a relieved Elisabeth passed the mobile phone back to Charlotte.

"He said he's going to try and catch a flight from Nice tomorrow morning." Charlotte smiled back and thanked her friend for her help.

"I am just so lucky to have you in my corner Elisabeth. I just don't know how I would have coped without you." The two women gave each other a spontaneously supportive hug. Suddenly Charlotte's body froze as she moved back from the embrace.

"What's the matter?" asked a startled Elisabeth.

"Oh no, I've just realised something," exclaimed Charlotte.

"If Eric has managed to access my FriendsBag profile then he could easily leave poisonous messages on my friends' pages. What if he's already done that?" Charlotte's mind began to race.

"What if he's left something about you being Luke's grandmother on your newsfeed and Diana sees it? Oh my God Elisabeth I'm so sorry he could have already blown the whole secret out of the water."

The two women quickly got up from the sofa and went into the study. Immediately Elisabeth switched on her laptop and logged into her FriendsBag account. She held her breath as the page opened up and she hurriedly scrolled through the newsfeed. They scanned each story and status from the past twenty-four hours, praying that Eric hadn't posted anything incriminating on there. Elisabeth let out a sigh of relief as she could see nothing that mentioned Luke.

"Perhaps it would be best if you just deleted me as a friend for a short while, just until the dust settles. That way there will be no connection between us that Eric can use against us," suggested Charlotte.

"Even if I changed my password there's no guarantee that he wouldn't hack in again and then start causing trouble for you and Christian's side of the family." Reluctantly Elisabeth removed the young woman from her friends list. Even though it was only a small click of her mouse, it still felt strange to break the precious contact that had at first been so difficult to establish.

"Anyway, who needs FriendsBag? We're true friends now and we can always stay in touch on the phone," added Charlotte in an attempt to soften the moment.

Elisabeth could feel her temples tighten and a dull ache begin to grow behind her tired eyes. The affects of drinking wine in the afternoon, Diana's unexpected visits and then the stress of Charlotte's bombshell that Eric had discovered the secret about Luke's biological father were all beginning to take their toll. The day's rollercoaster of emotion had been exhausting and she could spot the signs of an impending migraine. Charlotte noticed how jaded her friend looked and offered to make a soothing cup of Camomile tea as Elisabeth returned to the lounge.

"I'm so sorry you've had to go through all of that with Eric," said Charlotte as she entered the room with two cups of herbal brew.

"Well, it's not entirely your fault is it?" replied Elisabeth thoughtfully.

"He did seem a little calmer at the end of our conversation though, so I'm happy that I was able to help."

The two women chatted as they sipped their drinks. Elisabeth felt her headache slowly relent but the day's events had been extremely tiring and she was beginning to feel drowsy. The old woman had had enough excitement for one day and decided to retire for the night. As she got up from the sofa her muscles ached and her eyelids felt heavy. She slowly walked out of the lounge and into the marble hallway before making her way upstairs. Elisabeth showed her guest to the spare bedroom that she habitually kept made-up with freshly laundered linen, before wearily going to her own room.

Chapter 6

Elisabeth was rudely awoken by the sound of a black cab outside the gates at the front of her house; the clatter of the diesel engine roused her from a deep dream-filled sleep. She blinked opened her eyes and realised she was still fully clothed and lying on top of her duvet. How she hated sleeping in her clothes; it always felt so common. Elisabeth berated herself as she believed only someone not in full control of their actions would fall asleep without getting undressed. This was the second time that she had done it recently and such a slip in her standards was totally unacceptable to her. The tired woman's thoughts were disturbed by a soft knocking on the bedroom door.

"Hello Elisabeth, it's Charlotte here. I've made you a cup of tea," announced the young woman as she entered the bedroom.

"Oh, thank you," replied Elisabeth groggily as she turned to look at her bedside clock. She was surprised to see it was almost eleven-thirty. Her feeling of self-loathing increased, as not only had she fallen asleep fully dressed but she had not set the alarm clock or removed her make-up. Elisabeth's guilt was further compounded by what she regarded as the height of bad manners; she had been so out of control the night before that her house guest had been left to fend for herself.

"Oh gosh, I am so sorry, whatever must you think of me?" flustered Elisabeth as she quickly got up off the bed, hastily ran a brush through her hair and smoothed down her crumpled blouse and skirt.

"No worries," replied Charlotte with a smile.

"We both had a big day yesterday and it's good to let go with a bottle of wine once in a while," she added.

"By the way, I hope it's okay but Eric has just arrived in an airport taxi so I'll go and let him in while you drink your tea. I'll see you downstairs in a little while."

Elisabeth was heartened by the news. It appeared that she had successfully talked Eric around and at least he had been willing to come to England and listen to what his wife had to say about her illegitimate son. Why else would he have flown over from the south of France if not to talk things through face-to-face? Elisabeth went into the en-suite bathroom to freshen up and put on some clean clothes before making her way downstairs to greet her new visitor.

As Elisabeth reached the bottom stair she could see the door to the lounge was slightly ajar; from the hallway she could hear the young couple arguing in French. Even though Elisabeth's knowledge of the language was limited, it was clear that Eric was still furious with Charlotte.

'Christ what a bloody mess I've made. What a hornet's nest of problems I've caused with that damned letter,' thought Elisabeth sadly as she made her escape into the kitchen to brew a fresh cafetiere of coffee.

'I doubt they'll ever be able to come back from this and it's all because of me and my stupid meddling.' Tears began to well in the old woman's eyes as she could hear the arguing in the other room become more heated. She knew that she would have to summon the courage to enter the foray and meet the aggrieved Monsieur Benoit, but she would choose her moment carefully. Elisabeth's thoughts were interrupted by the unexpected trill of the telephone. She recognised the number in the caller display instantly.

"Hello Diana," whispered Elisabeth.

"Hello mother. Are you feeling better today?" asked Diana cordially.

"Yes thank you," she replied in a hushed tone.

"I was just calling to see if you'd still like to be picked up at two o'clock as usual to go shopping, and maybe we could call in and see Christian's new headstone together?"

Following the previous day's cool reception Diana thought it best to call the house first rather than just turn up. She was beginning to tire of her mother-in-law's bad moods and wanted to avoid any further quarrels.

"I am so sorry I had to cut you off yesterday Diana, I really didn't mean to appear rude." Elisabeth apologised for her curt attitude the day before and explained that Charlotte was a friend of hers from an online bereavement forum. She said the two grieving mothers had got together for a chat about their sons. Talking about Christian with someone new had just made Elisabeth more upset than usual and Charlotte's tale had also been extremely distressing.

"It was just all very delicate at the time," explained Elisabeth.

"I was just in the middle of comforting Charlotte when you called at the house. I couldn't just leave her to cry on her own in the lounge while I chatted with you in the other room could I?" Elisabeth poured hot water into the cafetiere and waited for the coffee to brew. The sound of the Benoits' argument coming from the lounge grew louder.

"Who is there with you now then?" asked Diana on hearing the booming tone of Eric's voice in the background.

"Oh, Charlotte stayed here last night. She's err . . . in the other room watching TV," she faltered as she softly closed the kitchen door.

Elisabeth could hear how fractious and loud the conversation in the other room had become and decided that it would be a good idea to give the couple more space to talk through their marital problems. After all she felt largely to blame for their predicament and she didn't relish the idea of becoming a verbal punch bag for Eric's wrath. Leaving them alone while she went shopping with her daughter-in-law sounded like a convenient escape plan. Diana arranged to pick her up an hour and a half later. Elisabeth hung up the phone and replaced the handset in its cradle on the kitchen wall before putting the cafetiere of coffee on a tray with three china mugs. She carried the tray through the hall and paused at the open doorway into the lounge. The arguing had stopped for a moment and the conversation appeared to have dropped to a calmer level. Elisabeth took in a deep breath to prepare herself for meeting Charlotte's husband.

Eric Benoit was an attractive man with a suntanned Mediterranean complexion. His shiny jet black hair was combed back from his face and his clean-shaven skin had no wrinkles. Although he was casually dressed in a pair of cream coloured Chinos, white polo shirt and dark blue deck shoes, it was obvious he had very expensive taste and took great pride in his appearance.

"Bonjour Monsieur Benoit," announced Elisabeth as she entered the lounge. Charlotte walked over to take the coffee tray from her friend as Eric stood up to formally shake the old woman's hand.

"Hello Madame Hambridge," he replied.

"I wish I could say it was a pleasure to meet you," his heavy French accent seemed to angrily punch the words from his mouth. Elisabeth knew that it was never going to be an easy encounter and she was fully prepared for his verbal avalanche of accusations.

#

Timeline: Friday 8th July 2016, 13:25hrs

Diana sat in her office replying to the last of her emails. It had been another busy morning at the estate agency and the young executive was in a contemplative mood. The business was doing extremely well under her guidance. She had taken on extra staff to cover the surge in sales and lettings and the past couple of months' accounts had reported a healthy rise in profits. On a personal level all of the legal paperwork for Christian's estate had been finalised and today she would see the last piece of the tragic jigsaw slotted into place by viewing the headstone with Elisabeth. The young widow had managed to bravely weather the storm following her husband's untimely death and she now felt a new more optimistic chapter was about to begin; even her mother-in-law had seemed to be in a friendlier mood on the phone today. But there was still something bothering Diana; a burning question that nagged at the front of her mind. Why had someone left a photograph of a young man on a motorcycle at Christian's graveside suggesting it was from a son he didn't have? She tried to put the niggling feeling to the back of her thoughts as she opened up the final email in her inbox. It was from one of her oldest and closest friends, Nicola Blunt.

Hi Di.

Hope all is great with you. Just a quickie to check if everything with the memorial garden for Hammers is going okay. Most of us donated on the GiveInPeace page and we wondered if you'd managed to find a suitable plot yet? Must catch up for drinks soon.

Much love.

Nicky XX

'What the hell is this?' thought Diana. There were no plans to create a memorial garden for Christian and the young woman had no knowledge of the crowd funding page. Her mind raced as she quickly looked at her watch to check the time. She needed to be at Clover Croft in just over half an hour to pick up her mother-in-law and she knew what a stickler for punctuality the old biddy could be, but she wanted to find out more about the mysterious fundraising page and exactly what Nicky and her friends had donated to. Diana grabbed her jacket, handbag and mobile phone and called her friend as she quickly made her way out of the office.

"Hello darling, how are you?" asked Nicky.

"Fine thank you," replied Diana, almost cutting off the question mid sentence.

"I just got your email about the GiveInPeace page?"

"Oh yes, we were all wondering how it was going. The plans sound quite exciting, and since it's been a few months, some of us were . . ."

"No you don't understand," interrupted Diana.

"I know nothing about it."

A confused Nicky explained that most of the followers of Christian's FriendsBag memorial page had been sent a link to the crowd funding site. Someone called Robbie Banks had set up the collection to say that the Hambridge family was going to buy a small plot of land at Himley Chase that would become a memorial garden; it would be somewhere for people to visit and remember the man who had given so much to his local community. Nicky remembered when she last saw the page a couple of months before; it had reached its target and raised in excess of two thousand pounds.

Timeline: Friday 8th July 2016, 13:55hrs

Elisabeth had listened to Eric Benoit's arguments; she accepted his accusations and knew she had little defence for her son's actions all those years ago. After an hour's tirade of insults his Gallic wrath appeared to be slightly tempered. He obviously had so much un-vented rage inside but, after an early start and bumpy flight that morning, he no longer had the energy to keep on fighting. Even though it had been Elisabeth's son who had initially set the wheels in motion for this nightmare situation, Eric's anger was firmly fixed on his tearful wife's deceit. Charlotte had no more words; there was nothing more to be said. It was clear that her husband would never forgive her and it appeared he had only made the trip to England to watch her squirm face-to-face. Elisabeth gathered up the coffee mugs and cafetiere and returned to the kitchen. Her friend followed closely behind.

"It's not going well is it," said Elisabeth supportively. Even though she hadn't understood the whole of the explosive conversations in French, the meaning had been clear and she doubted the meeting would end with Eric's forgiveness.

"No, but it's no more than I deserve I suppose," replied Charlotte.

"I think it would be for the best if I went out for a couple of hours to give you two some time alone. Maybe he will calm down a bit more if he doesn't feel so ganged up on," suggested Elisabeth. Charlotte smiled back and agreed that perhaps having the grandmother of her illegitimate son in the same room fighting her corner could be seen as antagonising to the already irate Frenchman.

"Okay then. Lady Diana will be here shortly to pick me up to go shopping. I'll make my excuses and give you two some breathing space."

Elisabeth had heard Eric's threats to cut off his wife without a single penny to her name; she would be abandoned and left to fend for herself. The normally self-assured confident Swan Blake now felt riddled with guilt that she had ruined her friend's life. She hoped to God the couple could at least come to an amicable agreement. Elisabeth opened her purse and took out five twenty pound notes.

"Here, take this to see you through, just in case you need to pop out for anything before I get back," she said, placing the money firmly into the young woman's hand.

"I'll get some more from the cash machine while I'm out shopping with Diana." Charlotte tried to speak but instead two big tears rolled down her cheeks. She smiled warmly back at her friend and mouthed a quiet 'thank you' as Elisabeth pulled her close to give her a friendly cuddle. Their embrace was interrupted by the short beep of a car horn outside. Elisabeth peered out of the kitchen window and saw Diana's red Mini parked at the entrance to her drive. She quickly gathered up her handbag, purse and keys before giving her friend one final hug.

Diana sat in the car watching her mother-in-law walk over the stone chippings towards her. She was surprised to see that the same unfamiliar silver car from the previous day was still parked on the drive. Elisabeth opened the wrought iron gates and stepped through the gap before quickly closing them behind her. She opened the car door, smiled, put her handbag into the foot well and then elegantly slid into the front passenger seat.

"Hello mother. Your friend is still here then?" asked Diana, nodding towards the vehicle parked on the gravel.

"Erm, yes," faltered Elisabeth.

"She's just leaving her car there for a couple of days while she's visiting friends in the area." The old woman was trying very hard to hold her nerve. She was keen to divert any attention away from her visitor as she couldn't be sure she wouldn't inadvertently mention Luke.

"Okay, let's go and see Christian's headstone first shall we?" smiled Diana as she swiftly pulled away from the house.

Suddenly Elisabeth felt a cold shock of pins and needles surge through her veins as she remembered that Luke's photograph and Charlotte's posy of flowers had been left at Christian's graveside the day before. She had slept in late with a hangover and had been so preoccupied with the Benoits' woes; the fact that the incriminating memento would still be there had totally slipped her mind. It was too late to cancel the trip to the cemetery. How could she possibly begin to explain it to the young woman?

Unbeknown to Elisabeth, Diana had spent a sleepless night thinking about the photograph and posy of flowers that she had discovered at her dead husband's graveside; why anyone would falsely claim to be Christian's son was incomprehensible. She had come to the conclusion that it was highly unlikely the picture had blown across from someone else's grave as it had been secured beneath a large and unusual pebble at the base of the headstone. Also the writing on the back had mentioned Hammers' nickname. It had definitely been put there deliberately, but who would want to play such a cruel prank? And now there was the additional mystery of the GiveInPeace page for a non-existent memorial garden. Who would want to desecrate the memory of her beloved Christian with a fund-raising scam? The young widow had a difficult dilemma; should she tell her mother-in-law or would it be best not to mention the strange things that had happened? Diana was at least thankful that she had visited the graveside alone the previous day and had had the opportunity to hide the flowers and photograph safely inside a bin bag in the boot of her car. She looked across at her passenger and smiled.

The old woman was quieter than usual and she looked quite anxious; almost fretful. Elisabeth's normally elegant demeanour appeared slightly ruffled, as if she hadn't quite had enough time to get properly prepared for the day.

'Poor woman,' thought Diana as she pulled her Mini into a parking space.

'First her husband Thomas dies and then, less than a year later, she's visiting the freshly laid headstone of her dead son. How could I even begin to tell her that some nasty piece of work is playing sick jokes on what's left of the Hambridge family? She gave another reassuring smile and took the bold decision not to say anything about the recent events to Elisabeth. Diana felt more than capable of handling it all herself.

The two women got out of the car and walked towards the grave. Elisabeth still had no idea how she was going to explain the flowers and picture left by the mother of her grandson.

There was no way she could bring herself to admit the truth to Diana. During the sombre journey to Hanford Town Crematorium Elisabeth had practiced in her head how she would feign surprise on discovering the posy and photograph. She would then helpfully suggest to her grief stricken daughter-in-law that the sprawling cemetery had hundreds of plots; someone must have left the tribute there in error. As they approached the shiny black granite of Christian's headstone, the old woman gasped in shock. The bunch of carnations, incriminating photo and large smooth pebble from a far away French beach were nowhere in sight.

"It's handsome isn't it;" remarked Diana, slightly surprised by Elisabeth's startled reaction. The grieving grandmother smiled back and breathed in a huge sigh of relief; Charlotte's secret was still safe for now.

Chapter 7

At the end of the inaugural viewing of the headstone, the two women bid a fond farewell to their beloved Christian and Diana drove Elisabeth to the supermarket. They returned home later that day with a car full of groceries and, as they turned into Clover Croft, Elisabeth started to rummage in her handbag for a remote control key to operate the electronic gates at the end of her drive. She never liked to keep Diana waiting. Even though Elisabeth didn't show her appreciation all that often, she was grateful for the weekly shopping trips and always tried to avoid any delays when being dropped off. Elisabeth was still searching inside her bag for the key as Diana pulled onto the stone chippings. The two women were surprised to discover that Charlotte's car was no longer parked on the driveway and the wrought iron gates had been left wide open.

"They must have gone out," muttered Elisabeth, secretly annoyed with her friend for failing to close the gates behind her when she left. The old woman valued her privacy and hated her security being compromised. The thought that a total stranger could have walked up to her front door without first being vetted at the intercom filled her with dread.

"They?" asked Diana with a puzzled look on her face. Elisabeth tried to brush off the careless remark and quickly got out of the car, but her daughter-in-law repeated the question.

"What do you mean they?"

"Oh, I mean Charlotte must have gone out," replied Elisabeth dismissively. She picked up a couple of carrier bags from the back seat of the car and swiftly walked up to the front door to try to escape her daughter-in-law's impending inquisition. Diana carried the remaining heavier shopping bags into the house and placed them on the kitchen counter top.

"Hey, look at this Mother, *they've* left you a note on the memo board," announced Diana, sarcastically stressing the plural. Elisabeth spun around to read the words that had been written on the black slate in chalk. The message was surrounded by a heart-shaped outline with an arrow pointing towards the cafetiere on the work surface beneath.

Thank you so much for your help.
We've worked things out.
Flying back to Cannes.
Much love.
Charlotte. XX

Elisabeth smiled. She was relieved that it appeared Eric had given his wife a second chance and the couple had decided to give their relationship another try.

"What was going on there then?" demanded Diana suspiciously.

"She wasn't just leaving her car here while she was out visiting friends was she?" Elisabeth felt her stomach begin to knot as she had to concentrate on what lies she was going to tell her daughter-in-law. She needed to keep her story as close to the truth as possible without revealing Charlotte's secret, but the slightest deviation from the earlier tale would be immediately noticed by the astute young woman.

Diana listened intently as Elisabeth explained that her friend wasn't coping well with her bereavement. She said that although Charlotte now lived in France she had actually grown up in Hanford. The grieving young mother had decided to come back to her home town in England for a few days to get a little perspective on life. The two women had met up for lunch the day before as planned and they had said their goodbyes when Elisabeth was dropped off back at home. Then Charlotte had unexpectedly returned to the house saying her husband had accused her of having an affair. Elisabeth said it was all a big misunderstanding and she had wanted to help her friend to sort out the problem. She had suggested the couple meet up on neutral ground and Eric had arrived at the house that morning. The old woman had simply given them the space they needed to talk things through.

"So, let me get this right," started Diana, her tone sounded like an engine that was about to rev up to full speed.

82

"You left two total strangers alone in your house while you went out shopping?" she exclaimed incredulously.

"No, it wasn't like that," replied Elisabeth defensively.

"Charlotte isn't a stranger to me."

Elisabeth was secretly upset that Charlotte hadn't waited until she had returned home from the supermarket so she could say goodbye properly to the mother of her grandson. She took in a deep breath to sniff away a small tear and wondered why her friend hadn't taken a later flight. It was a huge effort to hide her disappointment from her daughter-in-law.

"And what's this?" asked Diana, oblivious to Elisabeth's sadness, as she pulled out five twenty pound notes that had been tucked underneath the empty cafetiere.

"Oh I just lent her a little money to tide her over, in case she needed to pop out for some essentials, but obviously she doesn't need it now if she's patched things up with her husband," replied Elisabeth, proud and relieved that her new friend hadn't made off with the cash.

"So you just lent a hundred quid to this stranger as well? Oh well, if it's just a little hundred pounds that's okay then," continued Diana sarcastically.

"I told you, Charlotte's not a stranger," protested Elisabeth as small angry tears began to well in her eyes. Diana slowly shook her head and sighed, she could clearly see how defensive of Charlotte her mother-in-law had become, but she couldn't understand why the old woman had been so trusting of someone she had only recently met. Whatever the reason, Diana knew she would probably lose the argument and she felt nothing would be gained by fighting another battle against the formidable Mrs Hambridge.

"Well, at least leaving the money here for you is honest of her I suppose," conceded Diana reluctantly.

"But you really should be more careful about letting people you don't know all that well into your home though. I mean, what's the point in having all this security with the intercom and everything if you're just going to declare open house to any Tom, Dick or Harry? Honestly Mother, this Charlotte woman could have been anyone. Thankfully, this time, they appear to have been decent people." Diana pecked her mother-in-law on the cheek before walking back out to her car for the short journey home.

As soon as the Mini had left the driveway, Elisabeth called Charlotte's mobile. She tried a few times but kept being diverted to voicemail. Eventually Elisabeth realised that her friend had probably switched her phone off during the flight, so she left a short cordial message to say how pleased she was that the couple had managed to talk things through and she would be in touch the next day to check that she was okay.

#

Timeline: Friday 8th July 2016, 19:00hrs

At seven o'clock in the evening Diana eventually arrived home. The lavish penthouse condo she had once shared with her husband was at the top of a modern six storey block of apartments named The Folly. It was a striking circular building made from shiny steel and pale green opaque glass; an architectural landmark that stood at the pinnacle of a hill, on the outskirts of Hanford, overlooking a vast area of open parkland called Himley Chase. The imposing tower proudly watched over the valley below and it had earned a reputation for being a prime residential location for Hanford's elite. Diana parked her Mini in the underground car park before carrying her briefcase and a couple of carrier bags of shopping to the lift. Today had been an unusual day to say the least. The photograph and fresh posy of flowers discovered at Christian's grave the day before still played on her mind and the young widow still couldn't shake off the uneasy feeling she had felt following her conversation with her friend Nicky about the curious fund raising page.

Diana walked into her open plan penthouse apartment and kicked off her stilettos; her hot feet had suffered in the pinching leather shoes all day. The contemporary décor inside her home had been expertly designed by a Feng Shui master and its serene ambience created a calm sanctuary away from the stress of everyday living. It was a large airy space that bathed in shafts of softly coloured rays from overhead recessed halogen lamps.

84

The uncluttered lines of Swedish designer furniture were occasionally interrupted by brushed chrome floor lamps, as speckles of light danced on the highly polished Italian porcelain tiled floor beneath. Long flowing muslin drapes hung elegantly at three Juliette balconies, keeping the glint of the setting summer sun out of the room. The minimalist interior was highly functional and simply oozed peace and tranquillity. Diana padded her bare feet across the cooling surface of the tiled floor and entered the kitchen to begin unloading her groceries.

'I really should try to eat more variety,' she thought as she placed her usual half a dozen ready meals into the freezer. In reality Diana knew it was an empty promise as, since the death of her husband, cooking a proper meal from scratch had been the last thing on her mind. It was too much hassle to dirty the pots and pans just for one person; as a result, the grieving widow had mostly survived the past six months on pre-prepared microwave dinners. She opened a chilled bottle of Chablis and poured some of its fruity contents into an elegant wine glass before making her way across to the lounge area. She took a couple of sips of wine and picked up her mobile phone. It was time to bite the bullet and raise her concerns about the recent strange events. She took in a deep thoughtful breath before dialling 101. Her call was diverted to the Hanford Police control room and transferred once again, before being answered by a friendly sounding detective constable called Trudi Jones.

#

"This sounds like a familiar fund raising scam to me," said the policewoman at the other end of the line.

"I've heard of it before, and they're usually rife after national tragedies such as terrorist attacks; especially when lots of people have been injured or fatally wounded and their names and photographs have been released to the press." Diana listened in total disbelief.

The officer explained that the perpetrators of such crimes also found the names of people who had recently passed away by scouring family announcements in local newspapers. They would then set up a fund raising web page claiming to be

85

collecting money for the dead person's funeral expenses; some would carry a convincing back story to tug on the heartstrings of hapless donors, such as claiming the deceased had no life insurance and their family was now destitute. Links to the page would be mercilessly shared on social media sites and the scammers could just sit back and watch the cash roll in. By the time relatives and friends discovered the fraud it was very often too late to get the money back; the criminals would be one step ahead, having transferred the funds and closed the pages before the hustles were spotted.

"I know it sounds so cruel that anyone would try to cash in on someone's death like that, but I work in the Cyber Unit and we hear about this sort of thing all the time," added DC Jones. The detective thanked Diana for the information about the GiveInPeace page and said she would be back in touch after it had been investigated further. The bewildered young widow hung up the call and took a large glug of wine. She was shocked to discover such a heartless crime was so common.

Chapter 8

Timeline: Friday 5th August 2016, 13:00hrs –
One month later.

Four weeks had passed since Eric's visit and Elisabeth had still not heard from Charlotte. Her friend's mobile number no longer worked and emails kept bouncing back. Elisabeth assumed that emotions were still running high in the Benoit household, and no one would blame the young woman's husband if he had forced her to change her phone number and cut off all contact with the Hambridge family. But the grieving old woman firmly believed that, when the time was right, the mother of her grandson would get back in touch. The two women had grown very close in such a short space of time and not even the Gallic wrath of Eric Benoit could break such a bond.

Elisabeth had taken some comfort in visiting the online memorial page for Luke, but she was still unable to bring herself to comment on there; even though Eric now knew the painful truth about his son, she was unsure how the land lay between the troubled couple. She dare not risk causing Charlotte any more heartache by popping up out-of-the-blue and commenting on the page as Luke's biological grandmother; effectively dragging all of Eric's pent up anger to the surface again.

Elisabeth sat at the desk in her study looking through the photographs on the CD that Charlotte had given to her. The images had been thoughtfully titled in chronological order and mostly featured a smiling Luke.

'How full of hopes and dreams he must have been while he was growing up,' thought Elisabeth as she took a sip of freshly brewed coffee. Eric had provided him and his mother with a wonderful fun-packed lifestyle filled with wild camping trips, exotic holidays, speedboats and skiing adventures.

Suddenly Elisabeth's contented expression changed to a guilty frown, with an all-encompassing realisation that Charlotte could have lost it all, and all because of her meddling.

That young woman's very comfortable life in the South of France could have all been snatched away from her in a heartbeat.

'No wonder she has not been in touch with me,' thought Elisabeth regretfully. She knew the couple had been reconciled, but realised Eric had probably insisted this was on the understanding that his wife had nothing more to do with her dead child's family.

'I suppose I've no other choice other than to stay under the radar for a while then,' thought Elisabeth resolutely. The grieving grandmother blinked back a small tear that was threatening to fall down her cheek as she clicked open a browser window on her laptop. Even though she couldn't contact Charlotte directly, there was nothing to stop her keeping up to date with her friend's activities. Elisabeth decided to take a little comfort in trawling through the timeline on Luke's memorial page instead; if she could just see what Charlotte had commented on there lately then she would have an idea of how the young woman was coping.

The list of new greetings was disappointingly short. Where once they had rolled thick and fast, with dozens of sympathetic messages of love and condolence being added every day, there had been only four new posts in the past week. Three of these were from friends overseas who had only just heard the news of Luke's death, and one was a blatant advertisement for a new brand of ski clothing rudely placed on the page by an insensitive visitor. There was nothing on there from Charlotte.

Elisabeth was frustrated. All lines of communication with her friend had been severed. She had no choice other than to go back to the beginning and try to send a message through her FriendsBag profile. A quick search for the young woman's name in the list of followers on Luke's memorial page gave one listing for Lottie Benoit, but it was a different woman; the profile photograph was of a darker haired woman whose maiden name had been LeFevre, not Rook.

"Damn it!" exclaimed Elisabeth.

"There's bound to be more than one woman with that name. I suppose Charlotte or Lottie Benoit in France is about as common as John Smith is in England. Next Elisabeth scanned her grandson's friends list but she could find no link to her friend's profile. 'That's strange. Why would Charlotte un-follow her own son?' thought the grieving grandmother.

A fresh search on numerous social media sites only returned a list of other people with the same name. Eventually the old woman had to concede defeat, trying to re-connect with her friend was useless; Charlotte's FriendsBag profile had been deleted, every trace of her was gone. A terrifying thought crossed Elisabeth's mind.

'Oh my God I hope Eric hasn't hurt her.'

#

Timeline: Friday 5th August 2016, 14:00hrs

Diana pulled her car onto Elisabeth's driveway before making her way into the house to pick up her mother-in-law to go shopping. She was happy that during the past few weeks their relationship had returned to friendlier terms and they were now on a more even keel. She had decided not to mention the discovery of the photograph and pebble left at Christian's grave and instead chose to believe they had been placed there in error. She had even managed to put the upsetting business of the fake fund raising page to the back of her mind. The young widow had also decided to start a new healthier diet and, in a funny way, she was actually looking forward to perusing the fresh produce aisles at the weekly trip to the supermarket. Diana turned her key in the front door lock and walked into Elisabeth's house.

"Hello Mother, it's only me. Are you ready?" she asked cheerily on entering the marble hallway.

"Yes, I'm just finishing off some emails. I won't be long," replied Elisabeth, her voice sounded a little distant. Diana walked into the study and found the old woman sitting at her desk. She noticed a couple of crumpled paper handkerchiefs next to the laptop computer and Elisabeth's eyes appeared to be a little puffy from crying. She realised something was deeply troubling her mother-in-law.

"Whatever is the matter," soothed Diana as she placed a comforting arm around the sobbing woman's shoulders.

"Oh Diana, I am so worried about my friend Charlotte. You know the woman I met through the online bereavement group?"

"Yes, how could I forget," she replied, the sharp memory of that day when they had quarrelled stung through Diana's chest.

"Well, I haven't heard from her since she went back to France with Eric," Elisabeth continued, her voice wavering.

"But more worryingly than that, she is nowhere to be found on FriendsBag, it's as if she's totally disappeared." Diana hugged the old woman closer.

"I just hope to God that she's okay," added Elisabeth as she buried her face into her daughter-in-law's shoulder.

The young woman was shocked by the uncharacteristic outburst. Never before had she seen her mother-in-law in such a hopeless state. Even at the funerals of her late husband and son, Elisabeth had somehow managed to retain her impenetrable veneer; choosing to stoically bury all of her vulnerabilities deeply beneath the unflappable wings of Swan Blake. This was the first time Diana had seen the old lady display any unguarded sign of true emotion. She couldn't understand why the loss of the friendship of a relative stranger had affected her so deeply.

'What was it about this bloody Charlotte woman?' she thought.

"Well, you know how these things can fizzle out sometimes," offered Diana thoughtfully, trying to make light of the situation.

"Maybe she's just decided to move on with things and your friendship was simply a brief chapter in her life. People deal with grief in many different ways you know Mother. Just be happy that you were able to help her through a tough time." The young woman realised her comforting words were not having any effect.

"No, you don't understand. She wouldn't do that," protested Elisabeth.

"How can you be sure?" asked Diana quizzically, startled by her abrupt reply and strong defence of Charlotte.

"I just felt that we had more of a connection than that," she replied. The old woman suddenly realised that she had probably said too much. She would have to take a firmer hold of her feelings. Elisabeth knew that Diana had no idea what bond she had shared with Charlotte and, now that Luke was dead, there was nothing to be gained from her daughter-in-law ever finding out. She took in a deep breath and forced a small smile as she fought back more tears.

"I know it's going to sound silly but we really did grow quite close in a very short time. It just seems so wrong and out of character for Charlotte to cut off all communication like that. There must be something bad going on." Elisabeth paused and bit her bottom lip.

"Eric really was very nasty towards Charlotte when they met up here. I know her note said they had made up after their argument, but I am just really worried that he could have lost control or something and hurt her. Do you think I should report her missing or something?" asked Elisabeth, hoping her idea would get the young woman's endorsement.

"Don't be so ridiculous," snorted Diana.

"I know it sounds harsh Mother, but the police would probably laugh at you. I have people un-friend me all the time on FriendsBag, and people do occasionally close down their accounts you know. As I said, grief does strange stuff to people. She probably just needs time on her own." Despite her dismissive tone, Diana was surprised by how genuinely worried her mother-in-law appeared to be.

"God knows I've felt like that before now. Some days I just wish I could get away from everyone and the whole bloody world would stop and let me get off for a while; just so I can go and do my own thing," she added. Ironically for Diana, today was beginning to feel exactly like one of those times. The two women picked up their handbags and made their way out of the house to go shopping.

#

Timeline: Friday 5th August 2016, 16:30hrs

The air-conditioned aisles of the supermarket were a welcome break from the stifling hot summer sunshine outside.

91

Elisabeth ambled along the rows, aimlessly filling her trolley with trays of pre-cut fruit and bags of prepared salad. Diana had moved to another section of the store, so the worried grandmother was able to indulge her thoughts in Charlotte and their shared guilty secret. She couldn't help thinking how her earlier outburst could have raised Diana's suspicions. She knew that she would have to be more careful in future not to betray the trust of her grandson's mother.

Eventually the two women met up at the checkout and Diana loaded her groceries onto the conveyor belt behind Elisabeth's shopping. She felt quite proud of herself for having successfully bypassed the frozen ready meals counter; she had chosen the healthier option of fresh fish and organic vegetables instead. Diana placed the final two items from her trolley onto the belt and checked her shopping list on her mobile phone to ensure she hadn't forgotten anything. Suddenly she became aware of a small commotion at the front of the till. Elisabeth's debit card had been declined.

"I just don't understand it," protested the old woman as she keyed in her PIN for the third time.

"There's plenty of money in my account." Diana watched her mother-in-law snatch the declined piece of plastic from the reader and angrily search through her purse for a different card. Elisabeth's face flushed with embarrassment as the checkout clerk told her the second card had also failed.

"Mother, are you sure you've entered the right PIN?" asked Diana as she jovially smiled at the sales assistant, trying to ease the tension.

"It's easy to forget them when you're getting on in years," she teased.

Elisabeth was not amused by the remark and glared back at her daughter-in-law. She had never experienced such a humiliating ordeal before and the unwelcome reference to her age was not helping the situation. But it was no use, she tried three other cards from her purse and none of them worked. The cashier smiled back but her patience was wearing thin. There was a growing queue of customers in the line behind them; most of whom tutted and rolled their eyes with presumptive opinions, yet all were secretly entertained by the old woman's plight. After a few more failed attempts with the PIN machine Diana offered to pay for both loads of shopping with one of her cards; Elisabeth could settle up with her when they got home.

"Oh my God, I have never been so embarrassed in all of my life," flustered Elisabeth as she angrily loaded shopping bags into the boot of Diana's Mini. The bewildered woman was adamant that she hadn't been confused and she had entered the correct number on each occasion.

"There are thousands of pounds in my accounts and that stupid shop girl on the till did her best to make me look like a penniless vagrant," she protested.

"Okay, okay. I believe you Mother, but why don't you just go and check your balances at the hole in the wall over there while I finish putting the shopping in the car," suggested Diana. She was used to her mother-in-law's stubborn nature and she had felt sorry for the young checkout clerk when Elisabeth had vented her wrath in the shop. But this episode of forgetfulness was different from Elisabeth's usual belligerent demeanour and Diana believed it was a sign that the old biddy's grief and advancing years were beginning to take their toll.

Elisabeth slipped her debit card into the cash machine and confidently entered her PIN. After a few seconds the screen gave a list of options and the angry woman tutted as she sharply pressed the button to request a balance enquiry. The machine whirred and displayed the available funds; an unexpected over-drawn balance in her current account. A shocked Elisabeth stared at the screen in disbelief. Thousands of pounds were missing. Frozen with panic she felt very light headed; as if her lifeblood was draining down her body and out through the soles of her kitten heeled shoes. She grabbed hold of the edge of the cash machine to steady herself as she removed her card from the reader. Elisabeth took in a deep breath to quell a wave of vomit that was threatening to rise from her stomach. Her hands trembled as she put the card back into her purse and took out the one for her savings account. She entered it into the machine and quickly typed in the PIN. She was dismayed to discover the account had a zero balance.

Diana sat in her Mini watching her mother-in-law insert different cards into the cash dispenser. A short queue of shoppers had begun to gather behind Elisabeth as she carried on trying all of the cards in her purse. It soon became apparent that all of her accounts had been emptied and her credit cards taken to their limits. Eventually she stepped away from the machine and slowly walked back to the car.

"How did you get on?" asked Diana as Elisabeth slumped into the front passenger seat. Her face was ashen and large tears pooled in the fretful old woman's eyes as she sat silently clutching her handbag on her lap.

"Well?" prompted Diana impatiently.

"It's all gone," whispered Elisabeth as she swallowed back a hard lump in her throat. Diana looked back quizzically.

"All of my money, it's all gone. Every single penny," she wailed as tears began to cascade down her pale cheeks.

Diana took in a deep purposeful breath and rubbed her eyes as it slowly became obvious to her that her mother-in-law had become the victim of theft. Her mind raced back to the day Elisabeth had invited the mysterious Charlotte and her husband to stay in her house while she went shopping. Diana suspected that her gut feeling about the French couple had been correct and she had been right to berate Elisabeth for leaving the strangers in her home unaccompanied. But the young businesswoman knew trying to convince the old woman that Charlotte was anything other than a genuine friend would be a difficult challenge. Diana began to massage her temples as if she was trying to pluck a solution to the problem out of her brain.

"What the hell has happened to all of my money?" sobbed Elisabeth as she rummaged inside her handbag for a tissue. Diana gazed across at the pitiful woman. She knew that there was no real point raising her concerns about Charlotte and it would only serve to antagonise an already bewildered Elisabeth.

"Try not to worry Mother, it's probably just a banking glitch or something" soothed Diana as she struggled to hide her suspicions.

"We'll go home now and sort it all out over a nice cup of tea."

#

Timeline: Friday 5th August 2016, 17:30hrs

Back in the relative calm of her home office Elisabeth trembled with fear as she opened up her laptop and logged on to her bank's website. She felt a sudden surge of pins and needles pulse through her chest as the statements for three separate accounts confirmed that all of her money had been transferred and withdrawn over the past four weeks. It soon became apparent that her credit cards had been used to pay for large purchases that Elisabeth didn't recognise. The bank had also sanctioned a loan for fifteen thousand pounds. All of that money had been paid out, mostly through third party money transfer services and cash withdrawals. There it was in black and white, the cold realisation that every one of her bank accounts had been plundered; Elisabeth was in severe debt and every penny of her substantial life savings was gone.

Chapter 9

A fine mist of summer rain had descended on the town as Elisabeth and Diana entered Hanford Police Station; dark clouds had assembled in the skies above and the oppressive air outside felt as if a thunderstorm was on its way. The two women smiled supportively at each other as they walked into the reception area and headed towards the general enquiry desk. A young PC was sitting behind a heavy glass screen. He took their details and scribbled down a few notes before picking up a telephone to summon a colleague.

"Take a seat over there please and one of our officers will be with you shortly," he smiled, whilst pointing towards a row of hard plastic chairs that had been joined together beneath a window on the wall opposite. The two women dutifully obliged and took their places on the seats.

During the drive to the police station Diana had gently questioned her mother-in-law regarding the missing money and she now suspected that Elisabeth had become the victim of a scam. She knew that Thomas Hambridge had left his family well provided for following his death, with a large payout from a valuable life insurance policy and a comfortable widow's pension. The house at Clover Croft had no mortgage and Elisabeth had no debts. Diana knew that her mother-in-law would have had no need to take out any loans or exceed her credit limits; in fact the old woman had always been very careful with her money.

A tall man dressed in a smart blue suit and white shirt opened a door in the corner of the reception area and called out Elisabeth's name.

"Hello, I'm Detective Sergeant Duke," announced the officer as he walked over to shake hands with his visitors. Diana noted that he was friendly looking and quite handsome with kind eyes, but he had a tired expression and a heavy five o'clock shadow.

"Hello sergeant, my name is Diana Hambridge and this is my mother-in-law Elisabeth Hambridge."

The two women got up and followed DS Duke back through the door that opened into a brightly lit concrete corridor. They walked quickly behind the detective's long strides as he led them past numerous offices, interview rooms and waiting areas that were busy with the sounds of trilling telephones and raised voices. They took a lift to the first floor and finally arrived at a door that led into a long and narrow CID office. A quarter of the room had been cordoned off with padded blue acoustic screens to create a temporary dividing wall. This gave the sergeant and his senior colleague a workspace that was separated from the chaos of the main office. The other side of the room was assigned to a team of detectives and administrative staff.

"Please do both take a seat," said DS Duke, as he walked around behind his desk and gestured towards a couple of office chairs.

"Right then, I understand from my colleague downstairs that you think someone has stolen your identity?" he queried with a respectful smile.

"Well I'm not sure about that officer," replied Elisabeth, confused by the unexpected turn of events that had led her to be sitting at the heart of the town's police station.

"Of course you're sure Mother," snapped Diana incredulously.

"What other possible explanation could there be for all of your money disappearing like that?" she added.

DS Duke patiently listened to the embarrassed woman's story of how she had been unable to pay for her groceries at the supermarket, and how she had later confirmed with her bank that all of the money had been withdrawn from her accounts and her credit cards taken to their limits. Furthermore a loan for fifteen thousand pounds had been taken out in her name. The detective immediately carried out an online credit rating check for the fretful woman. Moments later it revealed the unwelcome news that other loans and numerous store cards had been opened up by someone claiming to be Elisabeth Hambridge at the Clover Croft address; with thousands of pounds worth of purchases made. The weary sergeant rubbed his eyes and scratched the itchy stubble on his chin. It had been a very long day and this was going to be another case to add to his growing workload. He smiled sympathetically at the old woman sitting in front of him, but Elisabeth simply stared vacantly into space. He could tell that this had all come as a tremendous shock to her and he wondered how severe the consequences could yet become.

"I need to ask first of all, has anyone had any access to your account details recently?" Elisabeth remained silent and shook her head. Her stare glazed over as tears welled up in her eyes. She was always very careful with her debit and credit cards and she was positive that they had always been in her purse. She kept a separate note of the PINs safely locked away in her bureau at home.

"You haven't lost any documents, utility bills, bank statements or anything like that?" he gently coaxed. Elisabeth stared at the floor and shook her head again.

"Have you maybe come into contact with anyone out of the ordinary recently? Unexpected door-to-door salespeople? Anyone asking you personal questions in a survey or anything like that?"

"I shouldn't have thought so," snorted Diana.

"I'm always with Elisabeth when she goes out shopping and I don't remember anyone like that stopping us in the street. Also there is an alarm, security gates and intercom at her home so nobody unexpected ever gets over the threshold," she added.

DS Duke paused for a moment and turned to face Diana. He didn't appreciate the interruption. At this point he was unsure if the young woman was simply being a supportive daughter-in-law or if she was involved with the fraud. It was not unheard of for people to play the role of a concerned relative or friend in order to deflect attention away from themselves and influence an investigation.

"Workmen in the house then?" he added, returning his gaze to Elisabeth. Diana noted his dismissive move and she angrily folded her arms, rolled her eyes and sighed heavily. It seemed obvious that the policeman didn't want her input and she was annoyed at being made to feel irrelevant.

Elisabeth knew that the detective was trying to be helpful but she could think of no one who could have stolen from her. In her mind she was sure nobody could have taken her cards or accessed her financial details. Maybe the bank had got it wrong, it was all a big misunderstanding; perhaps an over-worked anonymous bank clerk had deleted numbers from the wrong boxes; maybe it was a system error. Elisabeth was sure that pretty soon the mistake would be spotted and she would wake from this horrible nightmare, with everything returned to normal. She made a mental note to seek a generous apology from the bank.

Suddenly the tearful old woman's thoughts were disturbed by the one fateful sentence she had not wanted to hear; the burning question that her daughter-in-law hoped would help to solve the mystery behind the identity theft.

"What about your friend Charlotte from the bereavement group?" asked Diana. Elisabeth spun around in her chair to face the young woman and glared at her, as if she was trying to telepathically instruct her daughter-in-law to stop talking.

"You've got to admit it Mother, it was strange how she flitted in and out of your life like that." Elisabeth could feel her rage building beneath the fragile illusion of calm she had so far managed to cling on to. The heat of her fury was in danger of erupting, and Diana would feel its full force.

'How dare she even suggest that this could have anything to do with Charlotte,' she seethed under her breath.

"Charlotte?" queried DS Duke as he jotted down the name in his notepad.

"No, it's got nothing to do with her," snapped Elisabeth defensively as she took in a deep breath to try and regain her composure. The sergeant raised his eyebrows. Unbeknown to the two women sitting in front of him, the name Charlotte was becoming very familiar to him.

"Do you have Charlotte's surname?" he asked gently.

"Yes, it's Benoit," replied Elisabeth, adamant that the line of questioning would be a complete waste of time.

"Is she French or something?" he continued.

"No, she's English. Benoit is her married name. She was born here in Hanford and her maiden name was Rook," she added haughtily.

After a few moments of rapid tapping on the keyboard of his laptop, DS Duke reached over to pick up a sheet of A4 paper from his desktop printer, and sat back in his swivel chair. He paused for a short while as he checked the printed information once more. The sounds of buzzing phones and the hushed murmurings of police officers scuttling up and down the corridor outside hung in the air. Everything was beginning to merge into a low hum of irritating background noise as Diana and Elisabeth waited for DS Duke to speak. The experienced investigator with kind blue eyes was wondering how he could best break the unwelcome news that Charlotte Rook was an alias featured on the force's scam watch list. She had recently become the subject of an intensive investigation.

"It looks like your Charlotte could be what we call a 'long con' artist I'm afraid," announced the detective. Diana and Elisabeth stared back at him quizzically.

"That means she takes her time to draw in her victims," he explained.

"The report here says that someone calling herself Charlotte Rook has befriended lots of people on social media over the past year. She's wormed her way into their confidence by posing as a long lost relative and scammed money out of dozens of victims." He passed the print out across the desk.

"I knew it, I just bloody knew it," exclaimed Diana, a smug self-congratulatory smirk flicked across her lips.

"You see Mother, I just knew she was a wrong-un from the start," she added triumphantly, her suspicions appeared vindicated.

"No!" yelled Elisabeth. The old woman began to panic. The topic of conversation was starting to escalate out of her control.

"My Charlotte is not that con artist. I won't believe it," her protests grew louder. Tears welled in Elisabeth's eyes as she felt the overwhelming need to defend the innocent mother of her grandchild. She rummaged through her handbag desperately hoping to find a handkerchief.

"It was me who did all the running. I was the one who actively tracked her down online. I was the one who made the initial contact." She pulled out her mobile phone, house keys and purse and threw them all on the desk before resuming the fruitless search inside her bag.

"I was the one who called her every day. It was me, all me I tell you." Elisabeth punctuated each frenzied sentence by stabbing her index finger at her chest. Diana was startled by the animated outpouring; she had never seen Elisabeth so emotional before.

"Charlotte was extremely reluctant to talk to me at first. I had to virtually stalk her for a week to get her to accept my friendship on FriendsBag for God's sake." Elisabeth paused to take in a gulp of air as Diana and DS Duke listened to the verbal avalanche. The distressed old woman began to pant in an effort to quell the adrenaline pumping through her veins.

"But why was her friendship so important to you Mother?" asked Diana. Elisabeth chose to totally ignore her daughter-in-law's question and instead focussed her attention on DS Duke's face.

"And for your information sergeant she didn't worm her way into my life as you so delicately put it. My Charlotte has nothing to do with any of this scam nonsense, you've got the wrong woman in the frame and you're totally barking up the wrong tree," Elisabeth exclaimed, clearly irritated by not being able to find a handkerchief.

"I was the one who tracked Charlotte down on the internet and it took ages before I was able to coax her into talking about Luke." The grieving grandmother gasped and quickly placed her hand over her mouth. She knew immediately that she had got carried away in the heat of the moment and said too much.

"Luke? Who is Luke?" asked Diana. She knew the name rang a bell.

Elisabeth chose to ignore the question and stared at the sheet of paper on the desk. Diana waited patiently for an answer but her mother-in-law said nothing. DS Duke was surprised by Elisabeth's sudden silence following her emotionally charged outburst. He could tell that she was hiding something and he was determined to find out what it was. Elisabeth may have been able to fend off her daughter-in-law's question but the old lady would not be allowed to ignore him.

"Well? Who is Luke?" pressed the detective. Elisabeth felt a surge of pain at the sudden realisation that her unguarded comment had opened Pandora's Box; nothing could hold back the life-changing secret that was about to be unleashed. There was no escape from the policeman's question. Elisabeth raised her gaze to meet DS Duke's steely stare as she desperately tried to avoid eye-contact with Diana. In her heart she felt sure that the mother of her grandchild had nothing to do with the stolen money but she also knew she could no longer keep Luke a secret from the world. She took in a deep breath and opened her mouth to speak as fat salty tears streamed down her face.

"Luke was her son," sobbed Elisabeth, dropping her head in her hands.

Suddenly Diana remembered where she had come across that name before, as her mind raced back to the day when she had first seen Christian's headstone. The startled young woman swallowed hard and tried to dismiss the fear that was beginning to course through her brain.

'Surely the identity theft couldn't have anything to do with the photograph she had found at her late husband's grave could it? It must all just be a strange coincidence,' thought Diana as she picked up Elisabeth's mobile phone from the desk.

DS Duke reached into the top drawer of a small filing cabinet and pulled out a box of disposable paper handkerchiefs. He took several from the pack and deftly handed them to Elisabeth. The revelation that Charlotte had a son was of little consequence to the detective for the time being; it would just be another detail that he would add to the scammer's file.

"Did you ever give Charlotte any money? Pay for any big purchases, holidays, that sort of thing," he asked, shifting his line of questioning.

"No," replied the fretful woman as she blew her nose and sniffed back more tears.

"Charlotte lives in France and in fact when we eventually met up she paid for her own flight to England, the hire car and all the food and drink when we went for lunch," she added, fiercely defensive of her friend. Elisabeth was relieved that DS

Duke's attention had switched away from Luke and she was thankful that Diana hadn't asked anything more about him. In fact her daughter-in-law seemed to be rather distracted by scrolling through Elisabeth's mobile phone. The old woman was beginning to feel a little more relaxed; maybe her secret was safe after all.

"In fact Charlotte gave me back the money I lent to her," added Elisabeth proudly.

"You saw that didn't you Diana? Remember, the hundred pounds underneath the cafetiere that day. Even you said that she was honest," she added, slightly riled that the younger woman now appeared to be ignoring her. Diana continued to concentrate on the mobile phone screen.

Elisabeth could feel her inner Swan Blake emerge once more. She believed Charlotte was innocent but mentioning Luke's name unnecessarily had been a careless slip. If she remained calm, she would be able to help the police find the true perpetrator of the identity theft without anyone having to know about Christian's illegitimate son. DS Duke jotted down a few more notes in his pad as Diana eventually shifted her gaze and stared back at her mother-in-law in stunned silence. Unbeknown to Elisabeth the young widow was slowly beginning to piece the entire jigsaw together.

"Can you show me the FriendsBag profile page of this Charlotte woman please?" asked Diana, as she continued to scroll through the old woman's mobile phone.

"Why?" protested Elisabeth.

"Because I want to check something," replied Diana curtly.

"I can't. It's a long story but I had to take her off my friends list and then her profile was deleted all together," admitted Elisabeth sheepishly.

"Don't you remember, I told you she's vanished," she cried. A wave of panic began to build in the pit of Elisabeth's stomach again; she was petrified about where Diana's pursuit of the truth could eventually lead.

"What about her son then? This Luke boy?" The name stung the grieving young widow's heart as she tried to shake off the feeling that there could be a link to the floral tribute she had found at Christian's headstone.

"Christ Almighty Diana, you're like a dog with a bone," stalled Elisabeth, trying to dodge the question.

"Luke has a FriendsBag page doesn't he? So a link to his mother would be on there wouldn't it?" Diana persisted.

"Yes, she was, but I couldn't see her on there when I looked at Luke's profile the other day, just someone else who had the same name as her."

"Ah, so you had some suspicions about Charlotte then?" interrupted DS Duke. The detective had listened carefully as the bickering conversation unfolded. He had felt sure that Elisabeth was hiding something and Diana had begun to unearth it.

"No. I wasn't suspicious of her, I just hadn't heard from her for a while," replied Elisabeth, a hot flush of fear burned across her chest.

"In fact I was worried for her safety. I thought Eric might have done something to stop her from contacting me," she added. The policeman looked back quizzically.

"And who is Eric?" he asked.

"Scammer Woman's husband I think," replied Diana sarcastically as she rolled her eyes and began to look out of the open office window behind DS Duke. The gathering storm clouds outside began to rumble as large raindrops battered on the glass. The sergeant got up from his chair and turned to close the latch in an effort to escape the spitting rain.

"Why is everyone having a go at me, I haven't done anything wrong," protested Elisabeth. Diana and Duke paused for a second to gather their thoughts. The seasoned detective realised that the poor old woman was in denial about her friend's deceit and it was a fragile situation that would require careful handling. Diana was less understanding of what she perceived to be Elisabeth's sheer stupidity. Her simmering anger was coming to the boil and she found it increasingly difficult to restrain her emotions.

"Okay, so show me this bereavement forum where you met Charlotte then," demanded Diana.

"Surely she'll still be on there?"

"I can't." Elisabeth felt a wave of vomit billow in her stomach at the mere mention of the made-up website. The simple clever lie that had once been fabricated to protect Diana's feelings was now coming back to haunt her.

"The bereavement forum never existed," she whispered dejectedly.

"What?" asked Diana.

"So why did you lie to me about it Mother?"

A fine bead of sweat gathered on Elisabeth's top lip and her hands were becoming clammy. She knew that the time had come to reveal her family's skeleton. Sooner or later the whole story about her grandson would have to come rattling out of the closet. She took in a deep purposeful breath and wiped the back of her hand across her mouth.

"Oh Diana, I am so sorry," she began. Diana stared at her mother-in-law's tearful expression, fruitlessly searching for a clue as to what the old woman was about to say.

"I only made up the bereavement forum to shield you from the truth. So I didn't have to tell you about . . . about Christian's son," she faltered.

There it was, the secret that had been so deeply buried in a dusty envelope at the back of a post office for twenty years was opened up and laid bare for all to see. The tragic time bomb of teenage angst that had been hidden away from the world for two decades had just exploded in the muggy airless office at Hanford Police Station. The sound of cracking thunder filled the room as Diana jolted back into her chair.

"Christian's what?" cried the young widow.

"What the hell are you wittering on about now mother?" The memory of the tauntingly cruel text written on the photograph at the graveside flooded through Diana's brain.

"It started with the letter I received," croaked Elisabeth as she felt a lump in her throat begin to choke off her words.

"What letter?" interrupted Sergeant Duke. More thunder rumbled outside.

"The letter from . . . err . . . oh my God Diana I simply didn't know how to tell you." A hot spark of lightning fizzed through the sky as Elisabeth was forced to reveal how Charlotte Rook had written a letter twenty years ago to say that Christian had fathered her child during a drunken one night stand after a college disco. Diana listened intently to the confession, taking in each distasteful detail. The young widow sat forward in her seat and rubbed her tired eyes. She ran the palms of her hands over her face and slowly shook her head.

"No, no, no! Oh my God, you stupid cow," raged Diana as she looked across at the sobbing old woman.

"Surely Mother, even a silly old fool like you must have realised from the very start that it was all a pack of lies?" The detective patiently watched the spat unfold and took numerous notes.

"No, it's all real. I just didn't want to upset you," interrupted Elisabeth.

"You didn't want to upset me?" Diana was incandescent with anger and could not believe the wicked deceit.

"That's right. I wanted to protect you. I knew how hard you and Christian had tried for a baby for all of those years, and I thought if you knew that another woman had successfully carried his child, then that would make you feel like a failure," protested Elisabeth.

"It was something that happened twenty years ago, a time before Christian had even met you, so I wanted to protect you from all of that unnecessary pain," she added.

"You're unbelievable, you silly old cow," screamed Diana. DS Duke was startled by the young woman's fury. The heated outburst silenced the hubbub of activity behind the acoustic screens, as the rest of the CID office began to listen in.

"And why do you think we didn't have any bloody kids Elisabeth?" The grieving grandmother looked back quizzically and shook her head; embarrassingly aware that they had become the centre of attention.

"I . . . err . . . 'cos you couldn't get pregnant . . . or because you were more interested in building your career than giving my son children I guess," faltered Elisabeth as she lowered her gaze to fiddle with the soggy tissue in her hands.

"Well, you didn't bother following up any of those fertility places I told you about did you?" she added, trying to firmly shift the blame onto Diana.

The young woman felt the years of pent up frustration from protecting the matriarch's feelings violently shock through her chest. Christian had always lived in the shadow of his over-bearing mother and his long-suffering wife had resented the feeling of having to carefully tip-toe on eggshells so as not to ruffle the old woman's feathers. Today would be the day that everything would change. Diana decided it was time to claw back her power, to step out from beneath Elisabeth's control and give the meddling old busybody some long overdue home truths.

"Well let me tell you something Mommy Dearest. I wasn't the problem," began Diana with her trademark tone that sounded like an engine about to rev up to full speed.

"When I think of all those years I had to put up with your constant sniping and snide little comments about having a baby it makes me sick. Constantly quizzing me about our sex life; giving me little pep talks. Oh, and get this," continued Diana, whilst beckoning DS Duke to move in closer to hear the finer details.

"She even had the temerity to give me leaflets from a fertility clinic, just so I knew where to go to get my tubes checked out." Diana paused for breath as if preparing to deliver a final blow to the sobbing old woman. DS Duke looked on as he sensed the tirade was about to reach an explosive climax.

"When all along the real reason why I could never get pregnant was because your son was firing sodding blanks you stupid old sow." Elisabeth stared back at her daughter-in-law in shocked disbelief as she dabbed more tears away from her puffed cheeks.

"Yes, that's right, you heard me. I couldn't have a baby because Christian was infertile, not me." Diana sat up straighter on her seat and angrily turned her head to look squarely into the startled old woman's eyes.

"Oh yes, he asked me not to tell anyone, least of all you, because he didn't want you to think he was anything less than perfect," she sneered.

"But you were oh so quick to believe he'd knocked up some silly tramp of a college kid and then ignored his responsibilities." Elisabeth stared back silently as more fat tears streamed down her hot face.

"You were so desperate for someone to spawn your grandchild that you never even stopped for one second to question whether there was any truth in the bloody letter in the first place. How could you even think that Christian was anything like that?" she screamed as she shot another accusing glare. The barrage was relentless.

"One whiff of a Hambridge grandchild and you go charging in there, sucking up all of the scammer's lies, rewriting the past to mould it to fit what you want in life without giving a damned single thought for anyone else," cried Diana as she angrily searched through her handbag for a hanky.

"Do you still have the letter?" interrupted Duke calmly as he passed another paper handkerchief over the desk. Diana had momentarily stopped shouting. She blew her nose hard and began to breathe in and out loudly, as if summoning more energy from the stifling humid air in the office.

"No, I was looking for the letter the other week and I couldn't find it," croaked Elisabeth, sniffing into her own soggy tissue. Her mind raced back to the evening she had spent alone with a bottle of brandy, trying to strike up a conversation with Charlotte on FriendsBag. How her booze fuelled speculation had made her angry following the young woman's initial lack of response. Images of the crumpled letter being thrown into the waste paper basket in the corner of her lounge swept through Elisabeth's brain.

"You bloody selfish stuck-up old bitch," shouted Diana.

"She was blatantly scamming you Mother and you fell for it hook, line and sinker." The young woman's engine of wrath had re-started, her accusations just kept on coming.

"Heaven forbid, even her name isn't too far away from what she is; a charlatan. Did you not even notice C Rook spells the name crook?" DS Duke leaned forward in his chair and slowly placed the palms of his hands on the desk, lifting them up and down as if he was attempting to physically slow down Diana's verbal attack.

"Hey, hey, hey, don't blame your mother-in-law," his hands slowly fanning the air. An exasperated Diana turned to look out of the window again.

"Scams like these are all too obvious in hindsight, but when you're on the hook it's all very believable at the time," explained Duke with a soothing tone.

"But it's all real," protested Elisabeth.

"Charlotte had Christian's baby and there's nothing anyone can do about it," she pulled another couple of handkerchiefs out of the box on DS Duke's desk and sobbed uncontrollably. Diana was disgusted by the revelation that Elisabeth could ever believe such a lie about Christian. She was sickened by the old woman's deceit and shifted her gaze back to DS Duke.

"The lowlifes who carry out these crimes are extremely manipulative. They get right inside their victims' heads. It's almost like a form of grooming," explained the sergeant. Duke was a professional investigator and he knew that the only way he would be able to find the answers he needed was to calmly establish all of the facts.

Elisabeth told him she was convinced that Charlotte was genuine as she had contacted Royal Mail to confirm that the letter had been mislaid in a post office. She was adamant that it was simply a coincidence that the mother of her grandchild shared the same name with a criminal on the police database. Diana folded her arms angrily and snorted at the old woman's apparent ignorance.

"Can you remember the phone number you called that was in the accompanying note from Royal Mail?" began Duke. Elisabeth searched through her mobile phone and gave the officer the 0845 number that she had contacted to confirm where Charlotte's letter had been for twenty years. DS Duke wrote it down and said that he would hand it onto the fraud team for them to check it out.

"You have to remember these scam artists are highly accomplished at what they do. They can be blatant and they very often get an added kick out of using a risky play on words for their aliases. You're definitely not the first person to fall for Charlotte Rook's scam, and you probably won't be the last." He smiled back at the women in an attempt to lighten the atmosphere.

The detective went on to explain how hustlers very often believe that they are more intelligent than their victims. Grifters like to spice up their hustles by playing mind games. They would deliberately invent names that would be obviously suspicious to outsiders of their scams. But by drawing the marks into their carefully woven webs of deceit, over a convincing length of time, their victims didn't pick up on the little clues in the fictitious pseudonyms. Popular choices were often subtle, such as Charlotte Ann instead of charlatan; others less so subtle, such as Jo Kerr or Helen Bacque.

"There's a new one doing the rounds at the moment that my colleague in the Cyber unit heard recently. Robin Banks." Duke smiled awkwardly.

"Can you believe it? I mean how obvious can you get?" he laughed.

Diana squirmed at the mention of the nom de plume. Robbie Banks was a similar name that someone had used to set up the fraudulent fund raising page for Christian's non-existent memorial garden. She took in a deep breath to steady herself. The young woman needed to keep her startled fear under wraps as she didn't want to distract anyone from the main focus of the investigation by telling the detective about the second scam.

"Oh my God. Stop!" exclaimed Elisabeth.

"Helen Bacque was the name of the woman the council official was looking for," she added. Diana and DS Duke looked back at her quizzically. Colour began to drain from the old woman's face as she reluctantly came to realise she had been a target of the sophisticated hustle for months.

Elisabeth explained that a couple of weeks after Christian's funeral, she had answered a call on her house intercom. The visitor at the gate had said he was from Hanford Council and he was looking for someone by the name of Helen Bacque. When Elisabeth had told him that no one of that name lived at the address, he asked if it could have been a previous occupant. The grieving mother told him that her family had been there for at least thirty five years and no one of that name had lived there in all that time. She remembered the encounter well, as the official had asked if Helen Bacque could have been associated with anyone else living at the address and she had tearfully explained that both her husband and son were dead. She remarked that the name was ironic, as she herself had been to hell and back during that past year. DS Duke explained that it sounded as if the bogus official's visit had been a phishing trip to confirm

Elisabeth's family had been living at the house twenty years previously.

"The hustlers would have needed that crucial part of the jigsaw to claim the delayed letter had been posted to Christian at your address two decades before," explained Duke.

"So, someone had been planning this for ages?" asked a bewildered Elisabeth. The detective nodded regretfully.

"Yes, I'm afraid so. It sounds as if Charlotte managed to con her way into your affections and then into your home. She probably rifled through your private paperwork when you weren't around. Did you ever leave her alone in the house?" Elisabeth's expression glazed over as she tried to ignore the question. She still could not accept that Luke's mother had conned her.

"Yes sergeant, for a whole afternoon," interrupted Diana coldly.

"Can you believe it? The silly old fool left Charlotte and her so-called husband alone in the house for the entire afternoon while she went out shopping." Diana shot an accusing glare across at Elisabeth and shook her head. The sorrowful old woman bit her bottom lip and slumped down in her seat. She still couldn't quite believe what had happened and secretly hoped she would wake up to find it had all been a dreadful nightmare.

"What else can you tell us about the woman?" asked the policeman softly. Elisabeth thought for a moment as her mind wandered back to her visit with Charlotte to Hunter's Bar after their trip to the cemetery. How she had willingly shared photographs and stories of her home on the French Riviera and how she had revelled in a Mediterranean lifestyle.

"They live in a converted flour mill in a village just outside Cannes in the South of France. Charlotte said she'd renovated it and she showed me pictures on her FriendsBag profile," replied Elisabeth shakily.

"Ah! The mysterious FriendsBag profile that has now disappeared into the ether" sniped Diana, her anger beginning to bubble back up to the surface once more. Duke shot a glance back at her. He didn't appreciate the intrusion.

"Do you have any photographs of Charlotte?" he continued with his measured line of careful questioning.

"Come to think of it, no, I don't," faltered the old woman.

"So, apart from the original letter that has now gone missing, did she ever write anything else down, something we can get a sample of her hand writing from perhaps?"

"No. She did leave a note on my kitchen chalkboard that one time, but I wiped it off." Sergeant Duke took detailed notes and reassured Elisabeth that the case would be thoroughly investigated.

"So how does she get her money back?" asked Diana, now appearing a little less hostile towards her mother-in-law. She was reluctantly resigned to the fact that nothing would be gained by getting angry again.

"I'll give you a crime number and you will need to contact your bank again. They will tell you what steps to take from here." Duke jotted down the number on the back of one of his business cards and handed it across the desk. The sergeant was pleased that the two women had stopped arguing and he had at least managed to diffuse the overwhelming animosity between them for the time being. He hoped that they would be able to work together and help him to solve the case.

"At least it's all getting sorted out now," said Elisabeth thankfully; still very confused and refusing to believe the mother of her grandchild had anything to do with the scam.

"Well not quite," he replied.

"These people have had your information for quite a while now. In that time your details have probably been sold on to countless other criminal gangs. Information like that is big business, so you can probably expect other hustlers to come calling," he added.

"Ah yes, you mean she's on a suckers' list," muttered Diana as she shook her head and looked out of the window again. The thunderstorm had now passed and a little early evening sunshine was peeking through the last of the clouds.

#

Elisabeth climbed into the front passenger seat of Diana's Mini. As soon as the car door was closed her daughter-in-law started the engine and furiously pulled out of the police station's car park. The oppressive atmosphere inside the vehicle felt chokingly hot, so Diana switched on the air conditioning in an attempt to clear the muggy air. She hadn't uttered a single word to her mother-in-law since leaving DS Duke's office and both women now sat in an awkward silence. The earlier rain from the summer thunderstorm had flooded Hanford High Street and Diana joined a pulsating snake of stop-start traffic. The rocking motion of the car made Elisabeth feel sleepy. She closed her eyes and her deep breathing eventually slowed to a soft snore. Vehicles were taking it in turns to pass through a large lake of water that swept across the road and Diana was forced to stop outside the locked gates of Hanford Town Crematorium. The young woman's mind returned once more to the time that she had sneaked a visit to Christian's grave alone to see his new headstone. She scowled across at her dozing passenger. How stupid she now felt for giving her deceitful mother-in-law a second's thought. Why had she always let the controlling matriarch make her feel so guilty about everything? Why hadn't she stood up to the old crone before? Images of the mysterious floral tribute flowed through her mind.

'Oh my God, that must mean it was that scamming tramp Charlotte who left the posy of flowers and photo on the headstone,' she gasped.

"Did you take that woman to my husband's grave?" snarled Diana. The sudden outburst pierced the silence and shook Elisabeth from her impromptu snooze.

"What?" asked Elisabeth stalling for time. She was clearly startled by the question.

"Did you take that lying bitch to Christian's grave?" screamed Diana.

"Yes," she replied with a nervous croak.

Diana sharply turned the steering wheel, drove up to the entrance of the cemetery and screeched to a halt. Immediately she jumped out of the car and ran to the back to open the boot.

Elisabeth could hear a rustling sound coming from behind the rear seat as Diana rummaged around in a black rubbish bag. Eventually she closed the boot lid hard and returned to sit in the driver's seat, angrily slamming her car door shut. The poor little Mini was yet again suffering the wrath of its driver.

"Is this the boy that Charlotte claimed to be Christian's son?" spat Diana as she pushed a crumpled photograph into Elisabeth's face. The old woman sat in dazed silence at the sudden realisation that her daughter-in-law had known all about the picture and posy left at the graveside but had never mentioned it before.

"Well? Is it? Is it?" demanded Diana, her pitch rising to a sharp shriek.

"Yes, that's Luke, my grandson" cried Elisabeth, pulling the photograph nearer.

"No it isn't you silly old fool," screamed Diana.

"God give me strength." She could no longer control her incandescent rage.

"He might be the scammer's son but he most definitely isn't Christian's child. He could even be just some generic looking random lad off the internet. How could you ever fall for something like that? How could you ever believe Christian would sleep around and abandon a girl he'd got pregnant? What kind of nasty piece of work are you?"

Diana knew her venomous words would sting. If there was one thing Elisabeth Hambridge had been most proud of in her life, it was her unwavering love and support for her son. The fact that a few carefully placed lies from a sociopathic hustler could ever lead her to doubt Christian's honour was almost too much to bear.

"I don't care what you say, Luke was my grandson, Charlotte isn't lying," wailed Elisabeth defensively, as she gripped the photograph tightly in her hand.

"This isn't the only photo I have of him. Charlotte gave me a CD full of them," she added defiantly.

Diana switched off the car's engine and placed her elbows on the steering wheel, before burying her face in the palms of her hands. It seemed that her mother-in-law was firmly in denial and no amount of arguing with the old woman would change the rose-tinted view she had of Charlotte Benoit. She took a deep breath and began to think. Suddenly Diana remembered the writing on the back of the photograph. Quickly she snatched the piece of paper out of Elisabeth's hand and turned it over.

"Here you go! That scheming bitch wrote this didn't she?" shouted Diana. Elisabeth nodded. The grieving young widow realised it was a small start; a tiny piece of evidence that could help with the investigation. It was a sample of the hustler's handwriting.

#

Timeline: Friday 5th August 2016, 21:00hrs

Diana sat at the desk in her mother-in-law's study and pored over the images on the CD from Charlotte.

"These photos could have come from anywhere," said Diana.

"Look, if you do a reverse image search on Google you can find other websites where they've appeared." Elisabeth sat next to her, silently watching the cursor flick over the laptop's screen from one window to another.

"She probably just found a whole bunch of pictures of loads of boys at different ages that looked similar to one another and then whacked them all together into one nice fat fake photo story for you to get all teary-eyed over."

Elisabeth's tired gaze moved guiltily towards the leather-bound album on her desk. A fat salty tear fell down her cheek as she opened the back of the book and pulled out the plastic wallets she had filled with print outs that detailed Luke Benoit's death; newspaper cuttings and messages of sympathy from the young Frenchman's mourning friends.

"Oh my God Mother, you really did fall for it big time didn't you." Diana was shocked by what felt like a desecration of the family's photograph album; the precious Hambridge memories that lay between the laminated pages had been sullied by the addition of a scammer's lies. Diana opened up a new browser window on the laptop and typed in some of the web addresses that were printed on the bottom of the pieces of paper; she needed to see for herself how this elaborate and cruel scam had been created.

She quickly discovered Luke Benoit had been a real young man. He had genuinely died in a snowmobile accident in the French Alps, whilst on holiday and celebrating his eighteenth birthday. The hustlers had taken the tragic incident and invented a fake back story to falsely link him to Christian. It was a clever deception and one that had taken a lot of planning.

The fact that Christian's whole life story was effectively posted on his FriendsBag memorial page for any one to see, had given the con artists all the ammunition they needed to build a convincing connection. His hobbies, his nickname at school, his love of adventure sports, even where Christian had attended college and what he had studied twenty years previously; they were all important snippets of information that when gathered together, would prove invaluable to the grifters.

"They must have found Christian's memorial page online and soaked up every scrap of information left there by his friends," said Diana.

"All they then had to do was track down a gullible rich relative who hadn't got the brains they were born with," she shot a sideways glance towards Elisabeth.

"After a little bit of grooming online, hey presto you're happy to give them full access to your home and everything in it," she added accusingly.

The young woman was still extremely angry that Elisabeth had been so quick to believe the fabricated story fed to her by the confidence tricksters, but as she saw the look of utter hopelessness and regret in the crumbling matriarch's face, Diana realised that her mother-in-law had suffered enough for one day. It had been a sophisticated hustle and it looked as if the grieving mother had lost most of her money and all of her confidence.

"Oh, I am just so desperately sorry," sobbed Elisabeth.

"How could I have ever doubted Christian's morals? I brought him up to be better than that. He would never have shirked his responsibilities if he had known he'd got a girl pregnant." Diana realised that the confused old woman still hadn't fully accepted the whole of Charlotte's story had been a total fabrication; she still hadn't understood there had never been a college disco or fumbled encounter at the end of a drunken night. She simply could not accept that she had never been a grandmother.

#

Timeline: Saturday 6th August 2016, 08:30hrs –
The Next Day

Diana returned to the police station with the CD, photograph, pebble and dead posy of flowers that Charlotte had left at Christian's grave. There was a small hope that the samples of handwriting on the back of the picture and inside the condolence card could be used as evidence should the perpetrators ever be brought to justice.

"They obviously brainwashed the silly old fool," said Diana, as she placed the collected items onto DS Duke's desk.

"Yes, but that's how they work I'm afraid. Hustlers are like a pack of hounds following the scent of blood. One whiff of weakness and they're in there like a shot," he replied as he pulled a couple of plastic self-sealing bags from the top drawer of a filing cabinet.

"I'm sure Elisabeth's feeling pretty vulnerable at the moment though and she'll need the family's support to come to terms with it all." Diana frowned and shook her head in the realisation that she was the only person her mother-in-law had left in her life. It would be up to her to help the fragile old lady cope with the ordeal. The young woman watched the sergeant place the exhibits into separate polythene bags and carefully label each one with the case number and date. Duke looked up from his desk to greet a young blonde policewoman who had just entered his office. Immediately he introduced her to his visitor.

"Ah, this is Detective Constable Trudi Jones from our specialist Cyber Unit. Trudi, this is Diana Hambridge the daughter-in-law of the latest victim in one of Charlotte Rook's stolen identity scams." In that quick throw-away comment

Diana realised that Elisabeth had been only one of many other unfortunate targets of the sophisticated hustle.

"We've spoken before haven't we?" asked Trudi.

"A few weeks ago about a fake fund raising page?" added the young officer, as if looking for confirmation of where she recognised Diana Hambridge's name from. Diana nodded and felt a small glow of embarrassment flush in her face as she shook the constable's hand.

"Part of Operation Pearly Gates, sir," explained Trudi to quickly bring her boss up to speed. DS Duke raised his eyebrows at the revelation that there had been even more to the Hambridge incident than first declared.

"Why didn't you say anything about this sooner?" he asked.

Diana hadn't realised that the fake crowd funding appeal set up in Christian's name had become part of a much larger police investigation. She knew that she had her own reasons for not mentioning such a vital piece of information when she had visited the station with Elisabeth the previous evening, but in the bright morning light of the detective's office she felt her excuse seemed all too feeble.

"I simply wanted to protect my mother-in-law from the fact that someone had been making money out of her dead son's memory," replied Diana, unsure whether the hardened investigator believed her. DS Duke frowned, clicked the mouse on his laptop and opened up a new screen. DC Jones gave him the reference code for the fake fundraising scam and he quickly read through the notes.

Trudi picked up the CD from the sergeant's desk ready to take it for forensic testing. While her boss continued to scan his laptop screen, the young officer explained to Diana that all computers left a small unique piece of code on anything recorded on them; a little bit like a signature. This could be used to identify the device used to write the disc. The CD from Charlotte Benoit would be compared with the codes on other CDs and DVDs that had been collected from other victims of similar scams, to establish if it had come from the same criminal gang.

"We're also still trying to locate the IP address of the person claiming to be Robbie or Robin Banks who set up the fund raising pages," offered Trudi. Diana winced at the mention of the obvious pseudonym that she had failed to pick up on before.

"Sometimes we get lucky. The criminals get lazy and forget to wipe their tracks. It sounds as if this was a much larger and more sophisticated operation than we first thought though." The two women looked across at DS Duke, but he was still busily reading through the Operation Pearly Gates documents on the screen.

"What about Mother's video calls with Charlotte? Won't they have left a trail somewhere?" asked Diana, totally intrigued by the insight into the high-tech world of cyber crime that was unfolding before her.

"Well, when we get our hands on your mother's laptop then we should be able to find a record of when they were made and where they were made from," replied Trudi. Diana was encouraged by the welcome news; there appeared to be a little light glinting at the end of the long dark tunnel that she and Elisabeth had been drawn into.

"But even if we track down the IP address used by the scammer, there's no guarantee that it'll still be in use or lead us to the perpetrator," added DS Duke dismissively as he closed the window on his laptop. He was still clearly irritated by Diana's failure to tell him about the family's connection to a second scam.

"So if there's absolutely anything else you can think of that is connected to the case then it would be most appreciated if you tell me now; no matter how insignificant it seems to be." He hoped he wasn't going to have to coax every small nugget of information out of her. Diana smiled back and graciously noted the reprimand.

"No, there's nothing else and I am very sorry I wasn't able to tell you yesterday about the fund raising page." she replied cordially. The detective accepted the young woman's apology but he was keen to ensure that she understood why every piece of intelligence was important. Duke moved on to explain how the confidence tricksters worked.

Traceability was the grifters' worst enemy and they would go to great lengths to avoid being tracked. They usually set up fake email accounts using free wi-fi access in cafes and hotels to carry out their crimes; using pay-as-you-go burner phones and staying only for a couple of nights in one location before moving on. Their room bills were always paid for in cash or with stolen or cloned credit cards, making them almost impossible to trace. Hustlers often possessed the gift for speaking a few languages or at least altering their accents to suit a variety of different scenarios, and many were accomplished actors able to effortlessly drift in and out of character at a second's notice. Their transient lifestyles and chameleonic disguises made it very difficult for the authorities to catch them.

"They change their appearance more often than most people change their underpants, but their M.O. is usually pretty constant. It's as if once they find a formula that works they tend to stick with it for a while," smiled Duke.

"We're building up a nice stock of evidence about this particular crew and the profiling team are working on their next likely move," said Trudi.

"The net will close in on them eventually," she added reassuringly.

The handwriting on the back of the photograph could be compared with other samples on the police database and the Charlotte Rook case would now be cross-matched to information gathered through Operation Pearly Gates.

"These criminals get a bit cocky once their scams have worked a few times and that's when they start to get sloppy and make mistakes. When they do slip up, you can guarantee we'll be ready and waiting for them," said Duke with a confident wink.

Chapter 10

Muriel Grubbet sat at a small round table outside a pavement café, next to a soft sandy beach on the French Riviera. A large canvas umbrella shaded her from the glare of the hot afternoon sun as she took a refreshing sip from a long cooling cocktail. She was an average looking woman of slender build with no striking features. Her mousey brown shoulder length hair had been tucked up beneath a wide brimmed straw hat; her anonymous looking face mostly obscured by a pair of large framed designer sunglasses. The years had been kind to Muriel. Her flawless and smooth complexion bore testament to frequent trips to the beauty salon. Although not a vain person, she was definitely well maintained. The odd 'nip and tuck' and regular courses of Botox meant that she could easily pass herself off as a much younger woman when the need arose.

Muriel smiled contentedly as she switched on her mobile phone and idly waved at her husband in the distance. Eddie Grubbet was about to start walking back up the beach after his afternoon swim; he was standing just where the calm Mediterranean Sea met a wide band of golden yellow sand. A couple of rowing boats draped in fishermen's nets gaily bobbed up and down at the edge of the azure blue water, as they were lapped by the gentle surf. A hand-painted fishmonger's sign that pointed towards a small Poissonnier had fallen from one of the boats and was slowly floating out towards the horizon. Eddie laughed as he ran back into the sea and playfully frolicked in the waves to retrieve it.

Eddie was an attractive mature man with glossy black hair and a well-toned physique. His skin glowed with a healthy suntan and his pearlescent teeth dazzled in the Mediterranean sunshine when he smiled. He was a frequent customer at the vast array of male grooming parlours along the Riviera and, like his wife, he always took great pride in his appearance.

The Grubbets shared a comfortable life with all the decadent trappings of success and today had been another relaxing day for the couple, spent sunbathing and people watching. Eddie returned from his swim, carrying the wooden fishmonger's plaque in his hand and sat down on the café seat next to Muriel.

"Hercule's seafood sign nearly went AWOL again," he laughed, placing the piece of wood on the ground. He grabbed a large fluffy beach towel out of a bag beneath the table and began to dry himself off. Muriel looked back at her husband and smiled. They would give the board back to their friend when they dined at his restaurant later in the evening. She flicked open a saved web page on her phone to continue trawling the internet.

"What do you think of this one?" asked Muriel as she turned her phone towards Eddie's gaze and tapped the tip of an elegantly manicured finger nail on the screen. He quickly read the text in the window before rubbing his towel through his salty wet hair.

"Yeah, he'll do. He's about the right age to have fathered your illegitimate son twenty years ago" he replied.

The Grubbets were a pair of accomplished grifters and they were currently hunting for their next victim to help fund their lavish lifestyle. Eddie's wife had found a news report about a thirty-eight-year-old musician in England called Andrew Chiltern who had played lead guitar in a small-time rock band called Muscovado Crowz. The tragic young man had been in a coma for almost eight months following a car accident one week before Christmas. Andrew had been travelling home after a gig when he had been forced to swerve his van into a lamp post to avoid a drunken party of revellers who had foolishly stepped out into the road in front of him. The talented guitarist had suffered multiple injuries in the crash, including a heavy blow to his head which had caused trauma to his brain. His distraught parents had recently been told there was no chance of him making a recovery and they had reluctantly agreed to have their son's life support machine switched off.

A mercilessly wry smile stretched across Muriel's lips as she took another sip of her cooling cocktail.

"Yes, he looks perfect," said Eddie as he clicked his fingers to summon a waiter to the table.

"But we'll need to find a different dead kid to play the part of his son or daughter. The Benoit name is a bit of a hot potato at the moment." he added heartlessly. A young waiter arrived to take the couple's drinks order. Eddie closed his eyes and relaxed back in his seat to warm his sun-tanned chest beneath the Riviera sunshine.

"Yes, I was getting a bit bored of the whole 'son of an action man' thing anyway," added Muriel.

"I think I might enjoy becoming the tragic mother of a wannabe rock star's love child." The heartless hustler giggled as she melodramatically wiped the back of her hand across her brow.

"All I need to do now is find a dead young girl or boy who liked to play the ukulele or guitar to become Andrew Chiltern's long lost illegitimate offspring. It shouldn't be too difficult." The two grifters laughed as they planned how to unleash their next cruel hustle on the dead man's unsuspecting relatives.

#

A famous statesman once said the only two things that are certain in life are death and taxes. It was clear the Grubbets specialised in sucking as much money out of the former and never gave the latter a thought. Death provided a lucrative line of work for the couple.

Elisabeth Hambridge had been their tenth victim in as many months. The grieving mother was one of dozens of people whom the elaborate delayed letter scam had worked on. There was no reason for the grifters to believe it wouldn't work again on another bereaved family.

The Grubbets had followed strict criteria for their previous hustle to work. Muriel had tirelessly scoured the internet, carefully trawling for tragic news stories about young men who had met with an untimely death. Ideally they had to have been in their late thirties and died as a result of an adrenalin-fuelled adventure sports accident; something like a motorcycle crash, climbing fall or paragliding incident. It hadn't been a difficult search as the world wide web was full of distressing reports. The death notices that filled memorial pages in online newspapers were a primary source to find her marks. However, Muriel couldn't rely on those alone, as the acknowledgements from grieving friends and family seldom gave any hint as to the nature of the young men's deaths. In order for her wicked scam to work Muriel needed to establish that the deceased had been action men who had been fit and well just prior to their demise. Countless news articles in local newspapers across the country provided a useful catalogue of incidents that helpfully gave the grifter all the information she needed to get started.

For the sophisticated scam to work, Muriel's ideal target simply needed to be the elderly grieving mother or father of a dead thrill-seeking victim; most importantly they needed to be wealthy and their late son had to have lived at the family home 20 years previously. The dead action man needed to be aged thirty-six to forty-five at the time of his recent demise, so he would have been aged sixteen to twenty-five a couple of decades ago.

Muriel had spotted reports of Christian Hambridge's motorcycle accident in the Hanford Recorder online. He was just one name in amongst a list of fifty other incidents she had found in the UK that week. She had a well established procedure for hunting down her victims which involved trawling through a range of social media and ancestry search sites.

It always surprised Muriel how easy it was to find out the details she needed from the relative sanctuary of her sun lounger in the south of France. Victims' family members, dates and places of births and deaths were all documented on the sites for anyone willing to pay the subscription fees.

She soon discovered Christian's memorial page on FriendsBag and began to soak up all the subtle details she needed to know about his life and, crucially, that one of his affluent parents was still alive. She unearthed other important facts such as where he had lived as a teenager, when he had studied at college, all accompanied by many old photographs of when he was a student; all the valuable information she needed was readily supplied by his unwitting friends and family in their outpourings of grief on the social media site.

It had been easy to establish what Christian had been like as a student at Hanford College and what his hobbies had been. Many of his friends had helpfully referred to him by his nickname 'Hammers' or simply as Chris. The conniving con artist discovered how Christian's keen teenage interest in motorbikes had taken him to the Isle of Man to watch the TT racing each year, with lots of memories and photographs of biking and camping trips being shared on the tribute page. Other linked stories had established that the young man was the son of a wealthy estate agent and that he had recently inherited his late father's company. An online search of the Electoral Roll had quickly traced his widowed mother's address. Muriel's net had mercilessly closed in, as she anticipated that the elderly woman would be an easy target.

Soon after Christian's funeral the Grubbets set up their base in a local country house hotel in Hanford. Muriel's husband Eddie visited Elisabeth's house posing as a council official. He pretended that he was looking for a woman named Helen Bacque. The accomplished con-man wore a simple yet convincing disguise of a false beard and glasses; he knew that grieving people don't take much notice of an unexpected visitor's face, especially if the caller is twenty feet away at the end of a driveway. He rang Elisabeth's intercom and demanded to speak to the woman whom he said owed the council money for unpaid parking fees. The indignant Elisabeth had been keen to get rid of the rude man and insisted that he had the wrong address; no one of the name Helen Bacque lived there. In fact she confirmed that her family had resided at the house for the past 30 years or so. With that vital piece of information the Grubbets' meticulous plan was ready to be put into action.

Muriel wrote out a carefully worded letter and placed it inside an envelope. Next she created a fake twenty-year-old postage stamp on her computer and printed it out on a laser printer. She then methodically perforated around the edges to make it look as if it had been torn from a strip in the eighties. She wasn't exactly a master forger, but the stamped envelope wouldn't have to pass much scrutiny at first and it was doubtful that any one would ever check its authenticity until it was too late. Muriel then placed the sealed envelope into a shoebox that had been half filled with the contents of her vacuum cleaner. After giving it a good shake she removed the packet. At first glance it would easily pass for a letter that had been lost at the back of a dusty post office for two decades.

Eddie bought an 0845 number and set up call forwarding to his pay-as-you-go mobile phone. The Grubbets needed to create the illusion that the official helpline in the fake Royal Mail covering letter was a legitimate landline, just in case the recipient called the number to check any details. Muriel obtained a list of old post offices that had closed down in the suburbs near to where Christian Hambridge had lived and subtly mentioned the old branch in the convincing accompanying letter.

Finally Eddie wore a short blond wig, baseball cap and generic blue uniform with a clipboard and fake ID badge when he delivered the letter to Elisabeth's house. The disguise didn't need to be sophisticated as the hustlers knew that people rarely remembered delivery men's facial features.

When Elisabeth had predictably called the number in the accompanying note to research the circumstances behind the discovery of the old letter, she was unaware that she was talking to Eddie Grubbet. He had sat alone in the scammer's lair, with a pre-recorded tape of a noisy call centre playing in the background. Eddie adopted the persona of the camp sounding enquiry clerk to confirm the fake details of how the letter had been discovered.

The trap was set.

Luke Benoit had been a real eighteen-year-old boy who had died in a skiing accident in the French Alps. Muriel Grubbet set up a fake FriendsBag profile in the name of Charlotte Rook and sent a membership request to the young lad's posthumous memorial group. Luke's unsuspecting mourning relatives were only too happy to add her to his growing list of friends; they believed adding new friends was a good way to keep his name alive. Once the hustler's request was accepted Muriel altered the privacy settings on her fake profile to the highest level and changed her surname to Benoit. To the outside world she now had a legitimate link to the dead boy, but his real relatives were oblivious that someone was using their family name. Luke's grieving parents never looked through the whole list of friends so they probably wouldn't notice the name Charlotte Benoit née Rook lurking in there.

Because the real and innocent Luke Benoit had died in an adventure sports accident, Muriel knew that target 'fathers' for her scam would need to have been adrenaline junkies too; just like Christian Hambridge had been. It would add subtle credibility to the scammer's story if it could be suggested that the illegitimate Luke had inherited his biological dad's thrill seeking genes.

Following the delivery of the fake twenty-year-old letter, Muriel knew that the strength of a grandmother's love would surpass any reservations Elisabeth may have had about tracking down the mysterious woman. The grifter's 'Charlotte' profile would be easy enough for Elisabeth to find but, being a new page, it would have very little social history on its timeline and no interaction from any friends. This lack of content could look suspicious. Muriel devised a plan to explain it away by creating the sad story that someone had hacked into her old account and she had then had to start again afresh. This in itself would unwittingly serve to create even more sympathy from the old woman.

Once contact from the marks had been made, it was important for the scammer to let her victims believe that they were the ones pulling the strings; they were the people in control. A little teasing hesitation from Charlotte in becoming friends with Elisabeth had only served to convince the desperate grandmother that she was the one driving the online friendship forward. After a couple of weeks' careful grooming, the unsuspecting elderly lady was pulled further onto the hustler's hook by being made to believe that the two women shared a secret. Nothing could be better than an illegitimate but longed-for grandson that Elisabeth could never tell her dead son's widow about. This cruel twist made the grieving grandmother feel closer to Charlotte, as if they had a common bond, and it prevented her from speaking to anyone else about the unexpected turn of events.

Muriel knew that if any of the victims of her hustle ever joined the FriendsBag memorial page for Luke, then there was always the risk that they may be tempted to comment on there. If that happened then there was a strong possibility that the dead boy's real family and friends would see the messages and consequently discover the scam. Along with the dozens of other marks that had taken the Grubbets' bait, Elisabeth was instructed not to make any mention of being Luke's paternal grandmother on the page. She was told that any comments she wrote on there could lead to Eric finding out about Charlotte's deception, and that could potentially ruin the couple's marriage. Furthermore, there was an outside chance that Diana would see any comments that the old woman wrote on the memorial page; the remarks could ultimately lead the young widow to discover that her late husband had fathered an illegitimate son. Elisabeth was left in no doubt that such a revelation would devastate her daughter-in-law.

Meanwhile, Eddie had been busy setting up fake GiveInPeace fund raising pages for all of the dead relatives of the Grubbets' victims. He created simple and believable appeals in which he mostly asked for donations towards the costs of funerals and headstones or, as in the case of Christian Hambridge, a memorial garden. Members of the public donated money to each cause via the crowd funding website and, when the allotted time period was up or the grifter's target sum had been reached, GiveInPeace took their small fee and sent the remainder of the cash collected direct to the hustler. Each page drew in hundreds of pounds for the scammers, Christian's raised two and a half thousand.

Elisabeth was dragged further into Muriel's overpowering web of deception with numerous video calls with Charlotte. The hustler's trip to England would be the final 'convincer' that she was genuine. In the guise of Charlotte, Muriel would leave a posy of flowers, photo and pebble from Luke's favourite beach at Christian's grave, then take the grieving grandmother to a nearby wine bar and give her a CD memento of precious family photos. At the end of the impromptu lunch, the scammer would insist on paying for the couple's food and drink. These psychological manipulations made Elisabeth feel that her new friend was the real deal; a thoughtful, honest and honourable woman who was not simply a free loader.

Plying the old woman with a bottle and a half of wine meant, in an unguarded moment whilst Elisabeth slept off the boozy lunch in the car, Muriel managed to take all of the bank cards from her victim's purse. She dropped Christian's mother back at home, delivered the haul of plastic to her partner Eddie, and then returned to Elisabeth's house to break the news that her angry Gallic husband had discovered the lie about Luke's conception.

This was a tried and tested, extremely well researched scam that had worked dozens of times before. The heartless grifters knew from experience that Elisabeth would feel immensely guilty for having raked up all of the unsavoury details of Charlotte's past life. She would believe her son had treated the young girl badly all those years ago and, if it hadn't have been for her dogged determination to track down the author of that damned delayed letter, then the hard-done-by Charlotte would still have a happy marriage, a loving husband and a comfortable home in the south of France. Without Elisabeth's meddling the Benoits would have been able to continue mourning the loss of their son in peace.

The scammers' victim had been chosen with care. They knew Elisabeth would feel responsible for Charlotte's plight. The old lady would believe that, under the highly stressful circumstances of being cut off emotionally and financially by Eric, the only decent thing to do would be to give her friend somewhere to stay for a few days.

Placing a sedative in the old woman's camomile tea had been simple. After her generous host retired for the evening, Muriel Grubbet had been free to meticulously trawl through the whole of Elisabeth's home office, bureau, phone and computer. As the wealthy widow slept soundly in her bedroom, the shameless con-artist gained lucrative access to the elderly mark's bank accounts and gathered all the utility bills needed to steal her hapless victim's identity.

The following morning Muriel's husband arrived as planned, posing as the enraged Eric Benoit. The couple were able to quickly return the now cloned bank cards to Elisabeth's purse as

Muriel applied more psychological pressure to the elderly woman. It was no coincidence that the heartless hustler had visited her victim just before the weekend. From her daily video calls she knew that the Hambridge women were creatures of habit and Diana came to the house each Friday afternoon at two o'clock sharp to take her mother-in-law shopping. The scammer also knew that the impending visitor would un-nerve the elderly lady and Elisabeth would be keen to keep the Benoits and Diana apart. Elisabeth could not cancel the routine supermarket trip at such late notice as it would have aroused Diana's suspicions; especially after giving the young woman such short shrift the day before. Elisabeth would feel she had no alternative but to leave the Benoits alone in her house while she went shopping.

Muriel knew that Elisabeth would feel guilty if she abandoned her friend during her hour of need. She also knew that her benevolent host would try to compensate for her temporary desertion by giving Charlotte some cash to tide her over. The Grubbets were experts in anticipating human nature. Muriel knew that throwing a little money at a short-term problem was a coping mechanism wealthy people often used when faced with a personal dilemma. When Elisabeth predictably opened her purse and saw her bank cards and cash were all still present and Charlotte had not stolen them whilst she slept, this subconsciously strengthened her feelings of trust for the young woman. It strengthened Elisabeth's belief that the mother of her grandchild was honourable and a genuine friend. Encouraged by her guest's honesty, Elisabeth felt comfortable as she unwittingly gave the criminals open access to her home. The grieving grandmother was totally unaware that all of her cards had already been cloned and she had no idea of the impending financial catastrophe about to befall her weeks later.

While Elisabeth was out shopping with Diana, Muriel and Eddie Grubbet took full advantage of the opportunity and systematically searched through their victim's home office. They removed more paperwork from the bureau and downloaded financial files from the laptop; ensuring that they had everything required to open up the necessary fraudulent bank accounts. Most importantly for the hustlers they managed to find the envelope and crumpled fake letter that had been used to spark off the whole series of events. Finally, to keep Elisabeth and her protective daughter-in-law off the scent for a few days, they left the five twenty pound notes that the old woman had lent to Charlotte underneath the cafetiere. This final little touch had been a master stroke, as a victim of a scam is only likely to search for the perpetrator after they think they have been hustled. Returning the hundred pounds was a tactic to keep the marks further off the scent.

Muriel had removed the SIM from her pay-as-you-go mobile phone and closed down Charlotte's fake FriendsBag profile. Over the next few weeks the criminal duo had meticulously plundered all of Elisabeth's bank accounts and credit cards; taking out sizeable loans using the identity stolen from their victim's home office.

It was a beautifully executed scam that had worked well on almost a dozen previous unsuspecting victims. It had funded the Grubbets' lavish Mediterranean lifestyle and it was now time for the couple to invent a new tragic story using another innocent dead man's name.

Chapter 11

Andrew Chiltern was a likable young man who had been the lead guitarist in a popular small time heavy rock band. Muscovado Crowz had played together since forming a group whilst still at school in the early nineties. Following months of rehearsal and five years of gigging in every pub, club, fete and festival going in the area, the four friends had been spotted by a talent scout and band promoter. That fortunate encounter had led to gigs at bigger and better venues and the band was heavily promoted by the Hanford Recorder as being the next big thing to hit the hair metal music scene. The lycra-clad mini rock gods' brush with fame had been short-lived though; their debut single 'Banging in my head' only skimmed the edge of the charts and they were soon forgotten by the promotions agency. However their growing army of fans were more loyal. Twenty years later they still showed unwavering support whenever the Crowz played at the town's only rock bar.

The strong friendships within the band had been forged in the early days jamming and song writing in drummer Gary Stevens' garage. Their bond had been built on a firm foundation and incredibly, despite their fall from the limelight, the lads had remained together for another two decades until the fateful night following a gig at a Christmas party. Andrew had dropped off his band mates and was driving the loaded van back home, when a group of partygoers in boisterously high spirits stumbled out into the road in front of him. The talented musician swerved to avoid a collision and steered his rusty old Transit onto the opposite side of the street before hitting a concrete lamp post. Andrew's head took the full force of an unsecured heavy flight case that had flown through the air from behind his seat. The impact caused a catastrophic injury to his brain.

Following a week in the critical care unit at Hanford General Hospital, Andrew's distraught parents were told that there would be little chance of him recovering from his unresponsive state. They had initially refused to accept the prognosis and instead sought alternative therapies at private clinics to help their son recover consciousness. But eight months later the heartbroken Mr and Mrs Chiltern had reluctantly agreed with medical opinion and Andrew's life support machines were switched off. It was now more than eighteen months since the terrible crash that had robbed the world of his gifted talent. Today was the first anniversary of the young man's death.

A buzz of anticipation had begun to filter through the rock community in Hanford town. There had been an announcement that a memorial concert in honour of the late guitarist had been planned by the remaining members of Muscovado Crowz. Coincidentally that summer would mark the band's twenty-fifth anniversary since the schoolboys first got together in Gary's dad's garage. The Crowz thought the gig planned for later in the year would be a fitting tribute to their friend's memory. The search began for any local talented guitarists who could perform guest slots at the event. Social media feeds had erupted in a loyal show of support as advance ticket sales had been brisk. Grown men brought their eyeliner and skinny jeans out of retirement and a gaggling army of female fans fought over the last few remaining hair extensions available at the local salon. The six months' countdown to the Christmas show had begun; for one night only, Muscovado Crowz were going to be back in town.

The band welcomed the column inches in the local paper and online that promoted the gig in honour of their fallen band mate. The middle-aged rockers secretly hoped the sparks of interest would kick-start fresh interest in their flagging musical careers.

Yvonne Chiltern sat at her kitchen table reading that week's copy of the Hanford Recorder. She looked at the old photograph of her son featured on the front page. It had been taken during a sell-out show at the local sports hall about five years earlier. A few hundred hot and sweaty disciples had head banged the night away, while dozens of adoring fans stood at the feet of their idol as Andrew majestically strutted across the stage. She smiled at the proud memory of her beloved son and blinked away a dewy tear that was threatening to make its way out of the corner of her eye. Her thoughts were interrupted by the sound of her husband returning from answering a knock at the front door.

"Well, would you believe it?" he asked as he entered the kitchen and dropped a small package on the kitchen table.

"That was someone from Royal Mail." Yvonne picked up the packet. It was a sealed clear plastic bag with an official-looking sticker on the outside. It contained a small cream envelope addressed to the couple's late son and a covering letter apologising for its delay in the post.

"It says here it was posted twenty years ago," said Yvonne as she opened up the curious delivery to scan over the accompanying note. Alan picked up the empty cellophane bag and looked closely at the Royal Mail verification stamp with the previous day's date on. Yvonne quickly slit open the dusty paper envelope as Alan stood behind his wife, impatiently looking over her shoulder to read the letter inside.

Dear Andy,

I have tried to meet with you lots of times over the past few weeks but you haven't returned any of my calls and it feels like you're avoiding me. I think it's only fair to let you know I am pregnant and I am going to keep our baby.

I overheard Gaz say that Muscovado Crowz have been spotted by a talent scout and you're about to go on tour, so I realise that having a baby in tow wouldn't exactly be the best thing for your image. Also I know it was only ever meant to be a drunken fumble in the back of the band's van, and you wouldn't normally look twice at a fan like me, you could have any girl you want. So I understand if you don't want to have anything to do with me now, but I thought you should know about the baby to give you the choice about what to do.

I have a job in France to go to and I'll leave England at the end of the month. I'm giving you one last chance to get in touch. My coach leaves on Friday, so please, if you're interested, meet me at Hanford bus station before 1pm on the 4th of July so we can talk about it. If I don't hear from you before I leave, then

134

I'll understand you don't want to have anything to do with me or the baby. I will leave and you won't ever have to see me again.

Much love

Connie-Su Windell. X

PS: I hope this letter has reached the right Andrew Chiltern as this was the only address in Hanford I could find for your name in the phone book. xx

Yvonne and Alan stared at each other in shock and disbelief as they re-read the words that had been written by a scared young woman over twenty years ago. The couple knew the dates roughly aligned with their son's taste of the limelight. At the time of the alleged self-gratifying shag with an adoring groupie, Andrew had been a happy-go-lucky nineteen-year-old about to embark on an exciting career as a rock star. Both of his parents wondered how he would have reacted to the news had he received the letter twenty years ago.

Alan rang the 0845 number written on an accompanying sheet of paper. The call was answered by a clerk called Robin who confirmed a small number of undelivered letters had been discovered at the back of an old filing cabinet during the demolition of a post office in a nearby town. The stunned father hung up the phone and took his wife into his arms, crying and comforting each other they came to the slow realisation that even though their only son was no longer alive, there was a possibility that they had a grandchild out there in the big wide world.

#

Timeline: Monday 3rd July 2017, 18:00hrs –
Later That Day

Muriel Grubbet lounged on a king-size bed in a sumptuously furnished hotel bedroom, idly looking through some files on her laptop. She massaged her stiff neck and yawned loudly as she patiently waited for more incoming messages to appear on her newly created FriendsBag profile. Eddie had already taken half a dozen calls in relation to their latest delayed letter scam and the couple knew that Connie-Su Durand (née Windell) was going to have a busy evening. Their first victim had already made contact.

Hello Connie-Su
We know this is a bit of a long shot, but we've found your profile on FriendsBag and notice that your maiden name was Windell? We just wondered if you knew our son Andrew Chiltern from the band Muscovado Crowz? He passed away recently and we have been sorting through some of his old fan mail. The name Connie-Su Windell has come up in a letter and it sounds as if she was quite close to Andrew. If that sounds like it might be you, then we wondered if you'd like to get in touch at all and we can keep you up to date with various memorial things that are going on.
Best regards
Alan & Yvonne Chiltern
PS: If you didn't know our son, then please ignore our message and accept our apologies for the intrusion.

#

Timeline: Thursday 6th July 2017 –
Three Days Later

After a few days of sadistically playing hard to get, Muriel continued with her cruel scam and eventually replied to the Chilterns' heartfelt message; her lies knew no limits. She said she had known Andrew very well; in fact the young Connie-Su had absolutely adored the nineteen-year-old guitarist. She had secretly been in love with him but admitted she knew the talented musician was only using her for casual sex. After a long and emotional video chat with the grieving parents, the scheming hustler broke the life-changing news that Andrew had fathered her child whom she had called Henri. Alan and Yvonne had sounded ecstatic that they had found the right girl, but their bubble of happiness was soon deflated with the

136

devastating blow that Connie-Su's son had also tragically passed away.

Henri Durand had been an accomplished guitarist, a bit of a loner and a very insular child. The angst driven young Goth lived for his music and he had uploaded numerous self penned songs to the internet. In all of the short amateur videos published on his YouTube channel, Henri's long black hair, pale skin and dark sunken eyes looked back out at a merciless world. Despite his talent, the troubled singer songwriter had suffered from a crippling lack of self confidence; it had been an all-encompassing self-loathing that had festered into a black pit of morbid depression. The darkness had eventually driven him to take his own life after a Halloween party the previous year.

Yvonne and Alan sobbed as they were fed the hustler's tragic story about their troubled grandson. Muriel studied the pained expressions on her victims' faces as they chatted on a video link. She watched uncontrollable tears flood the elderly couple's eyes as they were made to promise never to reveal to anyone that Andrew had fathered Connie's illegitimate child; especially as Connie's husband Pierre could never know that Henri hadn't been his biological son.

#

Timeline: Friday 7th July 2017, 15:00hrs –
The Next Day

Muriel Grubbet sat at an antique hand-carved dressing table in a luxuriously appointed top floor suite at the Granary Mill Hotel. The country house estate had not been the first choice of accommodation for the hustlers. The Grubbets thought that the former stately home was a little too intimate and lacked the anonymity they thrived on, but it was the best Hanford had to offer. The Tudor building stood at the end of a long stone chip driveway and the plush bedrooms overlooked open parkland that was set amid beautiful rolling countryside. It was a tranquil location where many artists had been inspired and poets had become lost within the bucolic surroundings. But such natural beauty was largely lost on the scammer. Her main concern about the place was the risk that they would be recognised from when they had stayed there the previous year, using different names as Monsieur and Madame Benoit. It would be difficult to remain under the radar and escape without paying for their stay a second time.

Eddie had recently returned from playing a round of golf in the grounds of the hotel. As Muriel listened to her husband whistle contentedly in the shower, the ever-scheming hustler pulled her hair into an elegant chignon and put on an understated cream coloured blouse with a single string pearl necklace. Finally she adjusted the position of a chair from the dressing table to sit in front of a bedroom wall that was covered in Fleur de Lys wallpaper. The sumptuous décor had always provided the perfect backdrop for the scammer's fake French boudoir. She opened up her laptop and logged onto her video call account. Muriel was ready to lure more unsuspecting victims into the grifters' lair and it was time for Connie-Su Durand to turn up the heat on the Chilterns.

#

Timeline: Friday 7th July 2017, 16:00hrs –
Later That Afternoon

Alan and Yvonne were always delighted to see their friend's smiling face appear in the chat window. They were becoming quite attached to their daily conversations with the mother of their secret grandson. The elderly couple were both happy to see that Connie appeared to be more relaxed when talking to them and she had appeared more comfortable opening up about her life in France.

She told them that the Durand family lived in a comfortable villa in a small village on the outskirts of Saint Raphael in the south of France. Their home had once been an old schoolhouse. Pierre was a civil engineer and most of his time was spent travelling between various building projects along the Riviera.

Connie said that she had first met Pierre during a French exchange trip at school. They had kept in touch for a couple of years and she had moved to France after completing her A levels. She knew she was expecting Andrew's child but she had initially hidden her pregnancy from her French boyfriend. The young couple immediately rekindled their romance and they married the following year, shortly after Henri was born. Connie said she had then worked as a studio portrait photographer when she first moved to her newly adopted country, but soon after Henri arrived, she had found it difficult to cope with a hectic work schedule whilst juggling family life. The young woman decided to put her fledgling career on hold and happily devoted her life to being a full time stay-at-home mother. When Henri started high school, Connie opened up her own small photography studio.

Her son developed a passion for playing the guitar and song-writing, and it became obvious that Henri had undoubtedly inherited Andrew Chiltern's musical genes. Connie expanded her business by helping him to promote his talent. She videoed his performances and helped him to launch his popular YouTube channel.

Following her son's suicide she had begun training to become a mental health counsellor for troubled youths; to try and prevent another tragic loss of life. But her first love would always be photography.

The Chilterns had been impressed by Connie's positive outlook and envied her creativity and apparent ability to cope under adversity. It seemed that no matter what life had thrown at her, she had always managed to seize the day and make the most of things.

"If only you and Andrew had been given the chance to get together," Yvonne had once lamented during one of their online chats.

"My God what a beautiful collaboration of artistic talent the two of you would have been."

Muriel and Eddie Grubbet always planned their scams meticulously. They were long-con artists who were happy to play the waiting game. Muriel's fastidious attention to detail had created scores of successful hustles over the years, with a rewarding career that had funded the Grubbets' enviable lifestyle. Now in her mid forties she was not about to change the habit of a lifetime and rush into a situation that had not been thoroughly researched. It was imperative that she gained as much information as possible about Andrew's widow Lydia Chiltern; her victims' daughter-in-law.

The delayed letter con was an elaborate hustle that required a lot of planning and she could not afford to run the risk of a younger more scam-savvy relative ruining all of her hard work. The heartless grifter preyed heavily on elderly people and their innocent vulnerabilities; Muriel needed to ensure that Lydia was out of the picture and would not just turn up unexpectedly and see straight through the lies.

"Have you mentioned Henri to Andrew's widow yet?" asked the scheming swindler. Alan took in a deep breath, as if trying to hold back a tidal wave of distain for his daughter-in-law.

"No we haven't," he replied quite indignantly. Muriel immediately noticed a change in Alan's tone; even through the low resolution video call screen she could tell there was an undercurrent of ill feeling in his expression.

"You must excuse my husband," offered Yvonne apologetically.

"We don't get on with Lydia much, she . . ." the old woman's sentence was unceremoniously cut off.

"She's just a low rent slut who has always been too big for her bra," interrupted Alan. Muriel fought hard to quell a sly smile that was beginning to creep across her lips.

Yvonne felt she needed to explain the reason for her husband's outburst and why they had never warmed to their daughter-in-law. She said Lydia and Andrew had married after a whirlwind romance and the relationship had always been stormy. Lydia had been a drama student at Hanford University and Alan doubted her education would ever help her to find a proper career. He added that she only arrived on the scene when it appeared Muscovado Crowz were about to hit the big time and he had always thought she was a bit of a gold-digger; becoming the wife of a rock star would be far more rewarding than any small time acting job. The Chilterns firmly believed the feckless young woman had been having an affair at the time of their son's accident and, if Andrew had not have died, then it would only have been a short matter of time before the couple split up any way. Alan seemed to particularly resent the fact that

140

Lydia had benefitted financially following his son's death. In his words she was now sitting pretty with a mortgage-free house and financial stability courtesy of a large settlement from Andrew's life insurance policy. The elderly parents had not heard anything from their daughter-in-law since the generous payment was made almost six months previously. Muriel had been reassured by the elderly couple's obvious distrust of Lydia and, with the unwitting confirmation that there was no meddling younger relative on the scene, the heartless hustler decided it was safe to put the next phase of her scam into operation.

#

Timeline: Thursday 13th July 2017, 15:00hrs –
One Week Later

Hanford Town Crematorium's garden of remembrance was a calm haven devoted to the memories of hundreds of lives. A large memorial wall, be-decked with a host of floral tributes, had dozens of small pieces of brass plate pinned to it; each one lovingly engraved with prophetic words in tribute to the people who had passed away. The contemplative tranquillity of the garden was only occasionally interrupted by birdsong. Muriel, Alan and Yvonne stood in sombre reflection at the site of Andrew's memorial plaque.

In loving memory of Andrew Chiltern.
Your music will always play on in our hearts.

The young man's parents were secretly disappointed that there was no grave to visit. To them the small metal plate seemed inadequate to properly honour their son's loving memory and it was the only physical tribute they had. The grieving couple said they had dutifully carried out Andrew's final wishes; he had been cremated and his ashes scattered at Glastonbury soon afterwards. Muriel read the inscription on the young musician's plaque and placed a posy of flowers and a photograph of Henri on the stone floor beneath. A small tear trickled down Yvonne's face as she read the hand written note on the back.

"Making peaceful music together at last
with your ever loving son,
Henri. X

#

Timeline: Sunday 16th July 2017, 19:00hrs – Three Days Later

The Chiltern's home was a beautiful large detached building at the edge of Himley Chase. It had a wide block-paved driveway and an attractive double-fronted aspect with tall stone pillars that flanked each side of the oak panelled front door. A gated side passageway led to the back garden. Here Alan and Yvonne had created a beautiful oasis of calm with raised flower beds, a paved sun terrace and perfectly manicured lawn with distant views over fields and open parkland at the rear. The only area that had been neglected of late was a withered vegetable patch. It had been one of Andrew's projects and the family had successfully harvested fresh produce from it every year. But now it lay barren. The grieving old couple's plans to reinstate it had been put on hold until the following Spring.

Muriel was delighted that she had been invited to stay at the house for the duration of her visit to England and she had settled in very well during the past few days; convincingly playing the part of Connie, the mother of the Chilterns' grandchild. The trusting elderly couple had been most insistent that she should not waste money on a hotel when they had a choice of perfectly fine guest rooms in their house. Although they were obviously affluent people, Alan had always been proud of his restrained approach to spending money; a trait that he had acquired from years of strict budgeting and having to watch the pennies when he worked in the public sector.

When the Chilterns had first married it had been very important for the couple to keep a careful eye on their spending, even more so after their son was born, as Yvonne chose to give

142

up her full time job as a legal secretary and had devoted her life to becoming a housewife and mother. Despite their humble beginnings, the Chilterns had built a good life from decades of honest toil. Now, in the autumn of their years, they were looking forward to enjoying the benefits of a healthy retirement.

Muriel sat on a sun lounger on the patio terrace at the rear of the elderly couple's house. She idly soaked up the last of the early evening summer sunshine as Alan popped open another bottle of Prosecco and Yvonne carried out a tray of tapas snacks.

"The weather's not quite as good as what you're used to on the Cote d'Azur I bet Connie," said Alan.

"But it's not a bad way to end the day is it?" he added with a satisfied sigh. Muriel smiled back as her Champagne flute was promptly re-filled with frothy bubbles. The young woman clinked glasses with her friends as they drank a toast to the memories of Andrew and Henri.

"You have a lovely home here you know," said Muriel.

"It's wonderful to see so much greenery. That's something I miss back in Saint Raphael. It's just so hot there that everything dries out during the summer," she lamented.

The congenial atmosphere continued into the night until the happy gathering was interrupted by the unexpected trill of Connie's mobile phone. It was her husband calling. Muriel stared at the screen for a couple of seconds and rolled her eyes in feigned annoyance at the intrusion, before reluctantly pressing the button to answer the call. Yvonne and Alan began to respectfully chat between themselves so as not to overhear their friend's private conversation, but it soon became clear that the young woman was listening intently to an angry voice shouting at the other end of the phone line.

Suddenly the colour appeared to drain from Connie's face and she began to silently shake. From her shocked expression it was obvious to the Chilterns that their house guest had received some terrible news. Muriel clicked away the call and remained motionless on the sun lounger. Well-rehearsed fat fake tears began to stream down the hustler's face as she stared blankly up at the sky. She bit her trembling bottom lip hard to try and stop herself crying but it was no use; anyone could see she was deeply upset by what she had been told on the phone. Yvonne moved over onto the sun lounger and placed a supportive arm around the sobbing woman's shoulders.

"Whatever has happened?" asked Yvonne as she hugged her closer.

"You look like you've seen a ghost." She thoughtfully took Connie's phone from her hand and replaced it with a flute of sparkling wine. Alan picked up a clean serviette from the tapas tray and handed it to his wife to dab away the upset woman's tears. Connie appeared to have difficulty finding the right words and instead began to hyperventilate into the paper napkin. She took a large gasp of air before gulping down the remainder of the Prosecco in her wine glass.

"It was Pierre," she cried, sniffing back a hiccup and wiping away a small moustache of wine from her top lip.

"He said he's found out all about Henri not being his biological son and he doesn't want to have anything more to do with me," she wailed, burying her hot face into the comforting embrace of Yvonne's shoulder.

"He's threatening to cut me off without a penny. What am I going to do?" cried Connie as Yvonne gently stroked her friend's back.

Alan looked at his wife. His shocked expression betrayed his innermost thoughts. He realised that the grieving young woman's life potentially lay in tatters; her marriage was ruined, and all because the Chilterns had relentlessly pursued her. The elderly man instantly felt guilty. There was no escaping the belief that his young son had taken advantage of a besotted teenage girl and, years later, he and his wife had mercilessly hunted down the young woman. Connie was the injured party and her anxious letter should have remained buried in the nineties. Dredging up the past had brought mayhem and chaos to her otherwise idyllic life in the south of France. Alan knew it wouldn't be long before Connie placed the blame for her plight firmly at the Chilterns' door.

"Let me speak to him," said Alan as he picked up the tearful woman's mobile phone.

"No, it's okay . . . I mean . . ." protested Muriel, slightly alarmed by his decisive action.

"Just let's see if I can calm him down," insisted Alan with a distinct air of authority as he called back the last number on the screen.

"I used to do this sort of negotiation for a living," he stated. Yvonne smiled warmly at her husband as she refilled Connie's glass and put her arm back around the trembling woman's shoulders. She truly hoped Alan still possessed the mediation skills needed to handle such a delicate situation.

#

Eddie Grubbet stood at the bar in the residents' lounge of the Granary Mill hotel. This was a popular location for many of Hanford's business executives to visit when meeting clients. The grifter knew it could be a fertile hunting ground for unwitting targets ready to fall victim to his small-time hustles. He believed, at the very least, he should be able to steal another guest's room charge card and swindle a few free drinks. Eddie had chosen his lair carefully. The private nooks and crannies in the bar were privy to the hushed secrets of many business deals; the medieval wooden booths kept thousands of covert conversations totally confidential. He ordered a large malt Whisky and carried it over to a table in the corner of the room. A small self-congratulatory smile grew across his lips as he began to think how rewarding the Grubbets' current scams had been. His wife had thoroughly researched their prey and at least half a dozen marks had fallen for their latest delayed letter hustle. The country house hotel was a good base to work from to carry out the second phase of the plan, but Eddie had been apart from his wife for almost a week and, without his partner in crime by his side, he was becoming restless and bored of his own company.

A petite young woman with ash blonde hair walked into the lounge and sat down on a stool at the bar. She carried a slim briefcase and wore a smart grey trouser suit with a crisp white silk blouse beneath the jacket. She ordered a lime and soda before asking the bartender to confirm the time. She nervously fiddled with a shiny glass brooch on her lapel as she quickly scanned the room, as if searching for a familiar face. Eddie had a keen eye for detail and was a self-proclaimed expert in reading body language. He concluded that the young woman was there for a business meeting, rather than for pleasure, as she had ordered a soft drink and her clothes were far too formal for a catch up with friends.

'Or maybe she's one of those high class hookers meeting a client.' He laughed inwardly at the thought that such an arrangement could be happening beneath the noses of the country house hotel management. In his mind he gave her the irreverent nickname of 'Bar Bunny' and decided she would be fair game for one of his short-term hustles.

Eddie smiled at the young woman and gave her a playful wink as his phone began to buzz. He was a little surprised to see the number from Muriel's burner phone in the display. A call back from his wife, so soon after Pierre's feigned argument with Connie, had not been in their plan. Eddie was an experienced grifter with a sixth sense for spotting trouble and the unexpected call aroused his suspicions. He wondered if something had gone wrong, and he was unsure who would be listening at the other end of the line, so he assumed the character of the irate Frenchman once more and took a sip of Whisky before answering the call.

"Oui?" announced Eddie cautiously.

"Ah, bonsoir Monsieur Durand," began Alan. Eddie was momentarily surprised to hear the male voice. He took a larger steadying gulp of his drink to quickly resume his composure, before slipping back into the character of Connie's angry husband.

Alan's mature soothing tone sounded gentle as he tried to calmly explain the background of the situation and how he and his wife felt totally responsible for the recent turn of events. As Alan continued to apologise to Pierre for his son's careless actions decades before; the con-man spoke very little and listened intently to everything the pragmatic old man had to say. It became clear that the Chilterns were willing to help the Durands cope with the aftermath, and they would honour any financial responsibilities they had as Henri's grandparents.

After a few minutes Eddie drained the last couple of dregs from his Whisky tumbler and ended the call abruptly. He had been unnerved by the conversation and was unsettled by the fact that Alan Chiltern had spoken to him in fluent French. The hustler was thankful that he had chosen to remain in character as Pierre when he had answered the phone, but he had needed to finish the conversation as quickly as possible before Alan realised he was hearing a false Gallic accent. He had made it clear to Alan that although he was disgusted by Connie's slutty behaviour all those years ago, it was her countless lies and calculated deception over the following two decades that was impossible to forgive. The incandescent Pierre Durand was going to file for a divorce. His wife would only hear from him again through his solicitor.

#

"Hello, is this seat taken?" asked a young woman standing next to the wooden booth. Eddie slowly looked up from his mobile phone screen to see that Bar Bunny had made her way over to his table. He smiled broadly and gestured an invitation for her to sit down.

"I'm sorry to impose on you like this," she continued.

"It's just that I was supposed to meet my manager here but he's running late and I don't like to sit on my own in bars as it can give some people the wrong impression," she added with a small nervous laugh. Eddie breathed in deeply and caught a waft of her delicate floral perfume as she sat down next to him.

"Hi, I'm Daisy," she offered her hand to formerly introduce herself.

"How do you do Daisy? Call me Robin." He stood up to greet the attractive stranger and was momentarily transfixed by her sparkly blue eyes.

#

"I'm afraid there's just no reasoning with the man," said Alan as he broke the news to Yvonne that their house guest would be staying with them for a while longer. Alan looked across at Connie with a small quizzical look on his face. The hustler immediately sensed the change in his demeanour.

147

"What else did he say?" asked Muriel nervously, worried that she had missed something. Alan using her phone to call Eddie had not been in the Grubbets' master plan and she hoped to God that her husband had not let anything slip to arouse the old man's suspicions.

"It wasn't anything he said," replied Alan.

"It's just that when I called him the ring tone was a double sounding British one, and not the international single tone that I would have expected to hear when calling someone in the south of France."

Muriel felt a hot sting of adrenaline surge through her veins at the unexpected revelation. Would that one stupid detail lead to their scam being discovered? A wave of panic washed through her brain as she desperately scrabbled for a plausible explanation. She took a sip of Prosecco to moisten her dry mouth and to stall for a couple of seconds thinking time. The Durands' story would have to be re-written on the fly.

"Yes, he is in England," she began slowly, as she searched through her brain for a reasonable explanation.

"Pierre told me that he had initially suspected I was having an affair, so a couple of months ago he hired a private investigator to keep tabs on what I was doing," she continued, still trying to conceal her panic.

"He said the PI had compiled a whole dossier about me, where I'd been, who I'd seen," she added, before taking another stalling mouthful of wine. The heartless hustler felt cornered. She could envisage the whole of the Grubbets' elaborate scam unravelling before her eyes; she was trying to hide her fear of being found out as a fraudster and cleverly disguised her emotions as being terrified of her husband's wrath. She put down her wine glass and buried her face in her hands before sobbing uncontrollably into her open palms.

"Apparently the detective followed me out here to England a couple of days ago and Pierre came over yesterday to meet up with him in Hanford," wailed Muriel. Yvonne hugged the young woman closer and gave her a comforting pat on the back.

"Come on now my lovely, there's no need for all these tears." Yvonne looked over towards her husband as if asking him for unspoken guidance on how best to handle the delicate situation. The caring elderly woman firmly believed it was her son's fault that Connie's marriage was in trouble; if Andrew hadn't left the besotted groupie high and dry all those years ago then her life would have been very different today. Yvonne was determined that she and her husband would somehow make it all right.

"You've had a terrible shock. Why don't you go to bed and try to get some rest. Everything will look better in the morning." The callous con-artist smiled inwardly. She knew she was back in control as she proudly revelled in her ability to create such a convincing lie. All she had to do now was bring her husband up to speed.

#

The elegant Daisy sat next to Eddie in the residents' lounge of the Granary Mill Hotel. He noticed that she kept teasing her fingers through the ends of her bobbed blonde hair as she took delicate sips of her lime and soda. She placed her glass on the table and leaned down to pull a mobile phone out of her briefcase.

"Have you been to this place before?" she asked casually, as she scrolled through a couple of text messages on her phone.

"No," lied Eddie.

"Why do you ask?" he added curiously. Daisy clicked away the screen and slid the phone back into her bag.

"Oh, I just thought that if you had, then you'd be able to recommend a few good places to go or things to do during the evenings," she replied with a smile as she seductively uncrossed and re-crossed her legs.

"What about your manager?" asked Eddie, slightly aroused by the young lady's body language.

"Doesn't he have things planned for you to do this evening?" He was mindful that the young woman had earlier said she was not entirely alone at the hotel.

"Oh the boss is a bit of an old fuddy-duddy I'm afraid. I mean, take tonight for example. He was supposed to be meeting me for drinks but he's had to cry off at the last minute. Maybe his wife is scared that I'll lead him astray or something," she laughed.

Eddie fixed his gaze on the beautiful girl's hypnotic eyes as she continued to playfully fiddle with her hair. She was a welcome distraction from an otherwise dull evening and the wily con-man secretly planned that, by the end of the evening, she would become more than that.

#

Timeline: Sunday 16th July 2017 22:00hrs –
Later That Evening

Alan and Yvonne sat on two reclining chairs on the patio enjoying the last of the warm evening. Connie had seemed inconsolable following the earlier telephone conversation with Pierre and she had retired to her bedroom. The caring Chilterns opened another bottle of wine and talked long into the night. They both believed that Connie should be compensated in some way for the life-changing events that their careless son had created. The elderly couple had built a very strong online relationship with the young woman, Henri was an impenetrable bond between the three of them, and on meeting her in person they had warmed to her instantly. They agreed it was nice having her around.

"How did Pierre sound when you spoke to him on the phone?" asked Yvonne as she re-filled her husband's wine glass.

"Well, he didn't say much but he did seem rather resolute that he didn't want to have anything more to do with Connie, that's for sure," replied Alan.

"I thought at one point he was a little calmer and he did suggest he should come over to meet up face-to-face, but he changed his mind when I said we would protect Connie if he was thinking about trying any funny business." Yvonne sat up in her chair and bit her bottom lip.

"Mind you, I didn't realise he was actually so close to home when I made that bold statement," he laughed nervously.

"He's going to totally cut her off without a penny you know," added Alan. His wife appeared to be deep in thought; she had the facial expression of a woman with the weight of the whole world's problems on her shoulders. Yvonne felt as if she and her husband owed it to the mother of their grandson to look after her. She let out a small cough to clear her throat before tentatively speaking.

"I was thinking we could make it a more long-term situation," began Yvonne quietly. Alan gazed back at her with a quizzical look on his face.

"You know, with Connie staying here," she added. Alan brought his hand up to his face and began to rub his fingers over his chin, as if massaging an imaginary goatee beard. Yvonne was encouraged by the action as it was a habit her husband had when he was giving something favourable consideration. Eventually a small smile began to grow at the corners of Alan's lips.

"Yes, I agree," he replied before taking a small sip of wine.

"I reckon we owe it to her. She was the mother of Andrew's child, and after all she's been through, she deserves a decent place to live, at least until she gets back on her feet," he added. Yvonne smiled broadly back at her husband, relieved that he appeared to be as keen as she was to help the stranded young woman.

The Chilterns' only living family relative was Lydia, their daughter-in-law. Lydia and Andrew had never had children. Alan and Yvonne's wills had not been changed following their son's tragic death and the musician's wife still stood to inherit everything from the couple when they died.

"Talking long-term though, we need to get the wills changed pronto, 'cos as it stands at the moment that money-grabbing little trollop would get it all. Christ, can you imagine that; a second windfall from another Chiltern's death," stormed Alan.

"Exactly what I was thinking," replied Yvonne.

"God forbid this whole can of worms with Henri leads to Connie and Pierre divorcing, then I think we need to do something to help Connie out with a long-term plan. We owe her that much at least," she added.

"Yes. It certainly is something to think about. If we take her under our wing then she won't have to rely on the financial support of Pierre. And, at the end of the day, if we put her in our Wills then it'll leave nothing in the coffers for Lydia," agreed Alan as he clinked wine glasses with his jubilant wife.

#

Muriel Grubbet lay on the bed in the guest room at Yvonne and Alan's house; methodically going over the day's events in her mind. It was important to keep a careful track of everything that had been said as she knew she may need to call upon the information again later on during the scam. Her friendly hosts had been more than understanding when the manipulative hustler had retired to bed early. She had been shaken by Alan's unexpected phone call to Pierre and more than a little unnerved by the revelation that he had spoken in fluent French to her husband. Fortunately Eddie had a thorough knowledge of the language and he had been able to play the part of an enraged Frenchman very easily; the whole plan could have gone so badly wrong if Eddie hadn't been able to carry off that crucial piece of acting. The grifter breathed a sigh of relief that she had cleverly negotiated the tricky question of the British ring tone and her latest scam was still on track. Manipulative Muriel knew it was a careless slip not knowing Alan was bi-lingual and she would have to be more careful when selecting her marks in future.

She was a little concerned that Eddie had not arranged to visit the Chilterns' house the following morning, as that was how they usually operated. Their usual M.O. was for Muriel to become a trusted friend of the targets and then, at the earliest opportunity, gain uninterrupted access to their victims' personal papers and banking information. The Grubbets would plunder the documents before making a speedy getaway. Muriel was intrigued as to why her husband was not following the usual tried and tested arrangement. She knew that Eddie was a confident con-man who was able to swiftly adjust a plan to suit any change in circumstances. She was sure he must have had a good reason to delay his visit to the Chiltern's house.

The scheming scammer smiled inwardly as she reflected on how relatively simple it had been to make the elderly couple feel utterly responsible for Connie's plight; that in turn, it had led them to persuade the distraught young woman to stay with them. She was determined to make herself feel at home until Eddie arrived to carry out the next phase of the scam.

The Chilterns' guest bedroom was very large and beautifully decorated. Ceiling to floor muslin drapes hung at French doors that opened out onto a balcony. The windows had been left ajar and the curtains billowed in the warm summer breeze. A door in one corner of the bedroom led to a modern en-suite shower room. A comfortable king size bed was the star attraction, with a thickly padded cream leather headboard and matching foot board. Its crisp white Broderie Anglaise duvet lay beneath a cerise satin runner at the base of the bed, a collection of co-ordinating velvet cushions were piled high at the other end. Pretty floral wallpaper adorned a feature wall above the divan and the rest of the room had been finished in very pale rose tinted paint. The whole ambience created a calming sanctuary for the Chilterns' guests.

Muriel sat up on the bed and raised her mobile phone towards the ceiling; pointing it in a few different directions to try and find a signal. Finally she opened one of the French doors and realised a thick canopy of trees outside the window were blocking any path from the local phone mast. She stepped out onto the balcony to see if the reception was stronger outside. She sighed in relief at seeing the bars on the screen dance into life; she would be able to contact her husband and find out exactly what had been said during his conversation with Andrew's father. She began to dial Eddie's number but stopped suddenly when she overheard Alan and Yvonne chatting on the terrace below. She moved towards the edge of the balcony and knelt down to keep out of sight of the couple as she began to listen to what they were saying. A wide satisfied smile grew across Muriel's face as she realised the elderly marks were openly discussing altering their wills to solely benefit Connie, the mother of their grandchild. Lydia, their late son's wife, would receive nothing more.

Muriel drew in a small gasp and placed her hand over her mouth in excitement. The hustle had totally surpassed the grifter's wildest dreams as it appeared she would eventually stand to receive a fortune when the Chilterns died. Their house was worth at least a million pounds and Muriel felt sure that the elderly couple would have other pockets of cash squirreled away in shares, bonds and savings accounts. She realised it would be a longer con than usual, but such a reward would be well worth the wait. Muriel heard Alan and Yvonne clear away the wine glasses and fold up the sun loungers on the terrace below before going into the house and locking the back door. The old couple were now out of earshot and it was safe for the feckless schemer to call her accomplice with the unexpected good news.

#

"Yes Mu. I gathered they might be planning something like that from the over-protective way Chiltern spoke about you on the phone," said Eddie dismissively, with a long stretched yawn.

"That's why I didn't want to come over to their house tomorrow and cut off the opportunity too soon. I reckon we're onto a good thing here, and there will be a lot more to be had from these old codgers than a simple quick identity theft," he added. Muriel smiled warmly as a soothing glow of contentment enveloped her. Her loyal husband was a master at reading situations and he had never let her down. She realised that he had seen the bigger picture and his quick thinking would lead them to reap a far larger reward than they had previously imagined.

Apart from his conversation with Alan Chiltern, Eddie had spent an otherwise boring evening at the Granary Mill Hotel, people-watching from his booth in the residents' lounge. Unusually, the seasoned grifter had found no-one gullible enough to fall for any of his bar room confidence tricks. He was feeling a little dejected since Daisy, the blonde bar bunny, had also resisted his charm offensive. It was clear that she had tired of their conversation soon after it had started. The young

154

woman had eagerly answered a phone call from one of her colleagues who had invited her out on an impromptu pub crawl. Eddie's pride had taken a beating; was he losing his touch with the ladies? He had even failed to steal Daisy's room charge card before she left for her night out on the town. Unfortunately for the consummate hustler, he would be forced to settle his own drinks bill that evening.

Although he was only in his early fifties, Eddie wondered if his sexual prowess had begun to wane. He knew that grifting was largely a young man's game and, in one booze-fuelled moment of maudlin contemplation, Eddie had considered that maybe it was time to plan his retirement from his hustling career. All he needed was one final scam that would be lucrative enough to set the Grubbets up for life. Muriel's revelation about the Chilterns' changing their wills had lifted the con-man's melancholy mood a little; however there was one burning issue that needed to be addressed.

"So how are you planning on claiming your inheritance with a false name then?" teased Eddie as he took a sip of Whisky from a freshly poured tumbler. Muriel laughed at the question. She knew that her husband had contacts with at least a couple of accomplished forgers. A false passport and driving license to secure the deal would be the least difficult aspect of the fraud.

"I know you'll sort out the paperwork my darling, that's why I love you so much," whispered Muriel with a giggle.

"Yeah, I suppose the documents are relatively easy to come by," he replied.

"But I'm more bothered about you having to play the part of poor sweet Connie-Su Windell until the pensioners shuffle off their mortal coils. It's going to be a bit tough to cope here alone without you," he added thoughtfully, as his gaze was distracted by the arrival of an attractive raven haired woman who sashayed past his table.

"Yes, I'm missing you too sweetheart." Muriel's voice wavered a little at the sentiment before she took in a steadying breath.

"So how long do you think is reasonable for us to wait for them to die?" she added coldly.

Chapter 12

The Chilterns were delighted that Connie had settled in so well to their family life. The young woman had eagerly assisted Yvonne with the household chores, and she had become an almost indispensable asset to Alan in the garden, as she helped him to tidy up the flower beds ready for autumn. They had even begun to plan the replanting of Andrew's vegetable patch. Yvonne and Alan had been keen to take their friend's mind off her impending divorce battle with Pierre, and they were willing to give her all of the support she needed to start re-building her life.

Connie sat on a stool at the breakfast bar in the kitchen. She was talking on the phone and her frustrated tone became raised as she argued with a bank clerk on the other end of the line.

"What the Hell do you mean my credit rating isn't good enough?" she shouted. Yvonne walked into the kitchen to make a cup of tea and overheard the end of the heated exchange. Connie had become incensed by a negative response to her application for a bank loan. It sounded as if the person on the phone had done nothing to alleviate the tension.

"Well stuff you then!" exclaimed the irate young woman as she angrily clicked away the call.

"Bloody banks, they're all the same," she continued, as she watched Yvonne fill the kettle with water.

"When you've got money they fall over themselves to offer you credit cards; when you're on your uppers and need to borrow a few grand they don't want to know. I can't believe they'd make such a fuss over eight thousand pounds. I mean it's not like I'm going to fritter it all away on a whim is it?" Yvonne smiled back with a baffled expression on her face as she couldn't understand why her friend needed such a large sum of cash.

Connie explained that she felt guilty for taking advantage of the Chilterns' hospitality. It was time to look at moving on and she was thinking about re-starting her photography business. She reminded the elderly woman that she had once built a thriving company in France as a family portrait photographer. Her talented services had been popular with hundreds of people who had wanted to mark their anniversaries, birthdays and special occasions with a full colour memento printed onto canvas. Connie was sure that she would be able to achieve the same level of success in England, and she had spent the past couple of weeks working on a business plan. Alan caught the end of the conversation as he entered the kitchen and walked over to greet his wife with an affectionate peck on the cheek.

"What's all this then?" he asked, before dutifully filling a tea pot with boiling water from the kettle.

"Oh Connie was just telling me about her business plan weren't you dear," replied Yvonne. Alan looked puzzled. It was the first he had heard about it.

"I wanted to surprise you both by getting it all up and running first," lamented the young woman, recognising the old man's concerned expression.

"Look, it's all here in black and white but the bank just doesn't want to know," she added dejectedly. Muriel slid a slim stack of carefully typed A4 sheets of paper across the work surface towards the elderly couple. Alan picked up the document and slowly read through its simple financial proposal.

It appeared that the young woman had approached the bank for a short-term loan for eight thousand pounds. The money would provide start-up capital for her new business and would be used to buy some basic photography equipment, a laptop and software; the rest would cover initial marketing expenses and a couple of months' room hire at a local craft centre. The proposal was supported by impressive figures from Connie's old business in France when she would regularly have two shoots a day; the average session brought in the equivalent of three hundred pounds.

"If you had a couple of bookings a day, then a gross turnover of around three thousand pounds a week to start with sounds pretty good to me," said Alan, surprised by the healthy projected return.

"Yes, that's what I thought," added Yvonne as she read the document over her husband's shoulder.

"But the bank won't give me a loan as apparently my credit score isn't good enough. It's mainly because I have no assets in the UK and I'm not officially recognised as living here at the moment." Connie's frustration was clear to see as Yvonne and Alan continued to carefully study the business plan.

"I suppose I'll just have to wait until my divorce settlement eventually comes through then," she pondered. Alan carried on reading the paperwork as Yvonne poured out three cups of tea.

"The only problem is," continued the conniving con-woman, sensing that her latest short-time hustle may not come to full fruition,

"I know of someone selling some photographic equipment at a stupidly low price. They hadn't a clue how to run a studio and they've gone bust. They want to offload the gear before the bailiffs turn up and take it all away." The young woman took a sip of hot tea.

"They're even including their client database. It's the full set up I'd need to start the business and they only want eight grand cash for it all. It's an absolute bargain," she added lamentably.

"They'd have probably sold it all by the time I get anything from my divorce though. If only Pierre hadn't frozen me out of the joint bank accounts."

Alan and Yvonne looked across at each other, desperately trying to find a solution to their friend's predicament. Although they were comfortably well off, they didn't have ready access to those kinds of funds. Alan explained to the young woman that when he had retired he received his occupational pension and the elderly couple had invested their life savings wisely to give them a modest monthly top-up payment. It was enough to cover all of their household bills and pay for a couple of nice holidays each year, but it was nowhere near enough money to launch Connie's business. It was a classic case of being asset rich but cash poor. The Chilterns were in their early seventies and had to resign themselves to the fact that they were unable to help her financially.

Alan read through the document again and bit his bottom lip hard. He knew that one of his endowment policies was due to mature in a couple of months' time and he could maybe use that money to fund Connie's new venture. He had secretly planned to spend the windfall on a surprise for his wife, by trading in their old car for a newer model. However, as Alan mulled over the figures in his mind he soon realised that the money would not come through soon enough; Connie needed the capital within the next few days to take advantage of the short-term offer of the cheap photographic equipment and business opportunity. Alan was reluctant to cash in his investment early and risk having to pay a penalty charge.

The young woman was surprised by the pensioners' inability to lend her the money and she tried hard to hide her disappointment. Despite the setback she smiled and said she understood their situation perfectly; her lack of funds wasn't their problem and she wouldn't dream of imposing further on their generous hospitality.

Yvonne patiently read through the business proposal again, hoping to see if the costs could be reduced somehow, but it was a fruitless exercise. The three of them remained huddled around the breakfast bar trying to devise a plan to get Connie's photography empire off the ground. Suddenly a broad smile grew across the swindler's face.

"Here's a thought," began Muriel.

"What about if you took out a loan for me?" she said. The Chilterns were a little surprised by her idea, but in the backs of their minds they were still both feeling responsible for Connie's plight.

"And what if it didn't cost you a bean?" she added convincingly. Alan was now quite curious and asked her for more details.

"Well, let's say you use your really great credit rating and take out a loan for ten thousand pounds. You give me eight grand of it and keep back two grand yourself. You then use that money to cover the first six months' repayments. The business will be up and running in time for Christmas, and after that there will be all of the work I'll get for Valentine's Day, so it's a fair bet that by March next year I'll be making enough money from the photography studio to be able to take over the rest of the repayments myself."

"That's a rather brilliant plan," replied Alan. He was impressed by her business acumen and foresight. He believed it was a line of work that she knew well and she had planned her venture carefully to be operational in time to take full advantage of the festive season. Effectively they would be lending Connie the money she needed for the equipment without it costing them a penny; she would soon be turning over three thousand pounds a week. There would be plenty of profit; every one would win.

"And you can convert the study here into a studio space, which will save you the room hire charges at the craft centre," added Yvonne exuberantly, as they all clinked tea cups to toast the exciting new adventure.

#

Eddie Grubbet closed his heavy Samsonite suitcase and clicked the locks firmly shut. After one final look around his hotel room to check he had all of his belongings, he pulled the long leather handle of his laptop bag over his left shoulder and wheeled the suitcase out of the bedroom door into the plush corridor outside. The luxurious top floor suite of the Granary Mill Hotel had been his home for the past couple of months, and today he was happy to be leaving. Apart from a few distracting dalliances with unwitting lonely women in the hotel bar, he had lived a solitary existence while his wife stayed with the Chilterns.

To the outside world the tall, dark and relatively handsome man who made his way to the lift was simply one of dozens of other anonymous executives who used the location as a comfortable base for their deals and meetings. Eddie's glossy mane of jet black hair was smartly combed away from his face; held securely in place with a pair of designer sunglasses. With his cream coloured Chinos, crisp white polo shirt and dark blue deck shoes, he looked every inch the successful businessman about to embark on a well-deserved holiday.

Eddie needed the solace of his villa in the South of France; he longed to taste the fresh lobster at Hercule's fish restaurant;

to drink wine in his friends' vineyards again and to sense the familiarity of home. Most of all he needed a calm space in which to think through his audacious plan for how best to bring the Grubbets' final hustle to full fruition. Eddie emerged from the lift, crossed the hotel lobby towards the reception desk and handed over his room key to the checkout clerk.

"Thank you for staying with us Mr Banks," said the receptionist as she passed Eddie his receipt and returned his cloned credit card to him.

"Your taxi to the airport is just outside sir."

#

Timeline: Wednesday 1st November 2017 –
Two Months Later

Muriel Grubbet sat on the back seat of Alan's car and idly looked out of the windows at people passing by on the high street. The heartless hustler was waiting for the Chilterns to return from a visit to see their solicitor. The car was a new Jaguar. Muriel resented the fact that one of Alan's investments had matured and he had cashed it in to finance the luxury purchase. In her opinion she couldn't understand why people in the autumn of their lives would want to squander so much money on a sporty vehicle that they would never drive to its full potential.

'Doddery old fool going through a late life crisis I shouldn't wonder,' she lamented. Muriel knew that the expenditure would leave at least a twenty thousand pound gap in her eventual inheritance. She selfishly wondered just how much of her windfall would be left after the Chilterns had finished their spending spree.

Muriel took in a deep breath and the expensive smell of the leather hide interior filled her nostrils. She noticed that Alan had left the keys in the ignition and the temptation to get into the driver's seat and spirit the car away was almost all consuming.

'Maybe I should just cut my losses. After all I bet I could get a couple of grand for a nice luxury motor like this on the black market,' she thought as she picked up her mobile phone and called Eddie's number.

"Hello, it's me," said Muriel as her husband answered her call.

"Hi Mu, how's it all going?" It was good to hear his voice again. A wide smile grew across the scammer's lips. She began to laugh as she instantly dismissed the wicked idea of stealing the car. The seasoned swindler knew that this scam was panning out far better than the Grubbets had ever imagined and she had the Chilterns eating out of the palm of her hand.

Unbeknown to the unwitting elderly marks, the eight thousand pounds from the bank loan that they had given to Connie to start up her photography business had been used to maintain the Grubbets' property in the south of France. The calculating con-artist had managed to convince the Chilterns that she had become the victim of fraud; she claimed that she had lost the money when she was ripped off by an unscrupulous hustler who had managed to pass off a stack of empty boxes that should have contained the photographic equipment. Connie also said the useless client database had been largely filled with fake email addresses. The trusting pensioners had believed her lies without too many tricky questions. They had been drawn deeper into the liar's web of deceit. Yvonne and Alan had said that the local police didn't hold much hope that the fraudsters would be caught, so they were resigned to pay back all of the borrowed money to the bank themselves.

"I'm really missing you hun," said Eddie, hoping his wife felt the same way. Scamming the Chilterns had been a long con and the couple had not seen each other for almost four months. But the seasoned confidence tricksters knew that the prolonged absence was a small price to pay, as it would probably be their final hustle; the proceeds would be large enough to set them up for the rest of their lives.

"They're in the solicitor's office now, just putting the finishing touches to their new wills, then Connie-Su Windell will become the sole beneficiary of everything they own when they die," said Muriel.

"Just think about it Ed, their house, car, antiques, investments and all of their money and worldly goods will soon be ours," she added chillingly.

"I sure hope you're right baby," replied Eddie. "It's been a few months now and all the other delayed letter marks have been put on hold while you work on the Chilterns. That eight grand you got out of them won't last long you know."

Muriel quickly finished her conversation as she could see that the jubilant Alan and Yvonne were on their way back to the car. The elderly couple almost danced along the pavement before joyfully springing open the Jaguar's two front doors. Laughing and joking between themselves they eagerly got inside the car and turned around to face Muriel who was still sitting on the rear seat. They were thrilled that they had at last been able to do the right thing for the mother of their grandchild; Connie had now become their sole heir. It was the next best thing to actually adopting her as their daughter and they believed that Andrew would have wanted it that way. Even though their son had happily shagged his way around most of the country whilst on tour with his band, they knew that he had always been an honourable man. The Chilterns were sure that if he had known that Connie was carrying his child then he would have made sure the besotted young groupie was well provided for.

"Let's go out to lunch to celebrate," suggested a gleeful Yvonne.

"Yes, I think we should really push the boat out and go to that posh new Italian restaurant that's opened on the high street," agreed Alan.

#

Cibo Trapani was an elegant eatery that specialised in Sicilian cuisine. It was named after a medieval coastal enclave located on the western tip of Sicily. The chef had lived there as a child and, with a menu of mouth watering dishes, he had successfully brought an authentic taste of the historic Mediterranean island to Hanford. The restaurant had recently opened in the centre of town and its reputation for excellent food and cordial service had already begun to nurture a loyal and discerning clientele. It offered an up-market fine dining experience where executives with open-ended expense accounts entertained their clients, and romantic couples celebrated important anniversaries. The décor inside was sophisticated, if a little clinical, and it featured lots of taupe leather furniture with a dozen intimate tables covered in layers of crisp white linen and sparkling crystal glassware. The only area inside the building that evoked any feeling of old-time Italy was an over-sized sepia print of a crescent-shaped coastline that adorned one of the walls. Despite the cool, minimalist interior, there was still the familiar aroma of basil and grated parmesan in the air; so typical of Italian cuisine.

The Chilterns entered the stylish lobby area ahead of their guest and were immediately greeted by a smartly dressed host who stood behind a glass lectern. The man wore a deep burgundy coloured three piece suit over a starched white shirt. His breast pocket featured an embroidered logo with the Cibo Trapani name written in gold lettering beneath. A shiny metal name badge glinting on the man's lapel revealed that he was Marco Felini, the Maitre D'. The man had dark olive skin and a mop of shiny black hair that had been gelled towards the back of his head in a retro DA style. Even though Muriel stood a few feet away from the man, she could still catch waves of his heavy cologne waft over her as he stood behind the rostrum. Marco politely asked if the Chilterns had reserved a table.

The trio's trip to the restaurant had been an impromptu decision and Yvonne's initial excitement about the last minute lunchtime treat was now slowly deflating, as she heard her husband quietly apologise for not booking in advance. Despite only three of the tables being occupied, the manager sucked a sharp intake of breath through a set of veneered white teeth and studied the reservations list for a moment. Marco seemed to spend an unnecessarily long time perusing the bookings before acknowledging that he would be able to squeeze in the small party for lunch. He picked up three leather-bound menus and summoned a waiter to show the entourage to a table at the rear of the restaurant. A glow of happiness and relief returned to

Yvonne's face. Muriel smiled politely before shooting a secret glance of indignation behind the Maitre D's back.

'Pretentious little twerp,' thought Muriel.

'The place is only a quarter full.' The manager's self-important attitude and power to refuse them entry to the restaurant had riled her; furthermore she resented being relegated to dine at the rear of the room, out of the sight of people passing by the windows at the front. The quietly seething schemer consoled herself by making a mental note that Cibo Trapani and Marco Felini deserved to become future targets for one of her and Eddie's hustles.

Alan and Yvonne took their seats on one side of the table and Muriel sat opposite them with her back to the wall as a waiter took their drinks order. A sommelier quickly arrived and opened a bottle of chilled Prosecco before pouring the frothy bubbles into three Champagne flutes. Everyone at the table lifted their glasses to toast their absent family.

"To Andrew and Henri," said Yvonne, small tears of pride filled her eyes.

"May you both be playing beautiful music together," added Muriel, raising her glance towards the ceiling. Alan smiled at his companions as he took a sip of sparkling wine. He was happy in the knowledge that he and his wife had financially secured the future of their honorary daughter; it would have been what Andrew would have wanted for the mother of his child.

Muriel secretly celebrated the success of the Grubbets' audacious scam, as she now stood to inherit a fortune. The heartless hustler soaked up the Chilterns' hospitality and settled in to enjoy a leisurely lunch at the best eatery in town. From her seat she had a clear view of the whole restaurant and entrance. She could see the Maitre D' was busy welcoming a new customer into the lobby area. Muriel was still annoyed with his initial stand-offish attitude towards her party and she began to ponder how best to reap her revenge on the snooty Italian. She became even more irritated when she noticed how Marco positively fawned over his latest guest.

The new arrival was an attractive young lady who wore a smartly tailored pale pink Chanel suit and carried a matching leather clutch bag. She was obviously a regular visitor to Cibo Trapani, as the man behind the lectern greeted her with a small air kiss on each cheek before personally escorting her to a much coveted window table. The wine waiter immediately skipped over to deliver what must have been her usual order of a Cosmopolitan cocktail with a small dish of stuffed olives.

Muriel was well aware that a restaurateur's favourite trick was to seat what they perceived to be the most attractive or affluent-looking customers in window seats. They knew passers-by would subconsciously judge an establishment by its existing clientele; therefore the beautiful people in the window would attract more aspiring people inside. Although recognition was the last thing Muriel wanted, she felt snubbed that the judgmental Maitre D' had not considered her good enough to be given a coveted place at the front of the restaurant. She made a promise to herself to visit her personal beautician in Cannes for a full facial peel and Botox booster as soon as the Chiltern hustle was concluded. The scorned woman tutted loudly as she began to jealously seethe at the attention being lavished on the elegant young lady seated by the window.

"What's the matter dear?" asked Yvonne, surprised to see that her lunch guest appeared to be annoyed.

"Oh, nothing," replied Muriel, inwardly berating herself for the careless slip.

"It's just that I don't think it's fair that you and Alan don't command as much attention from the staff in here as other customers do. I mean I'm sure your money is just as good as hers," she added, rolling her eyes over in the direction of the young woman seated at the window. Alan turned around in his chair to see who Connie was referring to. Suddenly the expression on his face unexpectedly changed to a cold stare. He gently nudged his wife's arm to prompt her to take a look at whom he had seen across the room.

"Oh my God!" exclaimed Yvonne.

"What the Hell is she doing here?"

On hearing Yvonne's cry, the young lady looked up from her menu and immediately recognised the elderly couple. She seemed a little startled and nervously smiled back at the entourage. Alan and Yvonne frowned as they watched her get up from the window seat and walk over towards their table at the rear of the restaurant. The stylish customer was Lydia Chiltern, Andrew's widow.

"Are you having fun spending your inheritance then?" sniped Yvonne with a snide smile towards her daughter-in-law.

"I see you've finally bought some clothes that cover up your assets for a change," added Alan as he noticed Lydia's conservative attire.

"Hello Yvonne. Hello Alan," she replied politely, looking across the table to query who their lunch companion was.

"Connie, this is Lydia, Andrew's widow," offered Alan as he beckoned towards her. The young women smiled at each other and Lydia leaned across the table to shake hands with Muriel.

"And this is Connie. She's the mother of Andrew's son, Henri," added Yvonne with an almost jubilantly vengeful air.

Lydia was visibly shaken by the unexpected revelation about her late husband. Alan and Yvonne gleefully announced that Andrew had fathered Connie's baby almost twenty years before and they now fully planned to look after the mother of their grandchild. Muriel noticed that the Chilterns appeared to enjoy breaking the news to Lydia; as if it was the ideal opportunity for the grieving parents to avenge Lydia's adultery and poor treatment of their son. Yvonne said the young widow had made it perfectly clear that she had not wanted to have anything more to do with the family following Andrew's death; consequently Lydia would receive nothing more from them and Connie was now their sole heir. Alan didn't hold back his emotions either as he let his obvious pent-up resentment of his daughter-in-law bubble up to the surface.

"You need to think yourself lucky that we won't be going back through probate to get a share of Andrew's estate for his son," shouted Alan. It was a thinly veiled threat that obviously angered Lydia. Muriel sat back in her chair and watched the heated exchange unfold in front of her. Out of the corner of her eye she spotted the concerned looking Maitre D' sashaying between the tables towards the group.

"Is everything alright Senora Chiltern?" asked the burgundy suited man; a wave of his heavy cologne filling the air. He had heard the commotion brewing at the rear of the restaurant and had quickly made his way over to find out what the problem was and to ensure that his valued customer was being well looked after.

"Yes thank you Marco, I've just had some rather shocking news," replied Lydia, desperately trying to retain her composure.

"I'm afraid I'm going to have to cancel my lunch today." She smiled at the host and walked back to her table to retrieve her handbag. The upset young woman reached inside the bag and pulled out a twenty pound note to cover the cost of her drink and canapés. Marco reverently bowed his head before helping Lydia towards the front door. He gave her a fond farewell embrace as the Chilterns watched their daughter-in-law's every move until she was safely outside of the building.

"Good riddance to that little gold digger," sneered Alan as he finished off his glass of wine.

"She might have cleaned up her act with a posh new hairdo and tidy clothes, but she'll never be able to wash away the common little slut that's lurking inside. Once a trollop always a trollop," he added resolutely. Yvonne placed a steadying hand on her husband's arm in an effort to calm his outburst. The old woman was desperate to avoid offending their lunch guest, as she was mindful of the fact that Connie had once been one of Muscovado Crowz's groupies; she and Andrew had not exactly had an exclusive sexual relationship.

"But you didn't tell her that Henri is dead," queried Muriel, still a little startled by the unexpected encounter with Andrew's widow.

"She didn't need to know," replied Alan with a wink.

"Besides, I was having too much fun rattling her cage," he added.

"Yes, I bet you mentioning probate made her think a bit," laughed Yvonne in an effort to steer the conversation away from Lydia's questionable fidelity.

"She's probably gone straight round to her solicitor worried that we're going to claw back some of her inheritance for Andrew's son." The old woman giggled as she summoned the wine waiter to bring another bottle of Prosecco.

168

Chapter 13

To the outside world Muriel Grubbet appeared to settle in very well to her new life with the Chilterns, but she longed to shake off the shackles of constantly having to pretend to be Connie-Su Windell. As the months passed by, the doting elderly couple had become like a mother and father to her. Alan had cashed in their holiday fund and given the scheming swindler a generous monthly allowance to tide her over until the sham divorce from Pierre was finalised. It was leading up to Christmas and the conniving grifter knew that her honorary parents had planned a lavish celebration. But despite their generosity, and all the trappings of a comfortable lifestyle in Hanford, Muriel was missing her husband and her own home in the south of France.

The disappointing British summer had been followed by a dismal damp autumn. The leaves on the canopy of trees outside Muriel's bedroom window had long since withered and fallen; the biting cold winter was beginning to cut in hard. The manipulative hustler needed to feel the massaging warmth of the Mediterranean sun on her skin again; and the heat of Eddie's embrace. She knew it had been six months since the start of the scam and this long con was turning out to be a little too enduring. It was time for the Grubbets to speed up proceedings and bring the hustle to a close. Muriel lay back onto the king size bed in the Chiltern's guest room and rested her head on the soft velvet cushions. She picked up her mobile phone and tapped in a familiar number. She was instantly soothed on hearing Eddie's voice at the end of the line.

When Muriel had first overheard Yvonne and Alan's plan to make her their sole heir, she had quickly put the wheels in motion to arrange the forged documentation to open up a bank account in the name of Connie-Su Durand née Windell. Crucially her fake passport, birth certificate and driving licence had all passed scrutiny at the Chilterns' solicitors during the visit to change their wills. To the outside world it would appear that Connie had a legitimate claim to the whole estate after Alan and Yvonne passed away.

"We're going to have to make their deaths look like an accident or suicide," said Eddie coldly. Muriel felt a hot pain sting in her chest; a loud thumping sound beat in her head as the blood began to pump quicker through her veins. It was the adrenaline-fuelled moment of realisation that the Grubbets were about to cross over a line.

"Is there no other way Ed?" she asked.

"Nope," he replied casually.

"Not unless you wanna hang around for at least another ten years waiting for them both to die of natural causes."

Muriel could sense no emotion in her husband's voice and she became a little unnerved by his matter-of-fact tone. She knew that their life of criminal cons and audacious hustles had left hundreds of devastated people floundering in their wake; but no one had died. The woman secretly worried that she would not be able to cope with the couple's promotion to fully fledged murderers. Eddie appeared to be taking the development in his stride as he planned the fatal finale to scamming the Chilterns. Muriel desperately tried to ignore the fact that he actually seemed to relish the prospect of killing the elderly couple.

Her husband had devised a clear agenda and he had decided to work on creating the illusion that the Chilterns had committed suicide. It would have to be indisputable that Connie had absolutely nothing to do with their deaths, and she would need a water-tight alibi just in case any doubt was cast over the nature of their demise. Following a reasonable length of time to let the dust settle after the discovery of the bodies, the heartless hustlers would cash in their ultimate windfall.

"I'm just gonna need to know absolutely everything about the old codgers' normal habits and day-to-day routines," announced Eddie, as he began to finalise his foolproof plan. After a while the hesitation that Muriel had felt burning at the back of her mind was quickly extinguished. Eddie made it clear that he had everything under control; the Grubbets would soon reap the rewards of their wicked crime and no one would be any the wiser.

#

Muriel shivered as she stood in Hanford Town Crematorium's Garden of Remembrance. She was watching the Chilterns place a large wreath beneath the metal plate that commemorated Andrew Chiltern's life. It was the second anniversary of their beloved son's tragic car accident and the elderly grieving parents had arranged a small gathering for some of Andrew's friends to mark the occasion. One by one, the guests had placed their own mementos at the foot of the plaque and whispered their own private prayers of reflection. As the solemn group paid their respects, a narrow shaft of crisp winter sunshine broke through the clouds and danced on the path in front of them. Alan and Yvonne smiled at each other as they imagined it was a Heaven sent sign that Andrew was looking down on them and he approved of the event.

It was bitterly cold outside and Muriel was sure she could see a few flurries of snow hanging in the air. She hugged herself closely, desperately trying to retain any small amount of body heat that she could muster. She took in a sharp breath and waited for the last of the people to file past the memorial wall.

Yvonne wore a very thick and heavy coat with faux fur trim. She had turned up the fluffy collar and tucked it around her neck in a vain effort to keep out the biting chill, as she knelt down to read the tributes left for her late son. Muriel impatiently checked her watch for the third time. It had been almost an hour since the beginning of the service and the heartless hustler was becoming restless. Eventually she sighed with relief as Alan tenderly held his wife's arm and slowly led the contemplative entourage out of the cemetery.

The Chilterns had laid on a small buffet at a local hotel to finish off the day with their guests. Muriel knew that as soon as everyone was inside enjoying the warm sanctuary of the bar, the last few pieces of the hustlers' jigsaw would be mercilessly put into place. Today was the day that the Grubbets would play their final hand.

#

Timeline: Tuesday 19th December 2017, 17:00hrs

The memorial gathering to celebrate Andrew's life was well attended. He had obviously been a well-loved young man who had touched many people's hearts. Dozens of old friends filled the function suite at the Black Cross Hotel. Most of the guests chatted among themselves and cheerily clinked glasses in respectful memory of the late musician. The three remaining members of Muscovado Crowz were busy setting up a drum kit and PA system on a small stage in the corner of the bar. They would play an intimate gig in honour of the band mate they had loved as a brother. It would be the perfect warm-up for their upcoming memorial concert.

The hot air inside the hotel lobby hit Muriel's face as she followed the Chilterns inside. Alan undid the buttons on his Macintosh before hugging several of the familiar friends standing near to the entrance. Yvonne took off her heavy coat and seemed to be looking around for a suitable place to hang it up.

"Shall I take that for you?" asked Muriel helpfully.

"Yes, thank you Connie. I think there is a cloakroom over there," replied Yvonne as she pointed towards the ladies' toilets.

Unbeknown to the old woman, the quick-thinking hustler would grasp this opportunity to relieve her of the mobile phone that had been safely stored in one of the pockets. Muriel dutifully took Yvonne's coat and Alan's Mac to the cloakroom. Once out of everyone's sight she searched through the pockets and took out Yvonne's phone to switch it on. The heartless grifter smiled and shook her head to mock the elderly woman. Muriel could never understand why some people always kept their mobiles switched off. Her own device was a permanent fixture that she carried everywhere; it was her own personal

172

secretary that helped her to keep track of her swindling scams. Yvonne's phone was a recent model, loaded with all the gizmos for modern life, but Muriel suspected most of the functions had never been used. She laughed at the outdated concept that the old woman only ever carried a phone in case she needed to call someone in an emergency.

"Right, we don't want you to be able to use this later do we," said Muriel as she ran a few apps to drain the battery's power. Satisfied that the phone would quickly become disabled, she returned it to Yvonne's coat pocket and made her way back to the gathering.

"Connie, come over here," beckoned Alan as he saw her walk back into the room.

"There's someone I want you to meet."

Gary Stevens was a painfully thin man in his early forties with a receding head of severely dyed long black hair. He hid his thinning hairline beneath a black bandana that was tightly secured behind his head; a pair of mirrored aviator sunglasses covered the premature wrinkles around his tired eyes. Although a relatively young man, his frail body bore testament to a hard life on the road. His knotted knee joints were clearly visible through the frayed slits in his skinny black jeans and Gary's gnarled hands were beginning to show the first signs of arthritis, brought on from years of exuberant drumming with his band.

"As you know, this is Gaz; one of Andrew's oldest and best friends," announced Alan, assuming that the two people now stood in front of him were familiar old faces to one another. The old man had his arm around the drummer's shoulders; as if Gary's fragile body needed physical support to remain upright.

"Hi Gary," smiled Connie as she stepped closer to place a kiss on the rocker's face. He politely returned the embrace but looked at her quizzically.

"I'm sorry love, but have we met?" he asked nonchalantly as an awkward hush seemed to envelope the room. Alan was startled by the question. Had two and a half decades of gigging, drinking and other recreational activities on the road really taken such a heavy toll on the musician's memory? Why else wouldn't he remember the woman who must have featured quite a lot in the band's history at one point; the woman who had borne his best friend's child?

"It's Connie," offered Alan with a nervous laugh.

"Connie-Su Windell?" he prompted, hopelessly trying to nudge the ageing rocker's memory and break the uneasy silence.

It was an uncomfortable moment for Muriel but not an entirely unexpected one. Had the seasoned swindler not thoroughly researched her subject then the hustler's potential unmasking could have become a problem. But the Grubbets had everything under control; the small hiccup had been planned for.

As soon as Muriel knew she was going to be at the Muscovado Crowz reunion she knew there was always a chance that key members of the band would not recognise her. Muriel and Eddie had pored over endless online photographs taken at the band's gigs in the nineties. Dozens of fans had eagerly tagged their names onto the images of their faces taken from a lost era. The scheming duo had carefully noted that there were half a dozen girls who regularly appeared in the group photographs but were not featured as regular girlfriends of the band. None of the Muscovado Crowz's groupies had come forward to tag themselves. It had been a fertile hunting ground in which to find a suitable candidate to pass off as Connie-Su Windell.

Gary Stevens had started the band with Andrew Chiltern when they were both still at school. The drummer had been an immature sixteen-year-old at the time and his friend was a couple of years younger. The two of them had written most of the band's songs. Typically they had drawn on their personal experiences and vented their frustrations in the unsophisticated lyrics; songs filled with teenage angst and unrequited love. As the band members matured, their material blossomed into rocked up anthems about sex and money. Many of their lusty conquests' names would feature within the lyrics. Andrew and Gary would playfully tease their girlfriends and groupies by promising to immortalise them in one of the Crowz's next songs. Gary thought it was strange he could not remember his friend ever mentioning a girl called Connie.

"Oh I was always hanging out with you guys, but I looked a bit different back then," replied Muriel, an unwelcome slither of doubt that her carefully laid plan would backfire sent a small spark of adrenaline burning through her veins.

"I had short red spiky hair," she lied confidently. Gary thought for a moment as if methodically searching through a mental filing cabinet for any hint of familiarity. Slowly a small smile broke across his lips; he tilted back his head and laughed loudly.

"You mean the little red devil's delight?" he laughed at the memory of a particularly determined flame haired groupie who had followed the band in their early days. He hadn't known her name but he had a vivid recollection of her cleavage. Muriel nodded enthusiastically to enforce the blurred memory.

"Connie-Su Windell," pondered Gary, her name still didn't sound familiar.

"Blimey if you say it quickly enough it sounds like Connie Swindle," he added. Startled Muriel looked back at him before quickly switching her gaze to check Alan's response to the rocker's observation. A sick feeling began to grow in the pit of her stomach. Would this simple off-the-cuff remark unravel her whole scam and bring the hustler's world crashing down around her? Why had she used such a stupid play on words? Alan remained expressionless, silently staring at Gary.

"Did your parents hate you or something by giving you a name that sounds like a con-artist?" taunted the skinny man. Alan pulled away his arm that had been supportively hugging Gary's shoulders and watched the musician rock unsteadily from side to side. The older man rolled his eyes in disappointment. It appeared to Muriel that Gary's comment about her pseudonym had gone largely unnoticed, as Alan seemed to be more pre-occupied by the fact that the drummer had taken full advantage of the free bar and was now beginning to slur his words.

"Nope, I don't never remember Andy writing no song about no Connie," he faltered. Muriel winced at the double negatives as Alan gestured to his wife to bring over a chair for the frail rocker to slump onto. A small group of people had begun to gather around to watch the drunken outburst develop.

"Maybe he couldn't find anything to rhyme with my actual name so he invented the little red devil tag?" offered Muriel, in an effort to take back control of the heated exchange.

"Nah, not Andy. He could always find words to match his birds," replied Gary dismissively as the Chilterns helped him onto the seat.

"I mean, Connie is quite easy to rhyme with; there's bonny, honey, money," he rambled as he proceeded to mentally carry on through the whole alphabet.

"But he did manage to find one that rhymed with that bitch's name Lydia; but that doesn't take too much imagination does it," he laughed. The rest of the gathered entourage began to giggle with embarrassment as Gary sang the chorus of a scornful ballad that suggested the woman had a sexually transmitted disease.

"Lydia, sweet Lydia, I never will be rid of ya.
Like a dose of Chlamydia, you won't leave me alone."

The Chilterns chuckled at the revelation of their son's obvious distain for his own wife, but they were still annoyed by Gary's earlier insult about Connie's name. They had always known their son's attention-seeking band mate liked to stir up trouble, especially after a few drinks. It was as if he always resented the other members of Muscovado Crowz being in the limelight and he felt the need to compensate for always being trapped at the back of the stage behind his drum kit. The elderly couple had hoped the spiteful has-been would show a little more respect; today of all days.

"I'm going to tell the scrawny little stick insect to leave," whispered Alan to his wife.

"No, you can't do that," replied Yvonne.

"The band is going to play in a bit. And besides Connie doesn't appear to be too upset by Gary's banter," she added. The elderly couple were relieved to see the mother of their grandchild had apparently taken the quip about her name in her stride. They watched the young woman laugh and happily join in with Gary's third raucous rendition of the Lydia Chlamydia song.

Unbeknown to the Chilterns, Muriel had been desperate to deflect the attention away from her pseudonym and she was grateful that Gary seemed to possess the attention span of a goldfish; he had been easily sidetracked by bitchy gossip about his late friend's widow. The rest of the evening passed without incident and, despite Gary's alcoholic stupor, the Crowz introduced a few guest guitarists on stage who played a blistering set of the most popular numbers from the band's back catalogue.

Muriel breathed a sigh of relief that the drunken ramblings of the band's drummer didn't appear to have aroused any suspicions with any of Andrew's family and friends. The shameless scammer revelled in the role of ex-groupie and she was delighted that her homework had paid off. The information she had soaked up from dozens of tales posted on Andrew Chiltern's memorial page was proving to be highly valuable. It was a convincing claim that Andrew's song Little Red Devil's Delight had been written about her, as she regaled numerous tales of venues that the band had played at; all suitably seasoned with amusing stories of a few indiscretions.

"What about that time when that guy in the mosh pit at the Queen's Head jumped on the stage but caught his foot on one of Gaz's drum stands? He fell backwards onto the floor below and knocked himself clean out." Gary overheard the anecdote and began to laugh at the happy memory it evoked.

"The funny thing was, the band just kept on playing as the paramedics arrived to pull the poor bloke out of the crowd. I wouldn't be surprised if he'd cracked his skull," added Muriel.

"Well, you don't stop mid song just because a piss head falls off the stage do ya?" replied Gary with a wry chuckle.

"Anyway, we were only half way through playing 'Banging In My Head' which we all thought was quite fitting, considering that he'd just crowned himself."

The gathered group erupted into raucous laughter at Gary's endorsement of Connie's story. Andrew's friends began to warm to the woman and Muriel felt comfortable reciting a couple of the Crowz's most popular songs; two of their definitive numbers that had been carefully selected by the grifter from numerous research visits to YouTube. Soon the

177

crowd were merrily singing along to an impromptu acapella rendition of Little Red Devil's Delight.

#

Timeline: Tuesday 19th December 2017, 23:00hrs

Yvonne and Connie walked into the kitchen of the elderly couple's house. They had just returned home from the memorial party and Alan was parking his Jaguar in the garage. Yvonne filled the kettle with water as her friend sat down at the breakfast bar. Suddenly she noticed a pained expression on the young woman's face. Connie had both hands pressed on her stomach and she looked as if she was about to be sick.

"Oh my God Connie, whatever is the matter?" asked a worried Yvonne.

"I'll be okay," she replied weakly.

"I've just got the most dreadful tummy cramps." Muriel quickly got up from her kitchen stool and ran out of the room, rapidly crossed the hall and entered the downstairs cloakroom. Yvonne heard the young woman vomit a few times before the flush of the lavatory. The callous grifter washed her hands and face and emerged from the toilet looking suitably pale and withdrawn. She returned to the kitchen where Yvonne was explaining to Alan what had just happened. As she reached for the kitchen stool to steady herself, Muriel stumbled, lost her footing and fell heavily onto the marble tiles.

"Connie, Connie. Wake up!" shrieked Yvonne as she shook the young woman's shoulders. Alan stood behind his wife. He was on the phone trying to get through to the ambulance service as Connie began to come round.

"What happened?" she asked drowsily.

"You passed out love," replied a somewhat relieved Yvonne.

"Alan's calling for a paramedic," she added, trying to reassure her embarrassed friend.

"No! No I don't need an ambulance," protested Muriel as she slowly sat up on the cold kitchen floor and tried to regain her composure. The devious hustler began to explain that she suspected it was a simple case of food poisoning and it wouldn't be right to use the valuable resources of the emergency services; they would most likely be stretched to capacity at that time of year anyway, and the last thing they needed was a time waster with a dodgy stomach. Yvonne listened to her friend who explained the culprit was probably a prawn vol-au-vent she had eaten earlier at the buffet. Connie had thought it tasted a bit odd at the time, but she hadn't wanted to make a fuss on such an important day for the Chilterns. Connie said she had thought she'd be okay as she hadn't eaten the whole canapé, but when the stomach cramps had started a couple of hours later she had a fairly good idea what had happened.

"Honestly Yvonne, I don't need an ambulance; all those blue flashing lights outside the house and the neighbours' curtains twitching. I couldn't cope with all the attention. I'll just call a taxi," protested Muriel.

"You'll do no such thing," replied Yvonne firmly.

"Alan and I will drive you to the hospital to get you checked over instead."

#

It was the week leading up to Christmas and the Accident and Emergency department at Hanford General Hospital was busier than usual. It had become the unplanned end-of-night destination for dozens of late night revellers; many of whom had simply over indulged in seasonal spirit. The minor injuries team were stretched to full capacity, dealing with an array of cuts, bruises, fractures and drunken fracas. On arrival at the hospital Connie had been swiftly taken into triage to be assessed by a doctor. Alan and Yvonne were asked to wait outside and they dutifully took their places on an uncomfortably hard plastic bench next to the busy reception desk.

The area was filled with the sound of ringing telephones, beeping pagers and hushed conversations. The smell of disinfectant hung heavily in the air and that aroma was only interrupted by the occasional waft of coffee from the drinks machine. The bewildered couple sat in contemplative silence, anxiously awaiting the outcome of Connie's assessment. A friendly looking male nurse wearing a pale blue cotton tunic and trousers walked through a set of double doors that led from the triage area. He asked if anyone was waiting for Mrs Durand and Alan waved to beckon the young man over.

"Hi, my name's Dom," said the medic as he firmly shook the Chilterns' hands. Alan quickly scanned his eyes over the man's name badge.

"Would you like to follow me to somewhere quieter for a quick chat?" he added. Nurse Dominic Wells was a heavily built man with a shaved head. Although his demeanour was friendly, he had a direct approach to breaking news to relatives. He would often regret that he didn't have enough time during his shifts to give all cases his un-diverted compassion; an unfortunate consequence of under-staffing at the hospital.

Alan and Yvonne stood up immediately and followed in the nurse's striding footsteps. Neither knew what to say, as tears of dread began to well up in the elderly couples' eyes. Tragic memories from the night of Andrew's car accident flooded back as they were shown to the more comfortable surroundings of the relatives' room. It had been exactly two years to the day that the Chilterns had sat in the same clinical surroundings hoping for good news but fearing the worst. Was history about to repeat itself?

Yvonne's mind flashed back to the fretful night she had spent at the hospital perched on the edge of a hard plastic seat. A visiting choir from the local church had merrily sung carols in the reception area; their joyful renditions had drifted down the corridor, oblivious to the fact that the Chilterns were fearfully awaiting news of their son.

"How is Connie doing?" asked Alan, the question jolted Yvonne from her daydream.

"She's going to be fine," replied the nurse reassuringly.

"We think she's suffering from a rather nasty bout of gastro-enteritis and she is severely dehydrated so we've put her on a fluids drip." Yvonne ran the palms of her hands over her face to wipe away a tear of relief that had run down one cheek.

"Oh thank God. Thank you. Thank everyone," laughed the elderly woman as she sniffled into a handkerchief. Alan placed a supportive arm around his wife's shoulders.

"Can Connie come home now then?" he asked hopefully.

"Well, she has been pretty poorly with it so we'd like to keep her in the Clinical Decisions Unit for observation, just until tomorrow morning if that's okay," replied Dominic.

"We need to make sure any infection is under control and her fluid levels are back to normal so she doesn't incur any damage to her kidneys." The nurse smiled back warmly.

"Someone will pop back in a bit and take you to see her before she goes through to the CDU," he added as he walked out of the relatives' room and quietly closed the door behind him.

#

Muriel lay between the crisp cotton hospital sheets staring up at the white painted ceiling. One of her arms was attached to a saline drip; the other had a blood pressure cuff around it that automatically gripped into action every fifteen minutes to record her stats. She smiled inwardly, relieved that this particularly tricky part of Eddie's plan had worked perfectly. He had given her a vial of laxative to take to create the symptoms of food poisoning. However Muriel was concerned that hospital toxicology tests would uncover the drug in her system, so she had taken a more natural route. The day-old prawn that she had swallowed earlier had achieved the desired cramping stomach upset; her well-rehearsed fainting fit in the kitchen had convinced the Chilterns that she needed urgent medical attention. Her careful manipulation of the situation had seen her heroically refuse an ambulance but welcome a lift to the hospital in Alan's car. She was now in the safe hands of Hanford General and being cared for by an efficient nursing team. The swindling grifter was thankful that she would not suffer any lasting harm. She switched on her Ipod and selected a soothing track to play in the background whilst she waited for her visitors. Suddenly her tranquil moment of contemplation was interrupted as expected.

"Oh my God, are you okay now?" cried Yvonne as she and Alan burst into the curtained cubicle to crowd around their friend's hospital bed.

181

"I'm so sorry to have dragged you here," croaked the calculating con-artist as she warmly received the elderly couple's hugs.

"It must be the last place in the world you want to be, especially at this time of year," she added apologetically.

The Chilterns were immensely relieved that the young woman's ordeal was not as serious as they had first imagined, but they were also well aware of the irony of the situation. A function to celebrate the life of their late son had been the cause of another trip to the hospital; the same emergency department that Andrew had been taken to after his accident. It was the week leading up to Christmas and somewhere in the background of the bustling cacophony of sound in the A&E department Alan was sure he could hear the faint sound of a choir singing Silent Night, as cruel memories of that fateful evening came flooding back to haunt the elderly parents. The depth of sorrow in Yvonne's heart had been cruelly stirred; the draining utter helplessness that she and her husband had felt as they had watched doctors and surgeons valiantly battle to save their son's life washed through her mind.

"Oh Connie, I thought we'd lost you for one terrible moment back there," the bewildered woman began to wail. On hearing the fretful commotion Dominic quickly poked his head between the cubicle's curtains.

"Is everything alright in here?" asked the nurse as he beckoned a porter to bring a wheelchair over towards the bed.

"We're just going to take Connie through to Clinical Decisions now." He ushered the visitors to one side as he checked his patient's drip and blood pressure monitor.

"Come on old girl," whispered Alan, desperately trying to comfort his sobbing wife.

"Let's get you home and give Connie some peace. She'll be back at home tomorrow." The elderly man gave Muriel a hearty farewell hug before guiding his tearful wife away from the bed. The old couple both turned around to give a small wave and a nod of thanks towards the nurse before leaving.

"Aww bless, they were quite upset weren't they?" said Dominic, surprised by Yvonne's emotional outburst. Muriel slowly got up off the bed and slumped into the wheelchair. She was secretly delighted with how the Chilterns had reacted to her trip to the hospital. The Grubbets' plan was working like a dream.

Fortunately for Muriel, the A&E department was extremely busy. The hospital porters had been called away to help find more seats to accommodate the imminent arrival of the walking wounded from a pub brawl. Nurse Dominic decided it would free up the cubicle bed quicker if he took his patient to CDU himself, rather than wait for another porter to return. The short transfer in the lift upstairs was just long enough for the feckless hustler to sow the seeds of her water-tight alibi. She told the nurse that Alan and Yvonne had become a second mum and dad to her, and she had felt like a daughter to them. She quickly mentioned it was the anniversary of their son Andrew's accident and feigned a few crocodile tears, as she casually explained her honorary parents had probably felt so helpless at the shock of thinking they were going to lose another child.

"I hope the old biddies will be okay on their own," she mused.

"I've never seen them look so distraught before. They are both still quite fragile, and Yvonne's mental health doesn't cope with hospital stuff all that well. I guess a visit to the emergency department, especially on this date, must have brought such terrible memories flooding back for them both," croaked the drowsy grifter. Dominic smiled back supportively as he checked her drip one more time and handed his patient over to the Sister in charge.

Muriel was happy that her work was done. The seeds of doubt over the Chilterns' raw emotional state had been sown in Dominic's mind. He would remember just how upset the elderly couple had been. The helpful male nurse was totally unaware of the important role he would be asked to play at the inquest into the Chilterns' apparent suicides. The ruthless hustler smiled inwardly as, underneath the starched white cotton hospital gown, she clutched a mobile phone that she had stolen from Alan's pocket. She knew her victims would have no emergency lifeline to the outside world. Everything else was now down to Eddie.

Killing the Chilterns and making it appear as if the distraught couple had taken their own lives had been an audacious plan that required meticulous attention to detail. Murder was a serious departure for the Grubbets and it was imperative that Alan and Yvonne's deaths looked like a suicide pact. The heartless hustlers simply could not afford any suspicion of foul play, as that could lead to a robust investigation into any beneficiaries of their wills. Muriel and Eddie desperately needed to avoid any delays in claiming their fraudulent inheritance from the Chilterns' estate. Additionally they needed to devise a remote hands-off method of murder, as neither of them relished the prospect of getting up close and personal to witness the life-force drain from the elderly marks' faces.

Eddie had played and replayed the scenario in his head at least one hundred times, searching for any possible flaws in his plot. Tonight was the night when all of those weeks of careful planning would be put into action.

Chapter 14

Eddie Grubbet parked his hire car in the road outside Alan and Yvonne's house, a few yards away from the end of their drive. His clammy hands twitched on the steering wheel as a flicker of nervous anticipation fluttered in his stomach. The callous conman was feeling wired as he knew the homeowners would soon return from the hospital. It was at times like this that he wished he hadn't given up smoking. A calming cigarette had always quelled his anxieties before a big job, and the seasoned grifter knew tonight's activities would be the biggest challenge he had ever faced. He opened up the glove box and pulled out a set of keys that Muriel had posted to him earlier in the week, each piece of metal had been carefully labelled with the names of the doors at the Chiltern's house. The code to disable the house alarm had been noted on an accompanying piece of paper.

Eddie climbed out of his car and scurried across the blocked paved driveway towards the elderly couple's front door; carefully keeping within the shadows. He hid behind one of the tall stone pillars that flanked the entrance and pulled on a pair of latex gloves. The callous conman took in a deep steadying breath before turning one of the keys in the lock. Once safely inside the hall he crossed over to a beeping alarm box and swiftly entered the four-digit deactivation code. The room was immediately silenced and Eddie let out a satisfied sigh of relief.

Muriel had given her husband an in depth description of every nook and cranny in the house. Every ticking clock and each squeaking floorboard was meticulously etched onto Eddie's mental map of the building. There could be no surprises to throw him off guard; nothing to distract him from the important job in hand. He unlocked a door in the hallway that led into the integral garage. The heartless hustler smiled inwardly as he flicked on the light and saw that the well ordered space was largely empty. The concrete walls and floors were smartly painted and a few neatly stacked shelves of tools stood against one wall in the corner. The area was so unlike the Grubbets' carport at home in France which had become a dumping ground for unwanted garden furniture and boxes of junk. The Chilterns' garage was clearly awaiting the return of Alan's Jaguar. Eddie reached up to the fluorescent strip light above his head and removed the starter from out of the end. He switched off the light, returned to the hall and locked the connecting door behind him; leaving the heavy metal key firmly in the lock. A few seconds later he re-set the security alarm, walked out of the house and locked the front door, before quickly running back beneath the cover of darkness, to cross the driveway into the safe sanctuary of his parked car. The trap was set. All Eddie had to do now was hide in the shadows and wait for his unsuspecting prey to arrive home.

From Muriel's daily reports on how the Chilterns lived their lives, Eddie knew the elderly marks were creatures of habit. When they had been out together in the car, the predictable pensioners rarely used the front door. Instead they always entered the house from the garage. Alan Chiltern would habitually pull his Jaguar onto the drive and use a remote control to open the electronic metal up-and-over garage door. Like a well choreographed dance move, Yvonne would get out of the car, walk into the garage, switch on the fluorescent light and unlock the integral door to the hallway; while Alan drove in after her, switched off his car's engine and simultaneously closed the main garage door behind him. But on this fateful night things would be very different. It was a simple heinous plot and the Grubbets had discussed it hundreds of times.

Eddie checked the time on his phone as he saw a set of headlights approaching in the distance. It was nearly two o'clock in the morning and he was expecting his victims to arrive. He lay down across the front passenger seat of his car as Alan's Jaguar pulled onto the drive. The scheming conman's heartbeat quickened as he watched the up-and-over garage door open, before Yvonne walked into the garage and Alan drove in after her. A few moments later the door slowly closed. The Grubbets' evil trap was set.

Eddie's heart beat faster as he quickly started his car's engine and reversed onto the block paving. He came to a halt just a couple of inches away from the Chiltern's garage door and waited. He knew Alan would try to open it again as the elderly couple would not be able to get into the house through the integral door. Yvonne's key would not be able to unlock it, the garage light would not switch on, and the elderly couple would not be able to see what was causing the obstruction in the lock.

Suddenly Eddie felt the thumping sound of the garage door crashing into the underside of his car's rear bumper. The old man inside the garage was trying to lift the door up. Eddie left his engine running as he got out of the car. He laughed as he could see there was only a couple of inches space at the bottom of the rocking metal door. Eddie ignored Alan's cries for help as he got back in his car and revved the engine sending a thick choking plume of toxic gas beneath the door. Alan tried to force the garage door closed but it was no use, in the darkness he hadn't noticed the short piece of hose connected to the exhaust pipe outside that Eddie had sneakily fed through the small opening. The concrete chamber was filling fast with fumes as the terrified Chilterns hopelessly banged on the garage door. No one but Eddie would hear their desperate screams above the loud engine of the murderer's car.

"Get in the car and call 999," ordered Alan as he summoned every ounce of strength he could muster to try to bundle his wife back into the Jaguar away from the acrid air. But it was a fruitless exercise. The central locking mechanism on the car kept jamming. It suddenly became obvious to the terrified victims that someone else had an over-riding remote control key. Each time Alan unlocked the car the alarm would simply re-set. A heightened wave of panic swept over the couple as Yvonne shouted to her husband that the battery on her mobile was dead. Alan hurriedly searched for his own phone, but he couldn't find it in any of his jacket pockets.

Eddie remained seated in his car and pressed the accelerator again.

'Just a few more minutes,' he thought, as a sinister smile crawled across his lips. He knew in the choking darkness behind him, Mr and Mrs Chiltern would die together in each other's arms. It was a perfect plan. Their deaths would appear to be a straightforward case of carbon-monoxide poisoning; an apparent suicide pact.

The finale to the murderous plot would see Eddie eventually move his car away from the garage door and enter the gaseous chasm. The Chiltern's lifeless bodies would be placed inside the Jaguar, the car's windows opened and the engine switched on. Eddie could then leave the garage and close the main door behind him before slipping back inside the house to remove the incriminating key from the interconnecting door.

To the outside world it would look like the perfect double suicide committed by a couple of grieving elderly people. Connie would discover the tragic scene on her return home from hospital the following day. The suitably shocked and tearful young woman would emotionally suggest to the police that she believed the Chilterns had been unable to cope with the pain of the second anniversary of their son's tragic accident. Their visit to the hospital had obviously brought back painful memories and compounded their grief. Nurse Dominic Wells would be a useful independent witness who would confirm how upset the old couple had been.

#

Timeline: Wednesday 20th December 2017, 10:00hrs –
The Next Day

Muriel sat alone at a small round table in the hospital's coffee shop, slowly sipping a bottle of mineral water. She had been given the all clear by the doctors and they had reassured her that there would be no lasting damage following her bout of food poisoning. The heartless hustler had been discharged from the ward earlier that morning and she was happy in the knowledge that she had a suitable alibi for the previous night. Muriel picked up her phone and called her husband. It was the third time she had tried to contact him and, after six rings, she heard Eddie's familiar voicemail greeting again.

188

'Where the Hell are you?' she thought, as she nervously took another sip of water and ended the call.

The Grubbets' scam was not finished yet, and they still had to slot the final couple of pieces of the jigsaw puzzle into place before claiming their prize. Muriel would be the one to discover the bodies and alert the police, but the suspense of not knowing whether the Chilterns were still alive or not made her anxious. She had wanted to check with Eddie that the previous evening had gone ahead as planned, but now the scheming swindler had an uneasy feeling in the pit of her stomach. She took in a deep breath and called the elderly couple's landline.

"Hello, it's Connie here. Just to let you know the doctors have given me the all clear and I wondered if you could come and pick me up? I'll wait at the coffee shop downstairs by the reception. I'll also give you a bell on your mobiles just in case you're out and about. Love you both. See you soon."

The manipulative trickster knew that if Eddie's plan had worked, then the message would never be received, but she also knew that a call to her honorary parents would be the most natural thing to do under normal circumstances. Muriel left similar voicemail messages with a slightly more anxious tone on both Alan and Yvonne's phones; again knowing very well that they would never be answered by the Chilterns. They were the type of concerned calls that would have been made by an adopted daughter who was genuinely shaken by the lack of response from her parents; the type of calls that the police would expect to discover when they investigated the Chiltern's deaths.

One hour later, she had still not received a reply from Eddie. Keeping each other informed of developments was of paramount importance to the success of any scam and Muriel was beginning to get angry with her husband. She furiously snatched her mobile phone out of her pocket and began to punch in a text message.

Where RU? Did you do it? Call me now!

As the speech bubble on the phone changed colour to indicate a sent status, the uneasy feeling in her stomach swelled. A sudden wave of panic began to wash through Muriel's brain. She knew that radio silence from her husband had not been part of the Grubbets' master plan. Something must have gone terribly wrong.

#

Timeline: Wednesday 20th December 2017, 14:00hrs – Later That Day

The silver coloured minicab pulled up outside the Chilterns' house and Muriel stepped out onto the block paved driveway. A chill foreboding wind blew across the woman's face as she hurriedly made her way towards the front entrance. She glanced across at the closed garage door at the end of the building before slipping inside the hallway. Immediately the house alarm box began to beep its thirty second warning before she calmly typed in the four digit deactivation code.

The air inside the property was still and silent with not a single thing out of place. The curtains were still drawn shut which cast a cloak of darkness throughout the hall and living room. It had been a very overcast day outside, the type of day when there is no real burst of daylight, just a dull grey sky that had hidden any possible glimpse of the low winter sun. Muriel switched on the hall light and stared over at the closed integral door to the garage. Nervously she walked over to the doorway and shakily placed her hand on the door handle. Even though the heartless hustler had discussed the plan in finite detail with her husband, she was still unsure about exactly what scene was waiting for her in the garage.

The anxious woman took in a deep purposeful breath to try and summon enough courage to open the door. Slowly she pressed down on the handle and gently pushed, but the door remained closed. Muriel sighed and took a step back. The door was locked.

'I'm sure that wasn't in the plan,' mused Muriel.

'Maybe Eddie didn't go through with it after all,' she thought, secretly hoping that her husband had had cold feet. Muriel turned around and began to walk up the stairs. She smiled inwardly at the welcome reprieve; maybe her promotion to being a murderer had not materialised after all. She imagined that the Chilterns had received her message on their landline; they were alive and well and probably on their way to the hospital to pick her up. But Muriel's short-lived moment of hope quickly evaporated as the callous con-artist remembered that ensuring the integral door was locked before removing the key from the hall inside had been an important aspect of Eddie's plan. Her confused mind flashed back to the dozens of runs through they had plotted together and how her husband would stage the scene in the house.

"I'll check that they're unconscious, put them in the car, then go back into the house and take the key out of the door in the hall. It must look just like it would have looked if they'd have just driven back from the hospital and decided to gas themselves in the garage as soon as they arrived home." Muriel remembered Eddie's cold words.

"Just in case it all goes tits up at the hospital and you're not the one to find the stiffs in the car, it needs to look perfectly normal to anyone else who might happen upon them."

At the time Muriel had been thankful of her husband's astute attention to detail; something small like a key being in the wrong place would have been suspicious to anyone investigating the deaths. At that time, she had chosen to ignore the fact that Eddie's belt-and-braces approach to the murderous plot had taken into account the possibility that her food poisoning stunt could go wrong; if she didn't survive it then someone else would eventually find Alan and Yvonne's lifeless bodies. But now, in the aftermath of the previous eventful evening, and the fact that Eddie had not responded to any of her calls, Muriel's paranoia began to niggle.

'Christ Almighty, did he think there was a chance I might die too? What was in that vial he gave to me?' She shook her head and chose to put the thought to the back of her mind for the time being.

Muriel slowly turned around and walked back downstairs, fumbling in her coat pocket for her house keys. She pulled out the bunch of metal and felt for the long key to unlock the integral garage door. She swallowed hard and tried to moisten her dry lips as she turned it in the lock. The heavy wooden door creaked open and a wave of apprehension churned in Muriel's stomach as she peered into the shadowy darkness.

It was difficult to make out the shapes clearly, as the only available light was a small beam cast through the door from the hallway, but she was able to make out the dark outline of Alan's Jaguar. She reached for the fluorescent light switch but it failed to spark into life. Slowly her eyes began to adjust to the dim light and Muriel let out a small gasp. She could make out two figures were sitting inside the car. One looked like a man slumped forwards over the steering wheel; another smaller person alongside him had their head buried behind his shoulder. There was still an acrid stench of exhaust fumes lingering in the air.

"Oh my God, oh my God, oh my bloody God," squealed Muriel as she hastily slammed the integral garage door shut. The shocked woman was almost paralyzed with fear. Every fibre in her body tingled and fizzed at the realisation that she and Eddie had crossed the line; they had bluffed and hustled their way through a life of crime; the juggernaut of long cons and ill-gotten gains had now reached its fatal point of no return. They were murderers. Their evil plan had worked.

In all of her years as a grifter Muriel had never stayed around long enough to witness the carnage and suffering that her scams had created. She had never had to face the serious consequences of her actions before. But this last con was a whole new experience for her; dealing with death was an alien concept.

"Come on woman, just pull yourself together," said Muriel as she took in a deep breath to steady herself. To reap the rewards of the Grubbets' audacious plot she knew that she would have to ride out the impending storm. Eddie had carried out his side of the plan, all she had to do now was report the dead bodies in the garage to the authorities and confirm it was Mr and Mrs Chiltern in the car. Just one more step and the murderous swindlers would be on the home straight to collecting their ill-gotten gains. She allowed a small wry smile to crawl across her lips at the thought of how she and her husband had planned to spend the small fortune.

192

Muriel made her way upstairs to begin packing a case of clothes. She had arranged with Eddie that she would leave the house as soon as possible after the police arrived. The last thing she wanted was to hang around at the murder scene whilst the forensics team combed it for evidence to support or challenge the theory that the Chilterns had carried out a suicide pact. The sooner she could escape to the south of France the better.

'My God I hope they didn't suffer for too long,' thought Muriel with a short flash of empathy for her elderly victims. She entered the guest bedroom and pulled down her suitcase from the top of a wardrobe.

'So far, so good,' she thought, immediately switching off her emotions to concentrate on the task in hand. The feckless hustler imagined how smoothly the rest of Eddie's plan would unfold. The Coroner would be told that the Chilterns' visit to the hospital with Connie had been too much for the grieving parents to bear. Muriel had made sure that the helpful male nurse knew how upsetting it had been for them. The clinical relatives' room had brought back harrowing memories of the night spent in A&E following their son's car crash. The investigation would uncover how the distraught pensioners had come to realise that they would never be able to bear the immense pain of losing another child. Connie's sickness had driven them to a suicide pact, which would mean them never having to face such a loss again. At the inquest the unwitting Dominic Wells from the emergency department would be called in to confirm how distraught the Chilterns had been when they were at the hospital with Connie. The nurse would confirm that their concerned honorary daughter had been worried for their mental health and had hoped that they would be okay overnight on their own.

Connie would say she truly believed that they had come to terms with Andrew's death as the celebration of their son's life had been a beautiful evening; but maybe their visit to the hospital on the second anniversary of his accident had made them realise they would never get over the tragedy. Had the party been their swansong? As it would now appear to the outside world that a suicide pact was the only way the grieving parents could both escape their endless misery.

The Coroner would record a verdict of Death by Suicide in both cases.

Muriel allowed a small evil laugh to rise to the surface and extinguish her fears of ever being caught, as she thought about just how rich she was soon to become. The plotting sociopath picked up her mobile phone to try another call to her partner in crime. After six rings she heard Eddie's familiar voicemail greeting.

"My God Eddie where the hell are you? Call me as soon as you get this," shouted Muriel nervously.

The manipulative con-artist began to pack her belongings into the suitcase. She was a little sad to be leaving the cosy familiar surroundings of the Chilterns' comfortable home. Muriel had initially thought of staying on in the mansion to ride out the immediate aftermath of the tragic incident; but the draw of the Mediterranean winter sunshine was too strong for the hustler to resist. Besides, once the house and land had been sold on, the cold hard cash would buy the scheming scammer a superior lifestyle on the Cote d'Azur.

The Grubbets had decided that as soon as the authorities had been informed of the Chilterns' suicide then a suitably stunned Connie would say she was leaving to stay with friends in France. She would after all need time to recover from the immense shock of finding the lifeless bodies of the people she had fondly referred to as her new parents.

#

Timeline: Wednesday 20th December 2017, 18:00hrs – Later That Day

Muriel sat at the end of her bed and anxiously called Eddie again. It had been several hours since she had been discharged from the hospital. As the minutes ticked by, she paced around the bedroom occasionally looking out of the windows to see if there were any signs of her husband's car outside. There was a small chance that he may have lost his phone, it may have broken or run out of charge, so the only way he would be able to contact her would be in person. She looked outside again, but the road was in darkness. Muriel sat down on the edge of the bed as she picked up her mobile phone and angrily punched in Eddie's number again. She would need to check everything had gone according to plan, with no unexpected changes, before putting the final stage of the scam into action. But with no response from Eddie, she was becoming impatient.

It was imperative that Muriel made contact with her husband before calling the police, as both grifters knew good communication was always the key to a successful hustle. But why wasn't he picking up? It was then, in the tranquil serenity of the Chiltern's guest bedroom that Muriel thought back to the endless conversations she had had with Eddie to discuss the murderous plot.

Eddie had often said he was missing his wife; he had become bored at the hotel as there had been no one in the bar to play with of an evening. Muriel now wondered if that boredom had led him astray. The suspicions began to flow through the hustler's brain. This long con had been running for months and Eddie had recently returned to the country house hotel to finish the scam. But, with his wife living across town, Muriel wondered if Eddie had sought to massage his ego in the arms of a young conquest in the hotel bar. Her suspicions flew into over-drive, as she imagined his casual liaison with any young beauty could have developed into a relationship. The nagging doubt that had gnawed at the back of her mind suddenly jumped to the front of her thoughts: Exactly what had been in the vial he had given to her to make him consider Muriel may not survive the food poisoning stunt? Had he secretly planned for his wife to die so he could run away with a Bar Bunny?

Muriel was angry that her husband had still not replied, but her rage was fast growing into extreme paranoia. She knew she had to hold it together, otherwise the Grubbets' meticulous plan was in danger of falling apart.

"Ed, I can't do this alone. Those people are dead for God's sake and now you decide to do a disappearing act. You can't just kill them and leave me to face the music. This isn't the time to start testing me you idiot." Muriel remained on the line and took in a deep breath. She decided that she would carry out the final part of the plot, with or without her husband's support. She was feeling restless and needed to bring this chapter to a conclusion.

"I'm going to call the plod now to tell them I've found the bodies, so just call me back when you get this." A resolute Muriel snapped shut her Samsonite suitcase and dialled nine-nine-nine.

#

Timeline: Wednesday 20th December 2017, 18:30hrs

A tearful Connie sat on the bottom stair in the hallway of the Chilterns' family home. She had opened the front door wide in anticipation of the arrival of the police and ambulance. A bright intrusive blaze of blue lights flashed continually outside the front door as two paramedics and a doctor burst through the entrance. She peered across at the heavy wooden integral door that led into the garage. It was slightly ajar and a faint aroma of exhaust fumes meandered through the crack into the hall. The fretful woman limply pointed towards the open door to the garage and the trio quickly made their way inside. Muriel buried her face in her hands as she heard the medics shouting instructions in the background. She knew that any attempt at trying to resuscitate the lifeless bodies in Alan's Jaguar would be fruitless. Suddenly she lifted up her head and looked towards the open front entrance. She could see a shadowy figure approaching from the driveway. A tall man in a smart blue suit walked through the doorway swiftly followed by three uniformed police officers.

"Muriel Grubbet?" asked the man casually. The woman was shocked on hearing someone mention her real name, as a sharp sting suddenly burst through her veins. Dozens of scenarios raced through her mind in seconds, as she tried to think how she would cope with her true identity being unveiled at such a crucial time. Her first instinct was to distance herself from the lifeless bodies in the garage; if she could claim to have no direct connection with the Chilterns then maybe she would be able to slip away unnoticed while the police tracked down their next-of-kin.

196

"Mrs Grubbet?" prompted the man again. Muriel mentally flicked through her back catalogue of forged identities that she had used in the past. They were tried and trusted pseudonyms that had successfully enabled her to slip through Europol's net on numerous occasions; but more importantly they were names that she would still have IDs for somewhere in her handbag.

"Err, sorry non," replied the startled woman with a slight French hue in her accent. Muriel's heart throbbed loudly in her chest; the palpitations sent a pounding beat of blood storming through her brain. She was not used to thinking on her feet and she was finding it difficult to adapt to the unexpected situation. She had always admired Eddie's consummate ability to switch plans at a second's notice but it was a skill she had not honed. Without her fast-thinking husband at her side, Muriel was beginning to panic.

The man flipped his warrant card open and the heartless hustler could clearly read the name printed beneath his photograph. He was Detective Sergeant Duke from Hanford CID.

"I am 'Elen Bacque, a friend of Connie Durand, who lives 'ere," she offered nervously with a slightly over emphasised Gallic pronunciation. DS Duke slowly shook his head and smiled back at the hapless suspect before beckoning to one of the uniformed PCs to pass him a set of handcuffs. Unbeknown to Muriel, the wily detective was well aware of her true identity.

"Muriel Grubbet, I'm arresting you on suspicion of fraud and conspiracy to murder," announced Duke.

"Non, non, non! I am Madame Bacque," she cried.

"You do not have to say anything, but it may harm your defence if you do not mention when questioned something which you later rely on in court," continued Duke, unfazed by the woman's protests.

"Look 'ere, I can prove it monsieur," screamed Muriel, frantically searching through her purse for a set of forged papers. The policeman was undeterred by the woman's vain attempt to switch to her new character.

"Anything you do say may be given in evidence. Do you understand?" The words burned through Muriel's brain. She felt as if her lifeblood was pumping out of her body and out through the soles of her shoes. In all of her years as a hustler, being arrested was an occupational hazard she had always managed to evade. DS Duke's official caution contained the fateful words she had always dreaded to hear. Muriel felt the sharp click of the Sergeant's handcuffs before being led outside towards a waiting police car.

The continual flash of blue lights momentarily blinded her as she sat on the rear seat of the car. As the whole of the past few months played out in Muriel's mind she tried to work out where it had all gone wrong. It had been a fantastic plan, maybe the most lucrative one that Eddie had ever devised; it was to be a fitting finale to the Grubbets' grifting career. But it was now clear to the hustler that her husband was nowhere to be seen, their dream now lay in tatters and she had been left to carry the full burden of responsibility.

Two uniformed PCs got into the front seats of the police car. As the driver started the engine, Muriel looked up at the large family home she knew would never be hers. Fat tears began to well in her eyes as the car pulled away from the house. She turned around for one last look at the frontage. Muriel gasped in shock as she was sure she could make out the familiar figures of Alan and Yvonne Chiltern standing on the driveway staring back at her.

Chapter 15

It had been a risky manoeuvre but the elderly Chilterns had wanted to be instrumental in bringing Muriel and Eddie Grubbet to justice. Hanford CID knew that they would have to be patient as it could take months for the heartless grifters to fall into their carefully laid trap.

When Yvonne Chiltern first opened the fake twenty-year-old envelope she had initially been convinced that there may have been some truth in the claims of the innocent young infatuated groupie. She knew that her happy-go-lucky musician son had possessed the morals of a Tom Cat and there could easily be some truth in the story. However, when Alan had visited the old post office that the letter had allegedly been discovered in, the property developer who was still working at the premises had no idea what Mr Chiltern was talking about. To the disappointed grieving father's surprise there had been no discovery of a batch of old letters. Alan had then searched on line and found that the 0845 phone number was not a legitimate one for Royal Mail.

Muriel and Eddie Grubbet had been aware that Alan had worked as a civil servant but, despite the callous crooks' meticulous planning and attention to detail, they had failed to unearth the fact that he had in fact worked for Hanford Police. Their elderly mark had once reached the rank of Detective Inspector. Most of his work had been under cover in the vice squad, consequently he had no social media history. His name and occupation was only briefly mentioned in the newspapers once, shortly before his retirement, when he had appeared in a television appeal about a dead body discovered at Himley Chase back in 2004. Apart from that he had successfully protected his privacy.

Once the retired DI Chiltern's suspicions had been aroused, and he knew that the claims in the late letter were not genuine, he had mentioned his findings to his old colleagues in Hanford CID. On hearing the news, Sergeant Duke was astounded by how similar the latest scam was to another case he had worked on that had involved a wealthy widow called Elisabeth Hambridge. From the delayed letter and spurious connection with France, to keeping a secret from an angry Gallic husband, all of those similarities convinced the detective that he was dealing with the same crew of hustlers who had swindled thousands of pounds out of the earlier victim. The Hambridge case was still an open investigation as the perpetrators had so far eluded justice. DS Duke was determined that the latest delayed letter scam would be put to bed once and for all, so Operation Pearly Gates was reignited. Alan and Yvonne had agreed to work with the police and lure the unsuspecting grifters into their own irresistible web.

Just as Elisabeth Hambridge had tracked down the elusive Charlotte Rook and developed a strong bond with her, the Chilterns had pursued the mysterious Connie and struck up a seemingly genuine online friendship with her. Eventually they had encouraged the woman to stay with them. Unbeknown to the Grubbets, all contact between the elderly couple and the hustlers had been carefully stage managed; all conversations were closely monitored and recorded by the police at every point. Trudi Jones in the Cyber Unit noticed that the IP address associated with the video calls was the same as the one used by the hustlers in the Hambridge case. Duke had immediately dispatched a surveillance team to the Granary Mill Hotel. A covert camera in a glass brooch worn by a petite ash blonde PC at the bar had captured footage of Eddie Grubbet speaking in French to Alan Chiltern. Bar bunny Daisy's conversation with him in the residents' lounge had delayed the unwitting con-man's return to his hotel suite; just long enough for the team to plant their bugs inside the room. The confidence trickster had been blissfully unaware that his clumsy attempt to charm the young undercover police officer had been futile.

Sergeant Duke had needed to ensure that the Grubbets would receive long sentences for their crimes. He also wanted to establish what assets they had, as any proceeds from their sale could be used to compensate the victims of their crimes. During the covert operation to catch the Grubbets, he knew that there was a risk the scammers could become bored and move on to another hustle before the final sting. Duke assumed the

Chilterns would not be the only targets at that time, and he needed to lure the scammers away from any other potential victims. It was then he devised a plan to keep the swindlers focussed solely on the Chilterns and make the reward more tempting than just another simple identity theft.

The promise of inheriting a large fortune and never having to work again had been too much temptation for the greedy Grubbets to resist. But even Duke had been shocked by the hustlers' plan to kill their victims. He needed to protect the Chilterns from any harm, but everyone on the investigation team knew that the best method to ensure the duo served the maximum time behind bars, would be to catch the Grubbets in the act of attempting to carry out their murderous plot.

The high risk bait was laid.

The retired Detective Inspector Alan Chiltern had been more than willing to help his ex colleagues capture the criminals. He planted miniature cameras and listening devices in every room of his house, around the garden and in the car; effectively giving DS Duke a front row seat to the action. A team of private investigators had watched scheming Muriel stand on the balcony to overhear the deliberately loud conversation that Alan and Yvonne had staged, when seemingly discussed signing over everything in their wills to Connie. Each small detail had been carefully stage-managed to pull the evil hustlers further onto the policeman's unrelenting hook.

From the seemingly easy to obtain bank loan for ten thousand pounds, to the chance meeting with Lydia in the Italian restaurant, everything had been perfectly choreographed by the Chilterns and DS Duke. Muriel had been so driven by the end prize that she failed to realise she had been lured into a false sense of security with the elderly couple. She had no idea that Andrew's widow was an accomplished actress. The fact that Lydia had studied drama at college was another small detail that Muriel had failed to take any notice of. Instead she had blindly believed that Alan and Yvonne hated Lydia and they had chosen the mother of their grandchild over their own daughter-in-law. Even the gathering at the Black Cross and Gary's well-rehearsed piece of drunken drama at the memorial gig had been planted convincers to make the scammer feel at ease. Unbeknown to Muriel the drummer had utterly despised the confidence trickster. The fact that anyone could be so cruel to try to take advantage of his best friend's grieving parents had absolutely enraged Gary, so he had been happy to help the Chilterns and revelled in his new role as a drunken old rocker.

When Eddie had returned to the couple's villa in the south of France, another covert team had followed his every move. Duke was determined that the money-grabbing grifters would have nowhere to hide their ill-gotten gains.

As Muriel and Eddie devised their horrifying plan to murder the pensioners, the police had been listening to every conversation; they had intercepted all of the couple's text messages and phone calls; they knew every chilling detail. The detectives discovered that Eddie intended to trap the Chilterns in their garage and gas them with exhaust fumes. On the fateful night of the planned murder, Sergeant Duke and a hand-picked group of officers had been waiting for him.

The elderly couple returned from the hospital and parked their Jaguar in the garage as usual. Alan had then closed the up-and-over garage door behind him. Unbeknown to the hapless hustler, Alan and his wife had put on breathing apparatus. Their pitiful cries for help and furious bangs on the garage door that Eddie had heard had all been an elaborate act.

Eddie had been filmed outside the Chiltern's home entering and leaving the house. The murderous grifter was later caught red handed as he pulled out the hosepipe from beneath the garage door that had been attached to the exhaust pipe of his car. He had filled the garage with noxious gas and had clearly expected to have suffocated the Chilterns who were trapped inside. Eddie Grubbet was promptly arrested at the scene and later charged with attempted murder; his whole evening's activity had been recorded through a policeman's long lens video camera.

Muriel's agitated phone calls and text messages to her husband the following day had only served to further incriminate her in the whole plot. The shameless schemer had been keen to keep as far away from the crime scene as possible. During numerous conversations with Eddie, Muriel had insisted that she would not touch the dead bodies in the car. In fact she had refused to enter the garage after the murders had been committed. Eddie had always been more hands-on than her and she didn't want to get up close and personal with the results of their heinous crime. Consequently Muriel failed to realise that the corpses on the front seats of Alan's Jaguar had been nothing more than a couple of mannequins propped up over the steering wheel and dashboard. They had been carefully posed there by DS Duke following Eddie Grubbet's arrest. The Chilterns were safely out of sight back at the police station, awaiting the nine-nine-nine call from a suitably upset Connie who would report their apparent suicide.

#

Timeline: Wednesday 6th June 2018 –
Six Months Later

Diana Hambridge stood in her mother-in-law's kitchen and took in a deep purposeful breath. She sighed heavily as she took the old chalk notice board down off the wall. It had been two years since the whole dreadful Benoit saga had begun and she had just returned from the Crown Court. The woman she had known as Charlotte had been found guilty of thirty six counts of fraud and one of conspiracy to murder.

Muriel and Eddie Grubbet had amassed a fortune from their cruel scams and they were both ordered to serve equally long custodial sentences for the suffering they had caused; the Proceeds of Crime Act and subsequent sale of their home in the south of France would ensure some financial compensation for the grifters' victims.

Elisabeth Hambridge never recovered from the shock of the audacious hustle. The strain of the investigation had been too much for her heart to bear and she had suffered a stroke three months before the case came to court. Diana wiped off an old shopping list written on the chalk board and packed it away with the last few bone china mugs and a cafetiere from the kitchen work surface. They were all carefully placed into a cardboard box for the charity shop. The estate agent had sold the Clover Croft mansion to a young family and it was now

203

time for Diana and her frail mother-in-law to move on with their lives. As she secured the top tabs of the box with tape, Diana heard the unexpected trill of the landline echoing in the empty marble hallway.

"Strange, I thought I'd cancelled the phone contract," she muttered, as she walked out of the kitchen and knelt down on the polished stone floor to pick up the receiver.

"Mrs Hambridge?" enquired a softly spoken woman's voice.

"Yes," she replied.

"Oh hello, you don't know me but I went to college with your son." Diana retained her composure but sighed inwardly at the irony of the unknown caller's opening line.

"Who, you mean Christian?" she asked, desperately trying to conceal her suspicious sarcasm.

"Yes," confirmed the voice. Diana shook her head and coughed to stifle her annoyance. The stranger entered into a carefully prepared speech about how she represented a charity on the Isle of Man that helped to support motorcyclists injured in the island's TT races. The caller claimed Christian had always promised he would leave a sizeable donation to the worthy cause in his will. The organisation had become aware of his death and they were concerned they had not yet received the promised money.

Diana realised another hustler had acquired the Grubbets' list of vulnerable people to target; this was their initial contact. The young widow slowly shook her head as the voice on the end of the line explained 'Hammers' had been a loyal supporter of the charity and, as a keen biker himself, he would have wanted to ensure the intended money reached them.

"How much was Christian's donation going to be?" enquired Diana politely.

"Five thousand pounds initially, then ten pounds a month after that, so we'd need some bank details to set up a direct debit," replied the voice.

"Can you take a payment over the phone?" asked the weary young widow.

"Yes, of course Mrs Hambridge."

"Okay, just bear with me for a moment will you while I go and fetch my credit card."

Diana got up off the floor, picked up her handbag and the cardboard box for the charity shop and simply left the receiver off the hook. The young woman felt that keeping the scammer hanging on the line like that would be only a tiny victory, as a small tear began to fall down her face; she simply could not believe the bare faced cheek of the lying stranger on the end of the phone. She could still hear the swindler's voice babbling in the background as she made her way outside the house and firmly closed the front door behind her.

THE END

Printed in Great Britain
by Amazon